"A delightful culinary mystery that will keep you guessing right up until the end. A married couple are at the core of the story, which makes A Caterer's Guide to Love and Murder stand out as a different kind of cozy. I'm excited to see what new stories Jessica cooks up next!"

**Jenna Lynn Badger, author of the
Alpaca My Bags cozy mystery series**

"Anyone who loves Joanne Fluke's Hannah Swensen will love this book. The characters are gorgeous and comfortable. Perfect for cozy mystery lovers."

Blaise Ramsay, multi-published author

A Caterer's Guide to Love & Murder

Jessica Thompson

DARK
STROKE

www.darkstroke.com

Discover us online:
www.darkstroke.com

Join us on instagram:
www.instagram.com/darkstrokebooks/

Include **#darkstroke** in a photo of yourself
holding this book on Instagram and
something nice will happen.

To my husband and kids.
You made this possible.

About the Author

When Jessica discovered mystery novels with recipes, she knew she had found her niche.

As an avid home chef and food science geek, Jessica has won cooking competitions and been featured in the online Taste of Home recipe collection. She also tends to be the go-to source for recipes, taste-testing, and food advice among her peers.

Jessica is active in her local writing community and is a member of the Writers' League of Texas. She received a bachelor's degree in Horticulture from Brigham Young University but has always enjoyed writing and reading mysteries.

Jessica is originally from California, but now has adopted the Austin, Texas lifestyle and loves to smoke barbeque, shoot, ride, and wrangle. She enjoys living in the suburbs with her husband and young children, but also enjoys helping her parents with their nearby longhorn cattle ranch.

Acknowledgements

Thank you to everyone that has helped me! So many people have been amazingly kind and generous.

Thanks to Steph and Laurence, my publishers and editors, for taking a chance on an unknown kid.

Thanks to Whitney McGruder, my early editor who helped me get ready to share my work with the world.

Thanks to my Write Club, especially Heidi for pushing me to get really driven and start taking myself seriously.

Thank you to my readers and recipe testers for the honest, constructive criticism.

And most of all thanks to my Heavenly Father, my husband, and the rest of my family for being endlessly supportive.

I love you all.

I've been published! I love everyone right now!

A Caterer's Guide to Love & Murder

Excerpt from William P. Hobby Unit Interview, TDCJ Transcript 5 27 95
Completed by the University of Texas at Austin's Department of Psychology
Students: Mark Payne and Jamie Shimizu

. . .
Everyone was looking forward to the blessing of this planned, natural death.
They couldn't say it, but I knew. Even now, I still know that they wanted it. I was doing the right thing, but I knew the law wouldn't see it that way.

Chapter One

Are We Ready?

"Wow, this dough is sexy!" Violet's exclamation cracked through the echoing studio apartment. "I should make strudel more often!"

Her new husband, Jake, took a half-second to drag his sharp eyes away from his decrepit laptop where he was tapping out his latest military-themed mystery novel.

"What? Oh, that's funny, Vi. I thought you said . . ." he chuckled, then stopped and looked puzzled again. "Wait, what?"

The smell of yeast and fresh, green apples permeated the small space and caught Jake's attention now. Violet flipped her dark hair with a saucy grace that she reserved only for her husband and glanced over her shoulder without stopping her kneading.

"You heard me," she said with a smile in her voice. "This dough is sexy! If cars can be sexy, then dough can be too! Really though, feel this!"

She whirled on her heel with her ball of silky, elastic dough, making her A-line skirt inflate, and bounced it to the living room area where Jake had his papers erratically radiating out on the floor in a starburst. He leaned back in his black desk chair and poked the ball with a lackluster index finger and a neutral face. At first it was just to humor her, but then he really cupped the warm, round mass with almost reverent hands.

"Whoa! Totally!" Jake finally sounded piqued. His eyebrows raised and he cracked a hint of his signature, crooked smile.

Violet was practically giddy when she returned to slap the

4

dough on the lightly floured granite counter. Jake fell into repose again as he wrapped up the thought he had been ticking out on the keyboard. This was unusual. Normally Jake was more of a talker and Violet was a listener, except when he got her gushing about food. Now, she was practically vibrating with nervous energy.

"I think I need to stretch it out farther than last time. The video I watched got it so thin that you could see through it! It was amazing!" Violet said as she quickly duplicated the feat.

"Mmm-hm," was all that Jake uttered as he doubled over in his chair to hiss all his research into a rough pile.

Violet lapsed into silence and relaxed by a degree as he cleaned up the floor that she had just mopped that morning. She drew her weapon of choice, her favorite chef's knife, and raced through a bowl of peeled apple wedges, slicing them evenly in a blur of movement.

"Uh, Don called. Asked if we could hang out Saturday, so I told him it'd have to be the weekend after that. Cuz you and I are busy with that crazy catering job."

Any enjoyment and relaxation that Violet had accumulated escaped her now. She dumped her pile of perfect slices with exasperation.

"We're so behind already! I don't know how you convinced me to bake for us tonight. I should be making choux pastry!" Violet's annoyance and despair vacillated back.

"It's okay," Jake said. "You wanted to use up those apples to clear the kitchen while I wrapped up, and I'll be able to help you now. I just finished!"

When Violet wiped her brow with a shaking wrist instead of congratulating him, he tried to reassure her.

"It'll be fine! I know it's a big job, but you need to relax and look around. Everything is going pretty well!"

"I can't relax! This job isn't just big, it's make-or-break." Violet knew she was panicking needlessly. She took a deep, calming breath and went on. "Everything I've been working towards depends on this."

"There are things more important than work." Jake came up behind her and squeezed her shoulders. His fresh musk and strong hands reassured her more than his words. "Tomorrow we will be able to get tons done."

Violet wrestled with another deep, slow breath as Jake tried to distract her.

"That smells good. What are you making again?" He loved food, while Violet loved cooking.

"Crisp apple strudel," Violet sang, making a tentative attempt at being soothed as she fed Jake a spiced apple slice from her bowl of filling as she mixed. Then she pulled the bowl closer and spooned the mixture onto the flattened dough.

"I guess you're right," Violet said, returning their conversation to the subject that was making her OCD flare up. "I am hoping to hit the farmers' market in the morning and start shopping for the Jorgensen/Moretti wedding. Then I want to do more shopping, organizing, and make a detailed list of all the prep work we need to do. Then I can put you to work, Mister!" There was a slight smile in Violet's voice again, but the grin didn't spread to her eyes.

"I can cook some stuff while you're gone, too," Jake said as he kissed her shoulder.

Violet sighed with satisfaction and said, "Thank you."

Jake snickered deeply in a way that made Violet weak in the knees. "I could actually feel you unclench. Feel better?"

He asked it as he turned her around by the hips and pulled her close to him. His clear blue eyes sparkled, and Violet only answered with a prolonged kiss. He looked deep into her eyes as the oven beeped to indicate that it was preheated.

"What are your plans for tonight?" he whispered, rubbing his nose against the nape of her neck.

Violet cringed as their growing conflict rose close to the surface. She tried to act natural as she turned on him to face the counter again. His rust-colored 5 o'clock shadow rasping around to her other shoulder as she spun.

"I-I don't think we have time for that conversation right now." Violet tensed and cooled like a custard.

"Hey, it's not . . . don't worry. We don't have to decide anything tonight. I just . . . miss you."

Things between them had cooled off in the last month,

though neither of them wanted to address it. Since Jake had brought up having kids now, and Violet had hinted that she was not ready, intimacy was a minefield of a topic.

"Are you ready?" Violet tried to push aside the looming issue, but it ate at the corner of her already chaotic mind. As she rolled the strudel, her hands worked the inside and Jake's arms were around her while his big hands kept up with her on the outside edges.

She gathered her courage, "Well then, we'll have about an hour to do anything we want when I get this in the oven."

"Perfect."

Then, in one fluid motion, Jake stepped aside as he opened the oven door, and Violet slipped the cookie sheet in. Before the door had even closed all the way, Jake scooped her up as they walked away and turned off the lights.

As Violet's eyes inched open, she smelled apple strudel from the night before. It would make a delectable breakfast with some scrambled eggs. But that could wait. In the early morning glow that came sneaking in across the studio apartment to their bedroom area, Violet lay watching her husband. With her index finger she grazed his copper scruff. His tall frame was stretched out on his stomach with his arms over head, accenting his muscular shoulders, while his slow breathing was bordering on a snort.

He snored occasionally, but she didn't care. She loved him so much that she still got 'gaga' sometimes. They had been married for almost a year, but she was still amazed that a man this wonderful actually wanted to be with her forever. Everything had been a dream until recently.

Violet's eyes traced the curve of his back as she brushed her fingernails down his spine. When her gaze returned to his face, Jake's eyes were alive with startling intensity. His icy blue eyes were rimmed with red, but fully and immediately awake.

"When can we babysit Lindy again? Have you made any plans with Greta?" Jake asked, rolling to his side. Babysitting their niece was one of his favorite hobbies.

"I don't know, we haven't..." Violet left the sentence

7

unfinished. She knew where this was going.

"Kids are the coolest." He broached the subject without subtlety. "Do you think we're ready to start?"

Ready to have kids? Now?

He had aimed several times to bring up this subject lately, but never this directly.

The same knee-jerk reaction flew out that had put him off the last two times. "We don't have time for this conversation right now."

"Then make time." Jake monotoned as he rose to an elbow.

"What?" Violet tried to laugh off the uncomfortable tone. "We're busy!"

"Do you mean too busy to have kids or too busy to talk about having kids?" Jake retorted. Clearly he had been ready for this.

"Well, I don't know…" Violet stumbled to catch up with the topic.

"I want to know what you want, Violet." Jake's voice softened, then he pleaded. "Do you want kids?"

Violet let out another nervous snicker and threw herself out of bed. "No way!"

Now it was Jake's turn to look blindsided. "What do you mean? Why not?" He tried to laugh along, but the hurt showed on every inch of him.

"Our apartment, of course!" Violet could not keep a rebellious edge out of her voice. "It's a studio! And even the foot of our bed is the walkway at the front door! The only interior door that closes is to the bathroom!"

She could feel herself getting defensively rigid. Violet didn't mean to be throwing out this affront into Jake's face, but it was impossible to stop now that the flood gates had opened. It was automatic and hurtful. She wasn't sure that she was arguing her true feelings, but she didn't actually know what her true feelings on the subject were. Her mind only raced to poke holes in this attack.

Violet scrambled to regain control of herself and perched on the edge of the bed to hug Jake around the shoulders as she jabbed with a soft joke. "We can't have the baby sleep in the

sorry. I'm not ready, but, well, I don't know. I'm just not ready."

Violet sobbed into his shoulder now. He wrapped her in his arms that were still muggy from the outside air. He squeezed her so tightly that she struggled for breath, then released her and held her at arm's length.

"Hey, all that stuff you mentioned. You've got a point, but I still think we can do it. We are working on the catering business and that chunk of debt, sure, but I'm making money. And making enough that we can move anytime we are ready! It's really just…"

Jake visibly struggled for the right words while still trying to stay calm. Violet knew he was so anxious to have children that it was difficult for him. As a child, he had no direct, long-term father figures. Instead of making him apprehensive to take that journey himself, it made him eager.

"It's like all that doesn't matter!" He finally snapped, then gritted his teeth to regain his composure. His frustration melted into despondency. "Does this mean you don't want to, ever?"

"I can only guess that I will want to eventually," she said. But would she? Violet knew that she would someday regret not having kids, but she didn't want to resent them or Jake if she started before she was ready. "All I know is that I'm not ready now."

"When then?" Jake shook her slightly. His sad slate-colored eyes were especially translucent as tears gathered in them slowly.

"You can't predict these things, but…soon." It was all that Violet could commit to, and it seemed to appease Jake for the time being.

They agreed to revisit the subject after this upcoming, massive catering job. In Violet's mind, this weekend was everything, and nothing could distract her from this. Status quo had to be maintained until this business got to a stable footing.

But Violet needed to do some serious pondering before they could have that conversation. The idea terrified Violet. Kids?

As much as they loved their niece, she was a handful. Lindy was so particular about how things had to be done that she could be scary. As a baby she had screamed the whole time they would babysit. Jake was patient and bounced her by their big window the whole three hours, but how could they do that every day? And every kid was loud and messy!

As she walked around the kitchen, tweaking and re-tweaking the kitchen towel and perfecting the stacks of forks in the silverware drawer, Violet had to admit that Jake had a point. Violet couldn't sleep til the dishes were done, she couldn't eat at certain establishments with questionable food handling, and she couldn't sit down at her sister's house 'til she had cleaned it. Couldn't Jake understand that? He knew about her neuroses. He said he loved them! He also said that he always wanted to have kids. How could he reconcile those two loves?

Love is a strange beast, she thought now as she brushed her teeth before her morning excursion. How could he love her for being a 'clean-freak' and still want her to love a baby that would ruin everything stored under three feet? Mostly, how could Violet still love her husband as much as she did with a new person that she would presumably love even more?

A new thought struck Violet as she rinsed with mouthwash. Would Jake continue to love her if she didn't want to have kids? Could she maintain this status quo without giving Jake what he wanted? Could she lose him if she wasn't ready?

Violet stopped dead in her tracks. The farmers market was teeming, and she had almost walked straight into the taut leash between an energetic child and his obviously drained grandmother. The weather was finally getting cooler now that it was the first week of fall, but Violet could only think about how awful it would be to have to shop for work with a child in tow. Violet was already 'glowing', as her mother insisted she put it, without the extra work. Her dark hair seemed to absorb every bit of the glaring, late morning sun and it made her wilt like a spinach salad. Violet yielded to the older woman, dipped her head into a coy half-smile, and continued to dodge past them to get back to the loud river of people ebbing and flowing through the Downtown Austin farmers market.

She loved this market despite people lifting things over their heads and wafting their body odor in her face. Her skin crawled if she thought about the rank smells and germs, but she looked past the breath, the dogs, the heat, and all the perishable foods sitting out in the midst of it all.

This multiple-day catering job meant she needed to focus, shop, and buy produce now. She would need to fully stock her catering fridge that stood in the office of her tiny apartment before Thursday when the long rigmarole of successive parties would begin.

This whole wedding had to be perfect. Was she ready? Paul was the groom and his parents were long-time family friends. Violet's mother and Paul had teamed up to get Violet this job. Paul had even dated Violet's sister, Greta, fairly seriously for a while and now he was marrying a woman who was the closest to 'high society' that Austin had. Her family hosted events and held fundraisers several times a year, so if Violet could impress them, maybe she could book more catering jobs, even expand her business. She imagined hosting parties attended by Austin celebrities like Brooklyn Decker and Matthew McConaughey, but she was getting ahead of herself.

Violet forced her mind back to her task and stopped at a stall selling cocoa nibs.

This crowd would have taste, experience, and would know the difference between Ghirardelli, Guittard, Hershey's, and true European artisanal chocolate. Paul's grandmother was a bit of a food critic and had the money from her husband's business and some family money to support this foodie-habit for her whole family.

In Violet's mind, Paul's grandmother would be a sort of guest of honor, after the bride and groom, of course. She would be the person to impress. While both families were active in the community and could bring in a lot more business for Violet, Francesca LeBaron was a devotee of the culinary arts and a famous grump. It would be much harder to make a splash with her. She was not the type to tolerate mistakes just because you were a friend of a friend. Everything would have to be perfect, but if Violet could really impress her, she could hire more people, get the larger catering jobs, and abolish the small dark corner of accumulated debt to her parents that always lived in her mind.

Granny Franny, although Violet herself had never dared to call her that, intended to pass her money on to Paul and his brother, Luke. This would be good news for them eventually. When the money did fall to them, Violet knew that she was in good with them, and her little catering business would definitely benefit from their added income.

Would they be as socially and politically involved as their grandmother? Would she ever meet the Mayor or Lance Armstrong at their benefit banquets? And how much would their income grow? There may not be as much to pass on to her grandchildren as everyone thought. No, Violet knew she must seize this opportunity. Now.

Since Paul was marrying this girl, what was her name? Lori? Lauren? Lara? Something like that. She would have to ask Greta when she called her later. Now that he was marrying this girl, all his future money worries would just evaporate off like simmering alcohol. She was rich, cultured, and warmly beautiful. Violet guessed that Paul would be able to afford the life that he had always been trying to live. He might not even need his granny's money anymore!

As Violet noticed a sign and wrote down *lamb pastrami reubens* in her little lined notebook, her stomach rumbled. The scenery had been so captivating that she had forgotten to eat lunch. Lamb Pastrami Reubens were twelve dollars! The catering business didn't pay that well!

She continued upstream and finally arrived for the smells of fish sauce and onion at 'Coat & Thai.' Another patron turned away from the food truck with their signature Pad Thai noodles, floating the intoxicating aroma around her face and making her stomach growl afresh. She actually liked her own spring rolls better than most restaurants' versions, but the cool, crisp and sticky finger food sounded like the perfect refreshing lunch for the warm, piercing sunshine. She dipped her head

14

under the low edge of a tilted table umbrella and got in line.

"Four dollars," the pregnant, blonde cashier said bluntly as a sheen of sweat collected into a drop on her jawline. Ever since Jake had brought up the subject of kids, pregnant women seemed to be everywhere. Even this one seemed familiar somehow, like they had met before. Some time before she was haggard and uncomfortable from pregnancy.

The throng of foodies, hippies, restaurant-owners and tourist rubberneckers was especially stereotypical here at the farmers' market. Even the pregnant blonde that she had just spoken to had a tattoo and a piercing. Violet was too old-fashioned to fit in here, but she didn't care. Wearing a simple ruffled t-shirt and fitted jeans with her clean, shoulder length hair, she considered herself a plain, traditional Christian girl. Maybe even vintage. She had always placed cleanliness and skin care over make up and perfume.

Despite her height and being naturally attractive, she was always easily able to avoid attention when she wanted to, which was most of the time. An observant people watcher and an accidental eavesdropper, she preferred to think of herself as a good listener.

She watched these people swarming around the farmers' market, wondering how to serve as the invisible caterer but also to get noticed by the right people.

After the first bite of gummy rice paper wrapper, bracing lettuce, and tender shrimp, Violet felt much better. She swept her gently wavy, mahogany hair behind her ear before bending over for another taste. These rolls reminded her of an amuse bouche that her mom had made for a nice party. She had prepared snow pea wrapped shrimp instead of hiring a caterer. They had always believed in working hard and not spending money. Maybe she should serve one of these appetizers for this job? The more things she could prepare in advance and serve cold for the rehearsal dinner, family luncheon, bachelor party, bachelorette party and the wedding, the better.

It was going to be one formidable weekend. She had to be ready.

Crisp Apple Strudel (Apfelstrudel)

If you make the gingerbread cookies or cake, make it ahead so it has a chance to get stale and dry or else you have to dry it out in the oven. Otherwise you can buy gingerbread cookies and crumble them in a big sealed bag or pulse them in a food processor or blender until you reach whatever texture you prefer. This is a great use for a picked-over, old gingerbread house!

For the dough-
1 cup (120g) all-purpose flour
Dash of salt
2T vegetable oil
¼ cup (59mL) water

For the filling-
2 ½ lbs Granny Smith apples (this can be 5 big to 10 small apples or about 1.1 kg)
1 Tablespoon lemon juice
⅔ cup (135g) sugar
1 teaspoon vanilla extract
Dash of salt
Dash of cinnamon
½ cup (75g) raisins
2 Tablespoons apple juice (or filling juice from your apples)
Old gingerbread cookies or cake to make 1 ⅓ cups of dry crumbs or 120g
6 Tablespoons (85g) butter, melted
Powdered sugar to finish

1. Mix flour and salt for the dough, then add vegetable oil and water. Stir until it comes together, then turn it out onto a lightly floured counter and knead! Keep it up for 10 minutes to build the gluten and form an incredibly silky

16

ball of dough. You will need that gluten later when you try to stretch the dough, so don't skimp on the kneading! Cover and let rest for 30 minutes or longer.

2. Meanwhile, prepare the filling. Peel, core and cut apples to ⅛ to ¼ inch slices and drizzle with lemon juice. Mix in sugar, vanilla, salt and cinnamon.

3. As the apples release juices, pull out 2 Tablespoons and put it in a separate, small, microwave-safe bowl with your raisins. If your apples are especially dry, use apple juice, another fruit juice, or even water or your favorite booze. Cover this bowl with plastic wrap and microwave for 20 seconds. Let rest, still covered, on the counter until you are ready for them.

4. If you haven't already, turn some gingerbread cookies or cake into dry crumbs. Take an old gingerbread house, gingerbread cookies, ginger snaps, gingerbread cake, or even some cinnamon graham crackers and smash them up in a bag or food processor. If they are not especially stale and dry, lay the crumbs spread out on a cookie sheet and dry them in the oven for about 10 minutes at 400 degrees F (200C). If they are crisp and dry, you can skip this step.

5. Now for assembly! Preheat your oven to, or keep it on at, 400 degrees F (200C) and have ready a large cookie sheet or jelly roll pan.

6. Lay two silpat mats or a large piece of parchment paper out on your counter and smack that resting dough right in the middle of it. Roll out your dough as far as the rolling pin can handle, probably around 12 inches by 12 inches (30cm by 30cm), but you're still not there yet.

7. Now with gently fisted hands (imagine guys throwing pizza dough,) lift and stretch one area of the dough at a time. Focus on one corner while the rest stays anchored to the parchment paper, then move on to the next corner or side. If a hole appears, just pinch it closed and keep on keepin' on. Eventually, you will have a big rectangle about 16 inches (40cm) by 20 inches (50cm) of smooth, translucent dough.

17

8. Brush or smear the stretched dough with about 2/3 of the melted butter.

9. When your rolled strudel is finished it will be about 13-14 inches long (33-36cm). So parallel to one of the short sides, lay the crumbs down in a thick line about a third of the way through the length of the dough. Crumbs should stay about an inch (2cm) away from the long sides and form a bed for your apples that is about 6 inches (15cm) wide.

10. Now fold raisins into your apple mixture, then use a slotted spoon to pile the apple mixture on top of the gingerbread crumbs. Leave any juices behind in the bowl and do not add them to the assembly.

11. Stretch the dough over the filling, starting with the inches left at the ends. Stretch and fold in ends, then shorter side, pulling the dough so it wraps tight but does not tear. Now use the parchment paper or silicone mat underneath to gently roll the strudel onto and over the rest of the stretched dough.

12. When done, keep rolling and position gently until the strudel is laying crumb-side down in the center of the silicone or parchment paper. Use the paper or mat as a sling and move the strudel with the parchment or silicone mat onto the waiting cookie sheet or baking pan.

13. Brush with the remaining melted butter and bake at 400 degrees F (200C) for 45 minutes to an hour. You'll know it's done when it's crisp and a deep golden brown.

14. It's okay if it leaked juice. Dust with powdered sugar to hide the imperfections before you slice and serve.

15. This can be served warm after at least 20 minutes of cooling or served cold after sitting at room temperature for about an hour and then refrigerating for about 3 hours, but I like to have it at room temperature. If you are waiting more than a couple hours to eat this, better cover and refrigerate it after about an hour of cooling on a wire rack.

Shrimp Spring Rolls

Makes 10 rolls. This recipe is wonderfully flexible, so use whatever veggies you have! And leave out anything you don't like. I have even made these vegetarian. The only ingredient you need is the rice paper wrappers.

½ pound (225g) of shrimp, cooked, peeled, deveined, tail off. Any size will do.
½ package or 7 ounces (about 200g) of rice stick or other Asian noodle
2 1/2 cups (about 200g) shredded iceberg or bibb lettuce, or any lettuce that'll have crunch but not sharp edges
⅓ cup (50g) shredded carrot
⅓ cup (50g) shredded red bell pepper
⅓ cup (50g) sliced cucumber
⅓ cup (15g) cilantro
3 sprigs of mint
1 green onion, chopped
1 package of at least 10 rice paper wrappers. These are at asian markets and come as hard, white disks that are 6 to 10 inches (15 to 25 cm) across.

1. If you are using very large shrimp, split them in half lengthwise. If your shrimp is frozen, thaw it in the refrigerator overnight. If you don't have time for that, you can take the shrimp out of it packaging and put it into a bowl with cold water. Put that bowl in the sink and let fresh, cold water dribble into it from the tap. Excess water will run off the sides and down the drain. With this method, the shrimp will be ready in 10 to 15 minutes. Do NOT use hot or warm water, this will promote bacterial growth and/or overcook the delicate shrimp.
2. Prep your work area with a colander or strainer nested inside a large, heatproof bowl, a wet cutting board, a plate

with a wet paper towel, a spray bottle with water that you would feel comfortable drinking, and a clear sink that is ready to receive the colander

3. Boil 2 quarts (2 liters) of water in a large-sized saucepan or stockpot. You will be using this water for noodles and for the wrapper, so the stiff, shelf stable wrappers need to be able fit into the pot. First, boil your rice stick or other noodles according to package directions, or until soft. The only way to know is to fish one out and bite into it! When noodles are ready, pour into your colander with the bowl under it to catch your hot water. Then pour the hot water back into the pot.

4. Put the pot of hot water back on medium heat to return it to a gentle boil. When the water is anywhere between simmering and gently boiling, you can start dipping your rice paper wrappers. Using both hands, dip the first half of the wrapper into the hot water for about 5 seconds, then hold it above the pot for another 3 seconds while you let it drip and cool off enough to touch. Next gently flip the wrapper and grab the soft, dipped side keeping it spread out and preventing it from sticking it to itself. It will be hot, but should have cooled off just enough to handle. Now dip the second side.

5. The wrapper may still be slightly al dente, but it will continue to soften as you work. So now that the whole wrapper has been dipped, lay it out as flat as possible on your wet cutting board, rewetting it with the spray bottle as needed.

6. Now, picture that you are building a burrito with two closed ends that will be see-through on the outside. Working quickly, pile ingredients in a tight log shape in the middle of the wrapper with the more showy ingredients on the outside. I lay down carrot and red bell pepper, then rice noodles, then lettuce and herbs, then shrimp on the very top. In total the ingredients of each wrap should be about a half cup or a big handful.

7. When you are ready to wrap, pull up the side closest to you, use it to compress the filling, then press it gently to

20

the side farthest from you. The wrapper will instantly stick to itself and will not gracefully come apart. Next fold in the short ends, compressing the filling before you stick, then tightly roll up to meet the last unstuck side of the wrapper. Don't be discouraged if this takes a little practice. You will get it quickly and have some deliciously ugly practice wraps.

8. When you finish each spring roll, put it on a wet plate under a wet paper towel while you make the others. These dry out super fast, so keep spraying them with water and keep covering them with a wet towel until you are ready to serve them. Because of this, I make them the day of the event, but early in the day and store them covered in the fridge.

Spring Roll Dipping Sauce

Everything tastes good with these! A sweet chili lumpia sauce, a sweetened fish sauce with chopped peanuts, asian salad dressing, miso-based sauces, but the following is my favorite.

¼ cup (60g) peanut butter
½ cup (125mL) canned coconut milk (not coconut cream!)
1 teaspoon curry powder and 1 Tablespoon sugar OR 1 tablespoon satay seasoning available at any Asian market
1 teaspoon fish sauce

1. Over low heat, add peanut butter to a small saucepan and stir until it starts to thin out and get softer.
2. Add just a splash of coconut milk and stir. When it is thoroughly blended, add the rest of the coconut milk and continue to stir.
3. When it is all combined and warm, turn off the heat, stir in the seasoning and the fish sauce.
4. Pour into a low, small serving dish and serve alongside your spring rolls. This sauce doesn't keep well, so make just before serving.

That's why I planned it so well, you know, to look natural. I covered my tracks. Everyone would think it was a blessing that came naturally at just the right time. If anyone did look past that, then it would still look like an accident, or even a suicide. And then, even if they somehow figured out that this blessing was planned, I could make all the crumbs lead to someone else.

Chapter Two

Will There Be A Wedding?

Smelling the mint and cilantro and checking the prices under a large, white canvas tent, Violet felt her phone vibrate in her back pocket, then immediately heard it start to ring. Before she had even finished wiping off the grit that had settled on her hands from the herbs, she knew it was her sister, Greta. They talked almost every day, or rather, Greta talked and vented and ranted, and Violet edged in the details that she needed Greta to know. With Greta and Violet both being hired for the wedding, and with their habit of helping each other with production, they were lately having informal phone meetings more like twice a day.

"Hi Greta," sighed Violet into the phone.

"Vi! Do you have any time today to drop by and help with all these flowers? I don't know what I'm going to do! And I have another referral for you, this job in Bee Cave. Oh, I have to find some more buckets!"

Greta, though a little dramatic and scattered at times, was a great florist who supplied other establishments with arrangements, but kept no storefront. It was perfect that she worked a lot of private events, so Violet's catering business and the floral business were able to feed each other with opportunities. Good thing the sisters got along and could help each other when things got stressful. This new alliance with Austin's elite would be good for both businesses.

It would be a stretch for Violet to make some time for Greta today, but she kept in mind that this was when Greta was getting most of her work done for the wedding. Their unspoken quid pro quo also meant that Greta would help

Violet in a few days when she really needed it. Greta's floral arranging would slow down and even stop right when Vi's 'crunch time' ramped up in the hours before each of the parties. Violet would help Greta now with floral arrangements and organization, then Greta would help Violet later with service, aesthetics, and simple cooking tasks.

Violet also guessed that Greta needed extra support because she was emotional about this wedding, even if Greta insisted that she was fine. Once upon a time, just before Greta's short and eventful marriage, Greta and Paul had been each other's first loves. He was quite literally the boy next door, and it looked perfect, at least from the outside.

Although their breakup had been mostly mutual and they had decided to just be friends, Greta had been devastated when it all ended. Greta wore her heart on her sleeve, so Violet had heard plenty about it when they broke up. She would probably hear about it this week, too.

Greta may need extra support during those times when her denial-laced frustration over the wedding came out in different ways. Making sure the floral arrangements were done a little earlier than normal or giving Greta a tad more time to get ready would go a long way to heading off Greta's stress. As Greta herself had once advised Violet, "Everyone wants to look good in front of an ex!"

"Sure," Violet conceded into the phone. "Did the special ordered shipment for the wedding come in today?"

"Yes! Windsor just dropped them off and it's like a jungle in here! And I barely have time to chop the stems and throw them in water before I have to go get Lindy! It doesn't help that they are especially tender flowers and --"

Greta kept talking while Violet smiled to herself. She laughed a little bit every time she heard her sister's delivery boy's name. He was about the farthest thing she had expected when she first heard the name Windsor. With long, stringy hair and a perpetual slouch, he was the antithesis of royalty. When she saw him, she just wanted to hold him down and cut his hair, or at least wash it, but then she would have to touch that mop. She was still learning to shrug off dirty and messy things

24

like that, so she smiled to herself again and waited for an opportunity to interrupt and encourage.

"Ok, I can be there in an hour," Violet said when Greta paused to draw breath. Rallying her spirits, she said, "I just need to stop by my place first. Can I bring you guys some of the cookies I developed yesterday? They are a chocolate, chocolate chip and oatmeal dough, then rolled in cinnamon and sugar. They don't have a name yet."

She didn't have to listen for the answer. She knew it would be a polite, but eager, yes. Greta had been an unabashed chocoholic ever since she had given birth and finalized her divorce within the first year of her whirlwind marriage. Her four-year-old daughter, Lindy, was perpetually underweight, but one of the only things that they could always get her to eat was cookies.

"Thanks, Vi. You are a lifesaver! I'm just so overwhelmed I can't believe there are just so many events so close together! And big ones! And -"

Violet listened to Greta's frantic rant as she jumped back over to the food truck to buy Jake some lunch, too. Then she threw her tote bags and purse into her little, white hatchback, cranked the AC, and headed east.

***

When Violet turned the key to the front door of her downtown-adjacent condo on East 5th Street, she used the bags she was carrying to push the door open. After wildly flipping her hair out of her face, the first thing she saw was Jake. They had been married since Christmas, but she was still seeing fireworks. Even just sitting there in the living room area at the other end of their long, narrow studio apartment, he caught her eye. His face and short, red military hair were lit by the screen of his laptop and he was wrapped up in finishing the thought he was typing. Despite writing on the computer, he had a pen dangling from between his lips like a lazy cigarette and papers strewn around him on the floor again. This untidiness drove Violet crazy, but it was also endearing, and she knew it was what she needed. She was slowly and laboriously getting used to his ways.

As Violet shuffled past their bedroom and office areas and slid the bags onto the kitchen island, Jake finished putting his thoughts down with a little flourish of his forearms, came out of his writing fog, and walked over to kiss her. He inched her small waist closer to him with walking fingers while she untangled herself from all the bag handles. He wrapped his arms tight around her back for just a moment before kissing her quickly and taking a half step back to look at her.

Glancing at the bags, Jake said, "Oh sorry, Vi, you should have texted me. I could have helped you bring stuff in!" He lovingly scolded her. "And sorry about the mess. I'll pick it up."

They both knew that he was referencing their argument about children and cleaning, but neither of them wanted to land on that subject right now.

"Thank you, but just… whenever you are done. And it's okay, there wasn't too much for me to carry," Violet sighed with relief.

Jake tried to justify the already excused mess. "Cool. I had to dig something out of my file of story ideas 'cause I got a great tip from Don today." He walked around, stooping to pick papers up and went on. "It was something from one of our old cases that worked perfectly into my new story, so I was glad to get it down on the page."

Don had been Jake's friend from his military days, and they had worked together as MP investigators. Now, both friends had chosen not to 're-up', but had settled in Austin to put down some roots. Jake had chosen the quiet life on Violet's near insistence, and Don was still working cases, but for the Austin Police Department.

"Really, it's okay." Violet was worried about getting too close to the subject, but she ventured another apology for their big argument. "You really have been good about cleaning."

Jake glazed past this and was quick to answer as he came back to the kitchen. "Thanks. Cool. Can I eat any of this, or is it going in the other fridge?"

She shot him a coy smile, then she pulled out the improvised package of spring rolls that she had brought home for him.

"Bless you! For a couple of cooks, we sure have nothing to eat around here." He took the two cardboard trays sandwiched together, leaned in and kissed her again for a little longer, and settled down on the bar stool across the kitchen island from her.

"Yeah, sorry. I cooked all day yesterday, but I didn't make real food. Just desserts and bread. I have been keeping both refrigerators kinda empty because I will need room in both for all this wedding stuff. But they are about to start getting really full with stuff you can't eat. How about the cookies I made yesterday, did you see them? Are there any left?" She asked as she whirled into the huge catering fridge to start stacking things in.

"Yes, to both. I had a few, but I made sure to leave you some," Jake reassured her and took a huge bite of spring roll. "Those were great!" he said through a full mouth, and Violet was suddenly glad that she was not looking at him and all his chewing noises.

"Thanks. So you wouldn't change anything about them?" She spoke up to be heard as she dug in the depths of the refrigerator.

"Hmm," Jake thought while he chewed. "I liked the cinnamon, but it made me remember that my mom is not the biggest fan. So when you write it down I would have more variety for the coating stuff."

"Ooo, thank you!" she gushed as she spun to face him and glided some of the cookies into a gallon Ziploc bag for Greta. Then she let her mind wander into cookie coatings. She loved Jake's constructive criticism. His discerning palate was a welcome compliment to her cooking skills. The catering business was really her baby, but he helped a ton. Thankfully his job as an author made it so he could also be her partner, waiter, and sous chef, but still provide a modest second income.

As he finished the last bite of sticky rice wrapper, he watched her put away some more of the produce she had

27

bought. "Those spring rolls reminded me of our first date. Remember that little Thai place that we walked to with that Yum Nuer?"

"Mmmm." Violet joined in reminiscing, and quickly squeezed his hand with a smile before going back to loading.

Jake had introduced Violet to Thai food, and now it was her favorite. She had been in culinary school at the time and was tempted to focus on her career and not spend her non-existent free time on dating, but he bowled her over. That first time he had taken her to Thai food, on their first date, she could already tell that her life would never be the same. And not just because of the food.

Jake asked, "So based on the bag of cookies, are you going to Greta's?"

"Yup," Violent answered, still dreaming of limey, Thai-flavored strips of steak.

"What do you want to do tonight?" he asked as he reached out to hold her hand.

"Cook!" she smiled as she slapped a huge block of mozzarella on the counter with the other hand. "But you can wait for me until I get back from seeing Greta if you want to. She needs help with the flowers she got in today, but I'll be back around dinner time. Should I pick up some food on the way home?"

"Well, can we eat this?" Jake held up the loaf of crusty bread that Violet had baked the day before.

"Sure! I thought about making it into those pesto turkey sandwiches that you love, but you can do anything you want with it."

"Ok, then I'll make those," he decided with a curt nod. "Should I make it with the prosciutto? Fried a little in the pan? Toasted?"

"Yes please! Thanks! You make those better than I do anyway. I think I just can't bring myself to add as much mayo."

"Thanks, and you're welcome." He gave her his crooked, sly smile that made her swoon. "Just call me when you're on your way home."

"Oh well, on second thought maybe you shouldn't wait for me," she admitted, returning from the fridge again and standing up straight. "I have no idea what kind of state Greta will be in. With the flowers or her feelings. She might trap me there for hours talking about Paul."

"Do you think she's going to be okay doing the flowers for his wedding?" Jake asked doubtfully.

"Yeah. I'm just going to have to hear about it a lot. The more nervous she is, the more she talks. She was kinda heart-broken when they broke up, but she has moved on. Or, at least, that's what she says." Leaning in a little, she went on. "I am not so sure about Paul though. When they are in the same room and we are all talking wedding, he almost stares at her!"

They exchanged knowing glances with raised eyebrows as Jake quipped, "Sounds like this could get interesting!"

***

Violet strolled through the parking lot, past the little box truck that Windsor always drove overflowing with fast food wrappers and the smell of pot, and into the person-sized door to the warehouse. With the evening sun pouring in the door behind her and all down her back, it took a moment for her eyes to adjust in the big, dark warehouse. She didn't find Greta in the big central room, or her little office that stuck off from that, so she swept aside the sheets of plastic that made a sort of curtain to the colder room in the back.

There was Greta lifting a huge bucket of water full of vibrant, raspberry colored foxglove onto a table. Violet admired her arms for a moment. Greta was shorter than Violet, with a little bit of a mom-tummy, but trim arms and hips from heavy lifting and genetics. Her dirty-blonde hair and pretty face, that was remarkably similar to Violet's, had not yet turned to see the new inhabitant of the room. Violet hated the term 'dirty-blonde', or 'sandy blonde', so she described her sister as 'caramel blonde'. This avoided any unpleasant word associations. Sure, it still made you think of being sticky, but at least it didn't evoke dirt.

29

Violet opened with, "Okay, what do you want me to do first?"

Greta jumped a little, surprising Violet with her surprise.

"Oh, hi!" Greta forced a smile. Violet knew her too well to not see the honest distress behind it. "I have to leave in ten minutes to get Lindy from preschool, so…"

Greta deliberated while she erratically turned in a circle. "The heuchera! You can find a shorter bucket or vase and get those in water first." She continued her frenzied rotation. "Oh, then can you handle starting on stripping the lower leaves off of everything? But you need to wear gloves and be careful when you work with the foxglove."

"Sure, that's easy." Violet smiled, only understanding which flower was which because Greta had been good enough to point. "Don't you need to start on the table arrangements?"

"Yes, but we'll have to at least start those together, so it will have to be when I get back." Greta continued with an exasperated whine. "Katy is also going to come while I am gone, and she needs some sit-down jobs."

Katy was Greta's only full-time employee while everyone else was seasonal or part-time, like Windsor. She was a petite, cheerleader-type who was fresh out of the horticulture program at Texas A&M and was entering her third trimester of pregnancy. She could no longer do the grunt work around the shop like she used to. Greta was still grateful to have Katy's help, but she had been used to getting to do more creative projects herself.

As Violet came back from the stock room with a square plastic bin, Greta met her at the sink, sounding as though she was continuing a previous conversation.

"And this foxglove is so finicky! It was wilted when it got here, but I think I've gotten it to spring back. Remember! It's poisonous, so wear the gloves on the shelf over there and wash your hands really well when you are done working with it. Twice, even!"

When Greta paused to think about the flowers again, Violet revisited the previous subject. "So how has Katy been feeling?"

30

"Good, I think, but oh!" Greta exclaimed and turned to Violet. "Remember how Windsor and Katy were dating a while back?" Greta said with the gleam in her eye that a woman gets with a juicy piece of gossip.

Violet caught on to the sudden change of topic. "Sure. Why?" Violet asked while slowly turning to meet her sister's eyes.

"Nope. They're not anymore. It turns out they have been broken up for months! And I couldn't tell because Katy is not even sad about it! That is why she hasn't really been acting different. And when I asked why they broke up she said it was because he found out that she was already pregnant!"

"Whoa!" returned Violet, while both sisters raised their eyebrows and retracted their chins to show that they were silently judging. "So what happens to Katy and their baby boy? I had actually thought there was going to be a wedding!"

The two sisters stopped talking and tried to not look suspicious as Katy herself walked in the door. Though only six months pregnant, her slight frame was already showing quite a bit and starting to look uncomfortable.

"Hey Greta, nice shirt! Violet, thanks for coming and helping us." Katy shimmied herself onto a stool and let her hands work on flowers as she gave the two sisters an abnormally white, vacuous smile. The sudden silence when she walked into the room seemed to go right over her head.

"H-how are you feeling?" Violet asked again as she considered this the best conversation chip to use with pregnant ladies.

"Good, thanks. I'm excited for this wedding! The flowers are going to be so pretty, and I love Laguna Gloria!" Katy squealed sweetly while sweeping her super straight auburn hair up into a top knot.

"When are you due again?" The only other thing that Violet knew she was supposed to say to expectant mothers. She was especially stumped for polite conversation as every pregnant woman reminded her of her ongoing argument with Jake.

"About three more months, thanks," Katy chirped.

Recapturing the subject, Greta changed topics again and again, talking about flowers, food, the schedule for the

31

wedding, her last meeting with Paul…and then Greta suddenly stopped talking and froze.

Violet looked at her. "What is it?"

Greta shrugged again and color flushed her cheeks. She used a vague pretext of some heavy lifting and pulled Violet into the fridge to whisper alone. "It will probably amount to nothing, but Paul called me today. When he said that it wasn't about the flowers, there was something in his voice! I said that I couldn't talk, but . . . he said that he would call me back!"

Violet shrugged with one shoulder, not catching the significance, so Greta went on. "What should I do? What do you think he wanted to talk to me about? When he said that it wasn't about the flowers, he sounded so…tender!"

When Greta said the last word of her sentence, she suffused it with all the alarm and over-analysis that she had retained since middle school.

"What do you think that means?" Greta would keep asking the same question in new ways until Violet ventured a response.

"I guess you have to talk to him!" Violet shrugged again

Greta scoffed and bounced her weight onto one hip like this answer was totally inadequate while her phone started trilling. After retrieving it from her apron and gawking at it, she cried, "It's him, it's him! Will you listen in? Please? I don't know what he wants to talk about!"

Violet leaned against a frigid shelf and judged her mandatory eavesdropping to be harmless. "Sure."

"Hey there, Greta," Paul purred over the speakerphone and, right away, Violet felt guilty for listening somehow.

"Hi!" Greta tried to keep it light, but also led him on to the subject at hand. "What did you want to talk to me about?"

"Well, I was just thinking about the good ol' days." Paul hesitated, but edged slowly closer to his real objective. "Seeing you lately has just . . . got me thinking, you know?"

"Okay." Greta used non-committal words, but her tone was sweet and submissive. Telling a boy 'no' had never been a skill that she had chosen to cultivate.

"Like, that summer in college." His words dripped with real fondness. "Greta, that was pretty great."

Greta smiled until she saw Violet's reproachful sneer.

"I…uh, I don't think you should be thinking like that right before your wedding, Paul." Again, Greta's words hinted at a no, but her tone beckoned.

"I know!" Paul was agonized, but went on. "But we had some great times. And then we ended so suddenly."

Greta and Paul let that comment hang in the sweet-smelling air of the brisk floral refrigerator while Violet silently paced and ridiculed

"What went wrong with us?" Paul asked, but before anyone could have answered, he added, "Well, I guess I'm saying that…you'll always be 'the one that got away.'"

Greta received this with an even deeper blush that showed through her tan cheeks. "Oh, stop!" Greta tittered with a laugh that said the opposite of her words. Violet drew her eyebrows together, stared Greta straight in the face, and shook her head meaningfully.

"I guess I gotta go. And you…" Greta still beamed as she signed off with Paul. "Get your head back in the game! You're getting married in a few days!"

"Riiight," Paul drawled. "See you soon."

"Whoa! What? But…what is he doing talking like that!" Violet sputtered as soon as she was sure the phone had hung up. She couldn't help but imagine the hassle of a cancelled wedding. Eating the same food for a week while it slowly went bad and endowed her pristine kitchen with rank odors. The idea of fighting to still get paid, by the client or even insurance, filled her with dread.

Violet realized that those thoughts were selfish and needlessly fed her phobias, so she directed her attention back to her sister and gripped her arms. "Uh, so what were you doing flirting? Wait, first, *is* there still a wedding?"

"Yes, of course there is still a wedding!" Greta waved off the question. "Paul just wanted to talk about old times! I told him it was a bad idea! He has made his bed and now he has to sleep in it."

"You didn't exactly say that! Not with your tone, at least!" Violet scolded. "And you didn't say…when you were dating

33

you just did not work in the real world! Remember telling me that? Have you ever told him that? I actually think you might have been too similar! You both can't stop flirting!"

Violet had to stop herself from yelling at her sister and continued in a falsely calm tone. "Why didn't you say anything about that?"

"It just wasn't the time, okay? Oh shoot! Time! I lost track of time, I gotta go!" Greta did a double take at her watch. "Will you still be here when I get back from getting Lindy?"

"Um, yeah, then I…we need to get to work." Violet pointed at Greta with the floral shears she had just picked up.

"Okay, I'll be good. I promise." Greta winked and jogged out the door.

Chocolate Oatmeal Snickerdoodles

Makes about 24 cookies.

Why choose one classic cookie, when you can have them all in one?

For the cookie dough-
1 stick of butter or 1/2 cup (113g), room temperature
½ cup (100g) granulated sugar
½ cup (100g) brown sugar
½ Tablespoon molasses (10g treacle)
1 egg, room temperature
½ teaspoon vanilla extract
2 Tablespoons (13g) Dutch-processed cocoa
⅔ cup (80g) all-purpose flour
¾ teaspoons cornstarch
¼ teaspoon baking powder
⅛ teaspoon nutmeg
¼ teaspoon salt
1 ⅓ cups (120g) regular rolled oats
1 cups (170g) semi-sweet chocolate chips

For the Snickerdoodle dusting-
1 teaspoons cinnamon
¼ cup (50g) granulated sugar

1. Preheat oven to 350 degree F (180C) with rack in the middle position and line at least two cookie sheets with parchment paper.
2. Cream butter, sugars, and molasses together in a large bowl with an electric mixer until fully incorporated. Mix in eggs one at a time, then add vanilla extract and mix until smooth.
3. In a separate bowl, whisk together cocoa, flour, cornstarch, baking powder, nutmeg and salt. Now add these dry ingredients to the bowl with the wet ingredients and slowly stir in.
4. When well mixed, add oats, stir a little, and set electric mixer aside. Fold in chocolate chips until oats and chocolate chips look evenly distributed.
5. In a separate small bowl combine cinnamon and a ¼ cup of sugar. Using about 1 ½ tablespoons (about 20g) of cookie dough each (or a heaping cookie scoop), form cookie balls, roll smoothly in your hands, then roll each ball in the cinnamon mixture and place on parchment paper lined baking sheets.
6. Bake each sheet for about 12 minutes, or until the cookies are almost done but still a little shiny in the middle. While one sheet bakes, prep the next sheet for the oven. If you run out of cinnamon coating, just throw together more.
7. When cookies come out of the oven, let them sit on the cookie sheet for at least two minutes to set, then remove with a spatula and let cool on a wire rack.

Alternate dustings-

The Purist
2 Tablespoons (13g) Dutch-processed cocoa

The Night Owl
1 teaspoon instant coffee powder or coffee substitute and ¼ cup (50g) granulated sugar

The Crinkle
2 Tablespoons (14g) powdered sugar

Pesto Turkey Sandwiches

Serves 4

8 slices of prosciutto
4 ciabatta rolls, sliced in half for a sandwich or large sandwich-sized pieces of focaccia
¼ cup (55g) your favorite basil pesto
¼ pound (about 100 to 125g) real provolone, sliced, or mozzarella, or fontina
½ pound (about 200 to 225g) of good quality deli turkey, sliced
2 large tomatoes, sliced through equator
¼ cup (about 55 to 60mL) of mayonnaise

1. In a heavy skillet (preferably cast iron) heat the prosciutto slowly until it just starts to crinkle and render some fat, then remove from pan and set aside for later. Turn heat up to medium high.
2. One or two at a time, toast ciabatta pieces, inside faces down, in the prosciutto fat until golden, crisped and toasty. Set aside. When done with all the bread, remove pan from heat.
3. Assemble sandwiches! For each sandwich, start with ¼ of the pesto, then one slice of provolone, next layer on ¼ of the turkey slices, 2 pieces of warm prosciutto, 3 slices of tomato, a second slice of provolone, then a thin layer of mayonnaise on the top piece of bread.
4. When all sandwiches are assembled, reheat heavy skillet

over medium heat and arrange sandwiches in pan. You can cook them in batches if needed. Now cover and weigh down the tops of the sandwiches with a second heavy pan, free standing panini press, pot, or even a foil-covered brick. When bottom bread is toasty and bottom cheese slice is melted, flip sandwiches over and repeat the process.

5. When all the cheese is melted and both sides of bread are golden and toasty on the outside, remove from pan and serve immediately.

Beef Waterfall (Nam Tok)

Serves 4. 30-60 minutes. This can also be made with 2 pork chops or 2 chicken breasts. Beef is what is traditional.

⅓ cup (80mL) lime juice
¼ cup (60mL) fish sauce
1 Tablespoon (12g) white sugar
¼ teaspoon ground chile (Thai chile if you can find it)
1 Tablespoon tamarind paste (optional)
4-8 leaves of mint or ¼ teaspoon dried mint
2 Tablespoons raw, dry jasmine rice (or 2 teaspoons toasted rice powder if you can find it)
¼ to ⅓ head of lettuce, iceberg is most common
⅛ red onion, sliced paper thin
1 Roma tomato, cut into crescents
¼ bunch of cilantro, roughly chopped
⅓ large cucumber, skin half-peeled or scored with a fork and cut into crescents
1 lb (450g) flank steak or high-quality steak, or other tender meat
Cooked jasmine rice, according to manufacturer's instructions, for serving

1. Combine lime juice, fish sauce, sugar, ground chile, and tamarind paste in a medium-sized bowl. When sugar has mostly dissolved, taste and adjust this dressing. (Remember to "know your audience" and adjust the heat with the ground chile accordingly. Jake loves spicy food and can take a lot more chile powder, but if Lindy will be eating too then I leave out the spice entirely and just put a small bowl of ground chile on the table when it is time to serve.)

2. Finely mince or chiffonade the mint leaves and add them to the lime juice mixture. Let them sit and mingle while you make everything else.

3. If making toasted rice powder instead of buying it, place your dry, uncooked jasmine rice in a small pan and place over low to medium-low heat. Gently shake the pan every 3-5 minutes to turn the rice kernels as they toast and turn every shade of brown. Do not walk away! After some kernels have turned golden-brown, the final transformation happens very quickly. Some rice will still be white, some tan, some brown, but they will smell nutty and toasty. When the darkest kernels are milk-chocolate brown, quickly remove the pan from the heat and transfer all the rice out of the pan. Grind this toasted rice in a food processor, mini food pro, or mortar and pestle to a fine grit. The biggest pieces should be $\frac{1}{3}$ to $\frac{1}{4}$ of a grain. (It sounds like a pain, but this is really what takes this dish from a homemade knock-off, to restaurant-quality satisfying.)

4. Prepare lettuce in your favorite way for a salad. I like to wash and tear it into bite-sized pieces. Transfer lettuce to the bottom of the final serving dish.

5. In a separate large bowl, toss together all the other veg. Red onion, tomato, cilantro, and cucumber can be combined and set aside.

6. Grill the steak. I like to grill this on a BBQ or on a grill pan, but you can also do this under your oven's broiler or in a cast iron skillet. Get your grill or pan or oven broiler screamin' hot, on full blast, then grill the meat on each side for 4-5 minutes. When finished it should be rare to

medium, but I aim for medium-rare. Set meat aside to rest for 5 minutes.

7. While your flank steak is still warm, slice it across the grain as thin as you can get it. You can push down hard with your holding-hand to help get paper-thin slices. Working quickly, slice all your meat against the grain, then throw it and any accumulated juices into your lime-fish sauce mixture and knead it into the dressing with your hands.

8. Next, pour this saucy meat mixture and a teaspoon of your toasted rice powder over your vegetable mixture. Gently toss the meat, powder, cucumbers, tomato, etc. Then, pour this whole salad over your lettuce in the serving dish.

9. Garnish with more toasted rice powder and/or chile powder and serve with cooked jasmine rice.

They'd never look at me. I even collected it from outside while my neighbor was tearing out the stuff for his new firepit. Then I saved a bit and made most of it into a tea for later, all while wearing gloves. I even went on a walk and put the gloves in another neighbor's trash barrel. They would never know that it was me who blessed all of them.

Chapter Three

Where?

When Violet finally ascended the last stair, dragged her feet down the hall, and slid open the door to her condo, all was dark and quiet except the hood fan light over the stove. That one spot acted as epicenter of the whole apartment. The light from there spilled through the kitchen, touched the office and living room, and barely filtered around the row of closets to show Jake in their bed. Violet sat gently on the edge despite her tired feet.

Violet noticed his eyes were shut and his mouth was slightly open before she walked away to eat her sandwich. Then she showered and brushed her teeth in the adjacent bathroom, because she could never be too tired to skip her religious hygiene, turned off the light, and slipped under the sheets next to Jake. She wrapped one arm over his chest as it slowly rose and fell. Violet enjoyed being with him even when he was sleeping. His profile was barely silhouetted by the little bit of light from his cell phone on the bedside table and the wireless modem in the corner. Everything else could wait 'til morning while she enjoyed this peaceful, perfect moment.

If and when they had kids, there would be no more moments like this. They would get tired. Tired from sleepless nights and tired of arguing with each other about dumb stuff like who should take the diapers out to the dumpster and how often. They would grow distant and cold. Looking at him in the dark, she didn't want to move away from him. She was not ready for the honeymoon to be over. She was convinced that she could stay like this forever until he turned his head in his sleep and she got a face full of hot morning breath. She frowned briefly and decided to change positions. Violet rolled over, snuggling her back up against him, and fell immediately to sleep.

As the Soma Vida art gallery opened to Violet's view the next afternoon, she was once again reminded of how well she would probably get along with Laurel. The times when they had met or talked on the phone were easy and fun but always cut short by interruptions, usually from Paul's over-involved mother. They had even exchanged knowing glances over their cups of ice cream while others talked over and around them, hijacking the wedding plans and twisting them to fit their own tastes. Violet remembered thinking that the girl was really cool and that, in different circumstances, they could be friends. Being Laurel's future husband's ex-girlfriend's sister didn't make Violet feel awkward around her, but it would be a significant hurdle for most women. So Violet had resigned herself to the fact that Laurel probably would not be reaching out to her as a friend.

But this venue, which had been chosen entirely by Laurel, made her lament the loss of the prospective friend afresh. Unlike the location of the wedding and bachelorette party, Laurel had been completely free from her mother and other relatives to pick the location for tonight's rehearsal dinner by herself. Laurel had wanted it to be an elegant, but intimate affair with just 'family, finger foods and fine wine and coffee'. This location was all her, and perfect for what she had described.

It was perched atop one of those up-and-coming neighborhoods east of downtown filled with young people and nightlife, much like Violet's neighborhood. Now, during the day, it was filled with hot, natural light from large west-facing windows, but tonight, as the sun was setting, it would be suffused with comfortably warm rays as the air conditioner had a chance to catch up. By the end of the party there would be romantic, distant lights from downtown skyscrapers. The space was sparse and airy, not showy and elaborate like the other locations for the week. It was a small art gallery with pieces of intensely modern art illuminated by halogen spotlights on each wall. A nook on the north wall held a short hallway that led to the kitchen area and a spare room with a couch and more art. Everything was white and simple, and modern but content.

Violet loved it. The art was clean and understated, like Rothko, and even more importantly, the space was clean. Even the baseboards had been meticulously vacuumed. She grinned and giddily pulled up her shoulders despite her arms being full with boxes of food. The menu she had chosen fitted perfectly into this scene.

"This is going to be great!" Violet squealed, imagining an elegant crowd gliding around perfect food, with lively, classical music, tinkling wine glasses and soft laughter filling the air.

"Vi," Jake called as he came in behind her, his arms full with stacked trays of food. "Where do you want the rest of the boxes and stuff?"

"Oh yes," Violet said channeling her mind back to her long to-do list as she forced herself to delegate. "Put everything in the kitchen, and then when we are done with things, we can hide them in that back room. Then maybe move this table over there and...put this one by the windows?" She signaled with outstretched arms. She imagined the rectangular, dark reclaimed wood table with the platters of food and the glass table with the espresso machine and ice buckets, but left the oval birch table for whatever wines would be at the party. "And I'll get in the kitchen!" Violet said with a glance and a whirl and disappeared through the swinging door into her domain.

Violet stood in the kitchen retrieving trays of the Holy Cannoli cups with honey and orange smelling sweetened ricotta in tiny shortbread cups lined with chocolate and pistachios. Then she sprinkled them with mini chocolate chips, added a garnish of a purple flower and a leaf that Greta and Katy had called curly dock on each, and rearranged them on white ceramic platters that took the top shelf of the refrigerator.

Greta laced the air with sharp balsamic as she lanced marinated cubes of mozzarella, sweet basil leaves, and cherry tomatoes alternatingly onto fancy looped wooden skewers to make the Caprese salad skewers, then laid them all parallel to each other on a bed of more curly dock leaves and flat-leaf parsley and left them out on the counter in case there was not enough room in the cold.

Jake plunged sparkling water bottles into crushed ice, ladled 'Sweetish' meatballs into already warming sweet-and-sour barbecue sauce that smelled tangy and spicy with high notes of vinegar and pineapple juice, ground up espresso beans with a noisy electric grinder, and took care of all the heavy lifting that Katy was not allowed to do.

Katy acquainted herself with her charge for the evening, the rented espresso machine. With her head down and concentrating, she set to work learning this particular model. Making practice cup after practice cup, she served them to the rest of the crew and filled the air with bold, dark, eye-opening aromas.

Other members of the evening's 'help' were the photographer and the sommelier. While the sommelier had been expected early, he had still not arrived. The photographer walked in the door, stiffly owning the room, and immediately Violet recognized the smug, square jaw and short, well-dressed figure of Michael Bohles.

Violet's spirit deflated like a ruined souffle as she muttered to herself. "Ugh, is he the photographer? I can't believe they hired that arrogant, short-man-syndromed, little..."

"Violet. Good to see you." Michael interrupted with authority after Violet had trailed off. "I will walk around getting a feel for the space and adjust my metering. I know that nothing too special has been planned, but please have the food out as soon as possible anyway so I can take photographs of it." Then Michael started walking around the kitchen, hallway, and then stepped into the spare room.

"'Nothing too special', my butt!" Violet whispered in a mocking tone under her breath. Even there she didn't like swearing. After culinary school had taught her to swear like a sailor, she had decided it was too unprofessional. She regained her composure, on the outside at least, by reminding herself that Michael had always felt threatened by her. In their small high school, they had been the two most well-rounded yet most academic students, sharing the title of valedictorian. Even before that, he had always tried to undermine her. After she had once, plenty nicely, refused to go on a date with Michael Bohles, he had been bitter. It didn't help that he was short, and that she was tall. It felt as though Michael thought they were rivals, but Violet just wanted to be left alone. After college, when she had announced that she would go to culinary school, he had softened a little.

"Oh, trying to get your M-R-S?" Michael had said with a dry laugh.

This was the only time in her life that Violet had slapped someone, but at least it got him to leave her alone. It hurt Violet a little bit more that culinary school was indeed where she had met her husband. Michael and Violet had not spoken or run into each other until he moved back to Austin and started a side business of photographing events.

When Violet noticed that Michael was still in the unused spare room, she called around the corner. "Where are you? No one will be going in there, Mike!"

"Michael, please," he corrected her, strolling into view. "And I need to be ready for anything." Despite what he said, Michael immediately turned to leave the spare room and went back out into the main party.

"Should I start setting out food so he can start taking pictures?" Katy was wide-eyed in the kitchen for the moment and helping however she could.

"Pfft! He can wait! We will NOT be taking our orders from him!" Violet sneered. Michael was one of the only people that elicited this kind of disgust from her.

Katy gently rubbed tiny circles on Violet's shoulder blade and gave her a kind smile.

"Sorry, it's not you." Violet apologized. "MIKE and I go way back," she cracked a little smile, glanced at Katy and conceded. "I guess the tartlet things can go out, it is close enough to the beginning of the party and they might even be better at room temperature."

"That sounds nice," Katy said, energetically taking the tray out of the refrigerator. "And now you have more space in the fridge!"

As she walked out of the kitchen, Katy took one step into the spare room with the couch and then turned back saying, "What was he doing in there? I don't see anything different."

Both sisters shrugged and Greta turned toward them to stir the meatballs. "Both of you just don't worry about him," she said. "He was just being a jerk as always!"

Violet took a deep breath and let it go as she slid the newly garnished 'foxy lox' with chipotle cream cheese and a thick cut of smoked salmon arranged into a curled rosette into the hole left in the fridge. Katy turned around, pushed the door with her back, and carried the tray of cannoli cups out to the party. This was it. In Violet's mind, the party starts as soon as the first foods get presented.

Finally, just before the guests started arriving, the famous sommelier that the family had hired for the entire weekend wheeled in a dolly of crates full of wine. He was a tall, willowy, African American man with short, buzzed hair and an amazing skin care regimen.

"Fhew! Sorry y'all," he said to Violet's team. "My boyfriend was having a crisis! But I'm here, I'm here!"

"Great!" Violet said, not knowing what else to say. "Uh, can I help you set up?"

"Would you? Where do you want me? You're a doll!" he said with a downward flick of the wrist and an about face of the wine dolly.

As they stood at the birch table, they spread a pristine white tablecloth, then set out bottles of expensive wines onto perfectly sized little dessert plates. As the sommelier set out various wine goblets and crystal wine stem markers, Violet took a step back.

"This is so lovely!" Violet realized with wide eyes and emphatic tones.

He whipped towards her, assessed her, bounced his weight

onto one hip, and said, "Yeah girl! That's how Pierre does it! I like you. Now, wha's your name?"

Violet stuck out her hand, smiled and simply said, "Violet Whitehouse." After a dead-fish style handshake from him, Violet asked, "Pierre?"

"Oh girl, that's my business name. But you can call me Peter. Cuz that's what I'm known for." He switched his hips and Violet decided she didn't want to know what he meant by that.

***

Some of the first guests to arrive were too familiar to be considered actual guests. Violet and Greta's parents came straight into the kitchen to check on them. Their slim, dark-haired mother, Barbara, wearing a white blouse and subtle pink sweater, poked her head around the corner first and announced her presence with a big smile and a twittle-wave of her fingers.

"Hi Mom!" both girls said and took turns hugging her. "You look really nice," complemented Greta.

"Well, thank you. You girls look lovely, too," Barbara returned.

Violet looked down at her sauce-speckled apron, pristine white button-up shirt and black slacks that were her standard caterer's 'uniform' and thought, *Eh, I guess so.*

"Hey, how's it comin'?" asked their father, Robert, as he ambled in through the kitchen door and took each daughter in one-armed hugs. His best blue button-up shirt was pressed and warm but stretched slightly over his belly and Violet slightly stepped on his 'dressy' cowboy boots as she repositioned her feet for the hug.

"Good," they answered at the same time, again.

Greta carried the conversation as usual. "All the cold things are about ready and we just entered crunch-time, so we are really swamped with warm food and last-minute touches."

"Well, that's lovely," their mother said with hesitation as she looked around at the counters. "But 'swamped?'" Barbara said, putting down her purse and taking a step forward. "What can I do?"

"We really don't need anything, so you guys should just enjoy," Greta shrugged. "Ooh, and tell us what you think of the set up."

Violet leaned in. "I want to know what is working and what we need to change next time. Really, everything from the menu choices to traffic flow and where everyone wants to hang out. You guys can be my spies."

"You got it." Robert bellowed and gently led his wife out of the kitchen and over to the buffet table while Violet and Greta turned back to their cutting boards, picked up their weapons of choice, and got back to business.

Pastor Schmidt and Dr. Glenn, the family's pastor and their life-long family physician, were in the party the next time Violet ventured in to set out hors d'oeuvres. The pastor was a rotund man with jowls and a three-piece tan suit who was patting his belly and eyeing the food. The doctor was rattling on in a British accent and a loose grey suit, his cane shaking with his knobby hands. Both men spoke loudly, the pastor because he wanted attention and the doctor because he clearly couldn't hear past his tangle of ear hair.

When Laurel's parents came in, a hush fell over Violet and her staff. Violet was standing still for once and taste-testing an espresso when Laurel's father strode in, tall and every bit the Scandinavian. He was holding hands with Laurel's mother, Carina. Between the caffeine hitting her bloodstream and Carina's Harry Winston platinum jewelry, Violet was breathless. Carina reminded Violet of Melania Trump in a timeless navy-blue dress, thick eyeliner, nude heels, and a disapproving gaze. She walked just like her daughter, confidently owning her hourglass shape. Before the spell had broken, Pastor Schmidt had snatched the couple up and trapped them in his corner with a colloquy about the charity that his congregation had planned for the holidays.

Before Violet knew it, the party was about to begin. Violet, Jake, Greta and Katy raced back and forth from the kitchen to the main room of the gallery putting out last minute garnishes, lighting the Sterno under the chafing dish, and arranging the ice in the big bowl to receive the platter of open-faced salmon sandwiches.

Michael was constantly fiddling with his camera in the setting sunlight. Pierre manned his wine table, schmoozing and pouring gracefully. The gray wood floors soon came alive with shuffling and creaking sounds as guests came, hugged each other, and distributed themselves standing next to the furniture.

Exactly fifteen minutes early was Paul's grandmother. Francesca Ann LeBaron was a short but dignified woman with every vertebra in its proper place. Her shoulders were back, but she kept graceful arms and softly folded hands. Her charcoal gray, raw silk skirt suit looked expertly tailored and her indigo shoes looked uncomfortably expensive and pointy in all the right places. When Violet had seen her a few times as a teenager, she had thought that Mrs. LeBaron spent money like it was going out of style, but apparently, she could afford it. Paul's aging grandmother still held the bulk of the family fortune and was clutching to that money and not going anywhere anytime soon, despite her age and heart condition.

Violet touched her own hair as she became envious of her naturally white-gray bob and purple square glasses. In Violet's busy patrolling of the room she paused next to Pierre.

"Mm! Look at those shoes! Where did she get those? I have to impress this one! We have a history, you know." Pierre animatedly whispered to Violet. "She got me fired once."

"No! Where?" Violet slipped into gossip girl mode so fast that she surprised herself.

"Oh girl, it all worked out though. She probably doesn't even remember me; it's been a minute. So now I get to knock her dead!"

"Yikes! Good luck!" She whispered back trying to match his tone as he suavely walked up to the formidable lady.

Despite being close, Violet did not hear what he said as he held out a small tray with a flourish and a solitary glass of wine.

"Oh please." Francesca turned on him and scolded slowly

while taking the goblet and looking down her nose at him, despite the fact that he was much taller than her. "Do at least try to act like the man that God intended you to be while in my presence. You don't need to prance around like that." Then, she curtly strolled away to talk to the other guests.

Violet's jaw hit the floor. She had no idea someone, let alone someone educated and refined, could be so mean! How could she be so rude? Especially to his face! Violet knew that people were still people who needed love and respect. Wasn't this lady a member of Pastor Schmidt's flock? Violet held fast to the idea that belief in the Savior should make you more loving, even of people making choices you didn't approve of.

Pierre came back to the table, head held high, tears were just starting to well in his eyes.

"I'm so sorry!" Violet could think of nothing else to say, so she offered help in the only way she could conjure. "The party hasn't really started yet, and there is a little room off the kitchen, would you like me to cover for you a minute?"

"Where? Oh. You are a peach," was all he said before walking calmly out of the room.

Soon afterwards Paul's mother teetered into the party on excessively high, gold metallic heels. The contrast between her and her mother was almost shocking. While Francesca LeBaron had looked polished and age-appropriate, her daughter looked like she was clawing down her youth by trying to hold on to it. Antonia LeBaron Jorgensen wore a flashy, clingy red dress and her dyed blonde hair and collagen curled lips made Violet wonder how much it must cost to look that cheap! Her husband, with a plastered smile and fresh hair plugs, accompanied her as they made their entrance and came to get a glass of wine.

"Violet!" she said as she moved in to kiss the air next to her neighbor's daughter's cheek. "How is everything? Are we ready? Oh, and where is Pierre?"

"Oh, Peter. Uh, Pierre?" Violet asked, matching her hostess's tone before realizing it, quickly straightening her throat, and then continuing in a voice that sounded more like her own. "Sorry, he just got here and is still concentrating on setting up. But we are all doing great, and he will be right back."

"You're a dear. He is an old friend too, you know? Yes… he used to be the wine buyer at our club, until my mother got him fired over a big misunderstanding." She rolled her eyes and touched her manicured fingernails to her highlighted collarbone while they both turned to look at Mrs. LeBaron. She was critically tweaking the flowers in the arrangement closest to the door and making disapproving faces as she drank her glass of wine.

"But now he is more fabulous than ever! He is even a major sommelier in Paris during the tourist season, so, of course, I insisted that we hire him for the wedding!" Mrs. Jorgensen bragged. "I don't think my mother even remembers him."

"Cool!" Violet replied, then immediately regretted sounding so juvenile. "He has had the menu for more than a week, so I am sure he has some great pairings for you to try tonight."

"That's wonderful, Dear. Must make the rounds, you know. But thank you so much!" Mrs. Jorgensen cooed as she raised a bare shoulder, turned, and started greeting the closest guest.

Violet turned to see Jake leaning in the doorway to the kitchen, gave him a wide-eyed look and mouthed "Whoa!" then saw Pierre scoot around him and sway back into the room, oozing confidence once again. Pierre was stopped by Antonia and Violet could just make out him saying, "Just setting out the last exquisite bottle, hon," he spoke with lots of hand and facial gestures, showing off his delicate hands and gleaming white teeth. "Everything is ready and gonna to be amazing up in here!"

Foxy Lox or Lox with Chipotle Cream Cheese

Makes 4 mini bagels or big crackers. If you can't find canned chipotle chiles in adobo sauce, you can use a tablespoon of chipotle chilli paste or flakes

8 ounces cream cheese (220-230g soft cheese), room temperature
1 chipotle chile in adobo sauce, canned (one chile, not one can)
1/2 teaspoon of the adobo sauce
4 mini bagels or small pieces of pumpernickel, or 4 melba toasts or pumpernickel crackers (I get rye crispbread from Ikea)
6 ounces (150-200g) cold smoked salmon, kept long but cut into strips only about 1 ½ inch wide
2 Tablespoons chive or green onion, chopped fine
4 Tablespoons non-pareil capers or a few gherkin pickles

1. Finely chop chipotle piece and stir into cream cheese, then refrigerate for at least 1 hour, but can be done the night before to save yourself some grief.
2. When ready to assemble, toast bagels or bread if using. Bring cream cheese back to room temperature for at least 20 minutes.
3. Thickly spread or pipe bread or cracker with cream cheese, then arrange smoked salmon in a coil around a chopstick or skewer, starting with the wider end of the strips if one exists. Each cracker should get about 4 thin strips of salmon. Hold the loose end of the wrapped salmon and quickly stand upright on toast or cracker. If you want it to fill the surface of the cracker and look more like a flower, pull outer edge out and make it unevenly lay down and ruffle like the outer petals of a rose.
4. Garnish cracker or toast edges with capers or gherkins, then garnish top of coiled salmon with green onion or chive.
5. Serve very cold. Arrange on a chilled platter and serve immediately or set out on a plate that is over a bed of ice if it is going to sit for a while, like on a buffet.

It was ready. Ready for any time that I chose to use it. For the first time in a long time I felt powerful and in control. I could wait and find the perfect time to bless all of them.

Chapter Four

What Happened?

After a few last touches and some extra elbow grease from Violet, the party was actually ready just in time for the bride and groom to glide in the door. Paul looked the same as always -- lanky with dark eyes and fashionably curly dark hair, but now with a borderline goofy smile. He wore a dark grey suit and a pastel tie that matched Laurel's barely peach dress and earrings, not to mention the unmistakable flush in both of their cheeks, chins, and necks. What had just been happening? Violet was glad he was so deliriously happy, and it made her smile, too.

Paul's soon-to-be-wife was just as happy, floating around the room to kiss relatives. She was radiant. Violet had only met her once in an AC/DC t-shirt and ripped jeans, her naturally olive skin peeking through her 'favorite outfit', but tonight she was simply elegant. Her chin-length, angled milk chocolate brown bob was styled just right to match her tailored satin shift dress and kitten heels. She held a tiny, tasteful clutch and her beloved's hand. Clearly she had tastes more in line with her grandmother-in-law than her mother-in-law. Laurel waved across the room to everyone individually, including the hired help, so even in this moment it was clear that she was much more kind than her grandmother-in-law. Laurel's wide smile was so genuine, always, that it was warm and charming, but commanded the room's attention. Soon a relation pulled Laurel away from her greetings and Violet went back to the kitchen to get a towel.

When Violet emerged a minute later to wipe the food table for the second time that night, Luke suddenly appeared at her furiously working elbow. The groom's brother had never been her style, but he was definitely handsome and put a lot of effort into being charming.

"Violeeeeet, what's going on?" Luke murmured, too suave to be sincere.

"Hello Luke," Violet said more to the table than to him. "How are you?" she asked, to be polite, but didn't really want to hear about the latest rehab or girlfriend.

He had a curious combination of having nice clothes, but also looking like he didn't know how to wear them. Tonight he wore an expensive black velvet suit, but didn't wear a tie and had the top button undone. His long hair and perpetually smiling eyes had made half of the girls Violet's age melt in high school, even though he was a year younger.

"I'm back in town. We should get together," he rumbled in a half whisper, then bit his bottom lip.

Violet furrowed her eyebrows, cocked her head slightly to one side and said, "You remember I'm married, right?"

She looked at him for the first time as he raised his hands and shoulders innocently and said, "Hey relax. Bring him along!"

Luckily they were interrupted. The group had finally organized themselves, and Pastor Schmidt was asked to say a prayer. The portly man had stood up, buttoned his suit over his protruding belly, and was tinging the wine glass in his hand to quiet the room. He offered a well-planned prayer in a deep voice laced with a little extra modulation and showmanship. When it was over, the crowd descended on the food before the pastor could waddle back to his chair in the corner.

Violet escaped from Luke to the doorway of the tiny hallway and watched for a moment with wringing hands to see which foods were most popular, which ones needed to be replenished, and which dishes she need never serve again. After bringing out a second tray of cannoli cups and a third dish of meatballs, the merriment evened out to find its equilibrium. Violet retreated again, leaned against the wall in the little hallway between party and kitchen and took a moment to breathe.

Laurel and Paul unclasped hands for the first time that night and finally got to sample some of the food. Every time they tasted something they liked, they offered the second bite to the other person. It would have been sickening if it wasn't so cute. Finally, the room stopped watching the couple when Laurel disappeared, presumably to visit the ladies room.

Violet realized she was still smiling as Katy noticed Violet's relaxed hiatus. Katy gave her a bright, sincere smile then walked over with a tiny white mug on a saucer.

"Ready for another one?" Katy gently moved Violet's hands to cradle the saucer. "Things have slowed down over here, so I think I'll have one too."

"Good!" Violet remembered. "Definitely make sure you are resting enough. But are you allowed to drink that?"

"Just a little one." Katy winked. "I can have one coffee a day."

Katy waddled back to the espresso machine as the formidable Francesca announced, "I'm ready for my espresso now."

Although she hadn't said it to anyone in particular, Violet started forward, anxious to please, but noticed Antonia spring into action. Katy just finished brewing and hadn't even gotten to accompany the cup with a saucer when Antonia snatched the cup out of her hands.

"Oh, but..." Katy protested weakly.

"My mother is ready for hers," Antonia muttered over her shoulder at Katy and the espresso machine left in her wake. This was apparently enough of an explanation to silence Katy and send her back to her grounds and steam.

As Violet took a few tentative sips, Antonia suddenly stopped. She stood for a moment, watching her mother as Violet watched her. Francesca was in what she considered a conversation but could only be described by onlookers as a lecture, with Pastor Schmidt about finances. Something in their conversation made Antonia visibly pause right there in the middle of the room, passing the cup from hand to hand with visible agitation.

Just then, Paul walked past Antonia looking puzzled. He

had gone pale and looked lost in his own party.

"Oh, Paolo, Dear." Antonia had to shake his arm to get Paul's attention, but when she did, he looked relieved to have been distracted from his train of thought. "Paolo, could you take this to your grandmother? I'm not sure if I'm ready for her brand of socializing right now."

As Violet watched this scene and quickly drained her cup, the quick movement of Luke downing the bottom of his wine glass attracted her attention. It seemed like his suave exterior was a little too forced at the moment, so Violet continued to watch him as he slinked around the edge of the room. Violet knew what someone looked like when they were trying to be invisible because she employed the same tactics regularly. He was gliding, watching, not speaking, but mildly smiling, skirting the rim of guests.

Violet knew that he had gotten in trouble several times but had always escaped prison, although she hadn't known any of the particulars. Could he be getting into trouble right now? Or maybe trying to get one of the bridesmaids to get into trouble with him? At his brother's rehearsal dinner? Didn't he care at all about his family? Violet scoffed and was about to shrug it off as Luke finally stopped next to Dr. Glenn. Luke stood there looking too natural and bouncing his leg on a toe while Dr. Glenn finished what he was saying.

"Ah, yes, yes, I remember now. He wanted me to have a butchers so quick sticks that I, that I had to give it some more welly and..." Dr. Glenn droned on in his raspy, breathy British accent that was surprisingly loud, even after Luke reluctantly cleared his throat. Finally, Luke moved into Dr. Glenn's line of sight and gave him raised eyebrows.

"Quite right. Excu - excuse me, I have to see to a patient." Dr. Glenn headed straight for the nervous groom's brother where Luke spoke in hushed tones for several seconds.

Could Luke be sick? The aging doctor acted as if he knew why Luke had needed to talk to him, maybe even like they had already arranged to meet up during the party. Violet hated that her mind immediately assumed it was an STD.

Violet didn't want to know, but she found that her curiosity wouldn't let her look away. Practically everything Luke did was gossip-worthy, and right now it looked like he was up to something. Did Luke need something from Dr. Glenn? Did Dr. Glenn need something from Luke?

As Violet continued to watch, Dr. Glenn reached into his pocket then slowly and shakily handed a small, white square to Luke, which Luke immediately slipped into his coat pocket. When his hand returned, it shook Dr. Glenn's hand again.

Wait, was there money in that handshake? Violet wondered, but had no way to know. She replayed the hand-offs in her mind, but to no avail. Had Dr. Glenn just handed Luke paper? Perhaps a paper envelope containing something, like drugs? Or did she have it the wrong way around. Maybe it was a tiny envelope of money and Luke had given Dr. Glenn something secretive.

It better not be illegal! They are not going to ruin this party for me! She thought until the scene was disturbed.

Francesca LeBaron, Luke's grandmother, came forward out of the crowd and gracefully took Luke's bent elbow. She set down the espresso that she had been holding and locked both of her hands around his bicep. Although she was in the position to be led, it was clear through body language that she was the one doing the leading. Right towards Violet and the hallway she stood in.

"What just happened?" Francesca asked coolly. When he didn't answer, she calmly brought him back to the small hallway, past Violet, and up to the door of the little storage room in the back and in an ice-cold voice said, "Open the door, Luke."

Violet resumed her work and went to the kitchen, but their actions had settled it. Something was definitely going on. As she prepped more food, Violet tried to hear what Mrs. LeBaron and Luke were saying in the room next door despite the loud din of voices from the party.

Luke and Francesca said almost nothing before they entered the little room calmly with stiff composition, letting the door close behind them. Violet thought that was the end of it, but it was just the beginning. As soon as the door had closed, the old lady began an animated rant. Words could not be distinguished through the wall, but the muffled sound was clear to anyone in the kitchen or short hallway.

For almost ten minutes they yelled. Violet made sure that no one from the party came near by posting Jake at the entrance to the hallway. The only people that knew about their argument and had their spirits dampened were her staff. Katy and Violet stood silently shoulder to shoulder, setting food on trays and garnishing as they tried to listen in.

What was Mrs. LeBaron yelling about? Was she angry, anxious, or afraid? Were they working together? Any or all of them could be working together. Or two of them could be working against the other one, but who? It was very possible that Dr. Glenn or Mrs. LeBaron could be engineering the situation, but Luke was too harmless and dumb.

Finally, Francesca came out first, smoothing her raw silk suit and raising her chin. Right behind her, Luke meandered out looking care worn and languid. She stood serenely stoic as Luke retrieved her espresso, handed it to her, and tried to light a cigarette before Violet interjected.

"Oh, we can't smoke in here!"

Luke leveled his eyes at her and looked almost murderous as he glared at her, then, without a word, he swiftly walked out of the party and presumably outside.

Within five minutes, Paul's grandmother was back in the hallway. Katy had rejoined the party and now Greta stood washing dishes behind Violet, who was just grabbing another towel to frantically wipe another table.

Panting a little, Francesca asked without invitation as she came into the kitchen, "Please bring me a glass of tepid water. The water out there is much too cold." Her words made it sound like a request, but her inflection seemed to say, 'NOW'. The not-as-grand lady continued and sat on one of the kitchen stools, again without being invited, and began slipping medication out of her purse and into her slightly shaking hands. Somehow, Francesca seemed smaller than usual.

Violet was worried. She wasn't liking the party. Violet realized her priorities were in the wrong place when she noticed how rattled she was. Violet was reluctant to leave her on the high kitchen stool by herself, even though she had asked for water.

"Water. Room temperature." Francesca said again, more as a demand than a request, this time boring with her eyes into both occupants of the kitchen in turn.

"I will," Greta said as she turned to get a piece of stemware that had just been washed and put her back to them at the sink. Greta let the sink run for a few seconds, presumably letting the water get colder, then eventually slowly turned around with a goblet half full of water.

As Greta presented the glass, she made a concerned face and asked, "Is it your heart? What happened? Do you need your doctor?"

The family physician was currently in the party behind Violet, eating meatballs and congratulating the happy couple in a long, rambling speech that somehow ended on the subject of him 'putting a fiver on his slate at the pub' decades ago in London.

"No, no, don't fuss." Mrs. LeBaron dismissed Greta's concern with an upturned chin and a noisy gulp of water. Violet had heard about Paul's grandma's heart condition but had never seen it in action. Apparently, it was completely controlled with medication and a healthy lifestyle, as well as frequent and intensive visits to the doctor. Gathering up her purse and turning away from the kitchen counter, the rich, old lady asked, "But where can I not be disturbed for a moment?"

Violet interjected. "Uh, there is another smaller room over here. We have some things stored in there, but there is a couch if you want to use it."

"Perfect," Francesca said with the air of making an executive decision. "But don't come in. I want to be able to have some peace for an hour or so."

"Yes, ma'am," the sisters said in unison without a hint of irony. Then, as the door closed behind the slow moving, usually spry woman, they turned to each other.

"I hope she's okay! What was her heart condition called again?" Violet asked in a half whisper.

"I don't remember, actually I don't think I've ever told you, because I can never remember it myself. But she'll be fine. If she needs us, we are right outside the door, and her doctor is in the next room."

"And we need to prep the next plate of lox! And why are you not at your water station?" Violet began to stress again as she pushed Greta back out into the party.

"Relax. Katy said she could take care of the whole drink table now that the initial rush is over. So I made your next plate of lox before I started on the dishes." She turned to retrieve a platter out of the art gallery's fridge and turned back to Violet as if to say *you're welcome.*

"Sorry. You're right. Thanks," Violet admitted, and rushed out the doorway into the chatty party.

After wiping and replenishing the tables, Violet took a corner and began surveying the room again.

Dr. Glenn was still talking about the pub from his youth in ancient history. "Wh-what was it called again? The Fox and Hound? The Horse and Hound? Ah well. I-In my day the world and his wife would go every time they got a few quid, but now it's some bloody charity shop."

Luke was chatting up a beautiful girl that must have been Laurel's sister. Evidently he would survive Violet's rejection.

Antonia was laughing much too loudly with a sloshing glass of wine in her hand. She wailed. "I couldn't believe it! I said, 'No, the wedding has got to be somewhere nicer than that! I mean you deserve somewhere fabulous!'"

Pastor Schmidt was still planted in the chair she had last seen him in, with her parents standing on either side of him, lightly laughing into their goblets of sparkling water.

Paul and Laurel stood, permanently attached at the hand once again, and chatting with guests. It was barely noticeable when Paul turned to Laurel, said something, and handed her something that looked like a small white square.

What was with all the little white squares? Was that what Dr. Glenn handed Luke, a teabag? Violet doubted her own memory now.

Katy walked across the path of her eyes, rubbing her hands

on her apron, when Laurel reached out to touch her arm as she passed.

"Excuse me. Do you know if Mrs. LeBaron is alright? Will you please bring her an herbal tea?" Laurel asked pleasantly as she handed Katy what must have been a tea bag all along.

"Yes, ma'am," Katy said, dipping her face away from Laurel's before turning back to the espresso machine for some hot water.

Violet noticed that Paul had a strange look on his face again. Somehow blank and mournful, but he soon pasted a smile back onto his face and could almost pass for normal.

Violet shrugged it off and channeled her brain back on what was really important - her apparent planning failures. She deeply regretted Mrs. LeBarons discomfort and resolved to do more research into her important clients' preferences next time. If there ever was a next time! She was quickly losing her chance at cracking into Mrs. LeBarons set of people as future clients. She kicked herself for not including herbal tea as one of the beverage options for the evening.

Just then, she noticed that the saucer under one of the wine bottles was almost full of spilt wine, so she ducked into the kitchen followed closely by Katy carrying a steeping mug. As Violet wet another clean rag and squeezed it out over the sink, she was barely aware of Katy quietly opening the door into the room where Francesca LeBaron had commanded that she not be disturbed.

"Yikes!" said Katy a minute later when she backed out from the doorway of the spare room empty-handed. "Don't go in there! She really let me have it! She, like really, didn't want anyone to come in."

"Ooh sorry. I guess I didn't tell you!" Violet apologized. "She told us that she didn't want to be interrupted but I guess you weren't here when she said it. What happened? Are you okay?"

"Oh sure. I may be pregnant, but I can still take someone hollering at me!" Katy flashed a super white smile and bounced with surprising energy back out to the party.

Right at an hour after Francesca had commandeered the

storage room, Violet stood outside the door that she had been warned not to open. The rehearsal dinner was just starting to wind down, and it was time to start putting things away and cleaning up. This meant that Violet needed several boxes that she had left in that spare room. Katy had already gone in once and had apparently gotten an earful in return. As she stood still and deliberated, two people started a conversation in a heated whisper around the corner. Obviously they did not know she was there.

"Look, we had our chance."

"Just talk to me! Let me call you. I need to know that we didn't make a mistake."

"I don't think..." said the voice that Violet suddenly recognized as Greta's. Violet's mouth gaped as she hugged the wall and kept listening.

"Let me take you to lunch. That little place where we first kissed is still there!" Paul cajoled. "The weather's great. We could even sit at the same table, maybe recreate-"

"Paul! You are getting married in two days!" Greta's voice finally seemed to gather some gumption and resolve.

Paul pressed and almost whispered, "Then it's now or never. We only have this one...last...chance."

A split second of silence was punctuated by the sound of lips being unexpectedly separated from a kiss.

"I guess you've had some wine!" Greta joked then, sobered and straightened her throat. "We didn't work. We never worked. Even when everything was perfectly in line for us, we fought. We were just kids in college and we still fought all the time! We couldn't agree on anything, especially the big decisions! We wanted different things. We still want different things.

"The only thing we have is that we find each other attractive." Greta's determination seemed to waiver, until she shot out again. "That is not enough to build a relationship on!"

"I knew you still had feelings for me. What happened to us?" Paul sighed. "I am not saying I am not getting married, and I'm not saying I don't love Laurel, because I do."

Greta scoffed.

"All I am saying is that I would like some closure between us," Paul pleaded.

Violet hung on every word. She knew she shouldn't eavesdrop, but she was already in the thick of it and did not want to interrupt a conversation that seemed like it was going to resolve itself if left to continue.

"Look, Paul," Greta hissed in a calm whisper. "Whatever you are feeling now is just jitters. When things ended between us, you thought it was a good idea. It *was* your idea!"

"But…" Paul tried to interject but was cut off by Greta.

"We did not work. I do not have feelings for you anymore. You love Laurel. She loves you. Everything is working out for both of us." Greta paused to let her words sink in. "You say you love Laurel. Do you feel more for her than you feel for me?"

"Well…yes," Paul said cautiously, as if it would cause hurt feelings.

"Then that's your answer!" Greta emphasized, then sighed. "Don't worry. You are making the right decision marrying her."

"Yeah, I know." Paul sighed, then muttered with shame in his voice, "I guess it might have just been cold feet, but you are such a good friend."

"And I will stay your friend. Now go marry that beautiful, smart girl that is crazy about you and has more money than she knows what to do with!"

"Hey, that's not the reason…"

"I know, I know. It's not about the money. Just get out there!" Greta finished and pushed him back into the party.

Violet still stood frozen to the spot. Should she go hug her sister after what was obviously a tough conversation? Should she run away, maybe into the spare room, to not let her sister know that she had been listening? Should she look busy and pretend she couldn't hear their conversation? It was no good. Greta took a step farther into the little hallway and saw Violet. She started slightly, then sighed and started to tear up. All Greta said was a languid, "Hi."

Vi took a step forward and scooped her sister up into a hug.

They hugged for a long moment while Greta regained her composure. Only two tears fell onto Violet's shoulder before Greta gently pulled back, wiped under her eyes, sniffled, and said, "Okay…okay."

"Are you okay?" Violet asked, handing Greta the wiping towel she had tucked in her apron tie. Mentally she reminded herself that tears were not dirty, so she had no reason to be thinking about them being on the yolk of her shirt.

"Yeah. I just…yeah. It was just weird, ya know? I guess it's good that it happened, like for closure, but WEIRD." Greta took in a long shuddering breath. "He thought he still had feelings for me!" She went on to recount almost the whole conversation word for word. Greta knew that Violet had heard it all, but it was her way of dealing with the new information and old feelings.

By the time they were done rehashing, over-analyzing, and venting about what happened, the party was breaking up. The bride and groom were getting another round of hugs from guests that were once again holding their purses but walking less stably than when they had arrived.

"Sorry, we can keep talking, but I have to start cleaning!" Violet apologized as she turned, grabbed the doorknob, and walked into the spare room.

A virtual wall of warm air hit Violet in the face like she had opened an oven door. What happened in here? The dark, moist stench of vomit met Violet and sent her reeling back. Her skin felt like it was trying to crawl up her scalp and the back of her wrist instinctively flew to her nose. Questions flew to her mind and hung in the dank air around her head. *Who would puke in such a clean, lovely place?* and *why would they ever . . .* But she brushed them aside and flipped on the light. Francesca LeBaron was slumped down on the couch with her head back at a grotesque angle. Her eyes were open and glazed over. Her mouth gaped. She was dead.

Violet instinctively yelled for Jake and flew to the dead woman simultaneously. She tried to grab an arm to move her, but it was cold. The smell of vomit was much stronger now and it kept her from thinking clearly. Her mind whirled and she didn't know what to do. All she wanted to do was clean it, fix it, make it stop. In her panic, she wanted to do something, so she hysterically began CPR.

Ignoring the cold of the arm, she pulled to get the lady onto the floor. Francesca's glasses and one shoe fell with a clatter, but Violet didn't notice. She checked for a pulse and when there wasn't one, she did a few chest compressions then went to breathe into the once so formidable lady's mouth. She swept away a bit of food that was still there, pushed past the even more potent smell of stomach acid, plugged the woman's nose and sealed her mouth around the cold, lifeless lips. She only managed two breaths before Jake was there, he went to feel for a pulse too, but immediately pulled back and moved to stop Violet. He swept her back with his strong arm around her waist and whispered very close to her ear, "Please stop, STOP! There is nothing else we can do."

Violet disintegrated into tears from fear and confusion and frustration, but mostly from disgust. She dry-heaved in the persistent aura of sick and death and filth. Her frantic noises drew other people, first from the kitchen, then some guests from the party before Greta shoved everyone out of the kitchen. Through the door's muffled sounds, Violet heard Greta start to take charge.

Greta was always a calm and collected leader, never one to lose her head. "Katy, sit down and call an ambulance, and Dad, go get Dr. Glenn…then RUN and get him at the elevator! Everyone else please stay in the main room and our staff will get this sorted out. There has been a bit of an incident, so I think we will all need to stay here for a while until we sort this out."

Jake stayed with Violet and spoke so calmly that Violet couldn't understand how he could be so cool and even. She could still smell the vomit as if it clung to her, but now the long-term implications started to settle on her like sprinkled parmesan. Jake was holding her and making soft sounds simmer in her ears, but Violet increasingly thought of their business. She was ruined! They were ruined! Goodbye fancy parties with Blue October. Goodbye charity galas and hired staff. Goodbye dreams of a house and a dog and…

Violet reeled again. She was not going to think about that right now.

Slowly, Jake led her out of the room and over to a bar stool in the kitchen where he knew she would feel comfortable. Although she had stopped gagging, Jake continued to hold her and stroke her hair until she could sit on her own and get some fresh air.

He only left for a moment to open a window, and as Violet gulped in the cool, clean air, Jake must not have known what to say. "It's ok, it's ok. Can I get you a glass of sparkling water?"

Seltzer water was Jake's cure for everything, but in this case 'the Jake specific' sounded perfect. Before she could even answer, Katy came through the door with Violet's mother. Katy had her cell phone in one hand and sparkling water in the other. Barbara held another glass of seltzer and was leading Katy to the stool next to Violet.

"This is for you, Dear," said Violet's mother, handing over the goblet she had brought with her. "Are you alright? It must have been terrible to find a…body."

Violet almost felt guilty that the part that had bothered her the most had not been the body, or the fact that someone was dead. The death was sad and surprising, but mostly she was disgusted and regretted the mouth-to-mouth. Someone else's mouth, someone else's vomit, someone else's germs! It was too terrible for her to think about. She had taken a CPR class, thinking it was a good thing for a caterer to know, but the idea of someone else's mouth had bothered her. The thought that it was worth it to save someone's life had gotten her through the aversion, but to do it for nothing? For it to not even work? For it to be a mouth that was so rank and awful? She had to get her mind on something else, but there was little chance of that. She just continued to take deep, slow breaths and concentrated on her seltzer water.

Katy raised her left arm a little and flapped at the wrist to quiet the room and get everyone's attention as she still held the phone up to her ear with the other hand.

"911 says to not let anyone leave and to have everyone stay away from the body."

"I guess a detective is coming," Jake said to himself. "That's standard procedure."

"What?" said Katy to the room instead of the phone, looking confused.

"Why?" interjected Greta. "Wasn't it her heart condition? I mean it's obvious!"

"Even if it was!" Jake tried to clarify over the once again growing din of voices from this small group. "Even when its natural causes, the police department still has to have a detective make sure that's what happened. Every death, every time."

"Don!" Violet finally felt well enough to speak and bounced up to her feet a little too fast.

"Yeah, I'll ask." Jake gently held her hand, led her back down to sit on the stool again, then turned to commandeer the phone from Katy and stride out of the room.

Dr. Glenn was located downstairs and led to the room with Francesca. Since he had been her personal physician and knew all about her heart condition, it was thought that he especially might have some insight into what happened. He examined her, despite Violet's reminder that no one was supposed to touch anything.

From her perch on the stool, Violet was able to watch Dr. Glenn disappear into the aperture with all eyes fixed on him. Just behind Dr. Glenn, Laurel helped to lead him in, then immediately returned from the room with a full mug which she vainly tried to conceal in one hand hung casually at her side. While everyone was focused on the doctor, Violet tried to hide the fact that she watched Laurel calmly walk to the sink, pour out the contents, then wash it with dish soap. Twice.

"Oh dear! I'm g-gobsmacked!" said Dr. Glenn as he came out of the room. "Hard cheese, I suppose. Her-her heart finally gave out on her." He continued as he leaned on his cane and slowly walked over to claim the third and last bar stool. "I thought something might-might be wrong when she left the party, but-but I was having quite the knees up and-and she just disappeared, not a word. I-I thought if she were having some trouble, she'd say. She-she knows her onions about her condition, you know. Even when she-she laid her hand over her heart and touched the table I thought she was-was just trying to skive out of the party…"

Violet had calmed down sipping the effervescent water and was trying to decode all the doctor's British-isms as he rambled on. When he finally paused for a moment Violet pulled her face out of the water goblet.

"We even asked her if she needed you, and she just took another pill," Violet said, pretty sure she had figured out the gist of what he had said.

"Ah yes, she was a real-real corker of a lady. She didn't like to ask for help and she knew what-what to do. At her last appointment with me, oh, about a fort-fortnight ago, I told her to take another doofer when her heart was feeling particularly, uh, knackered. That is to say, if-if she was short of breath or fatigued. Then, to sit in a-a dark room and try to relax. I know this was not her first time having a go at this, so it-it wasn't the pills! I-I did not cock up! And besides, when she honked into the bin, the-the pill she had just taken came right-right out. It hadn't even dissolved! She-she…"

"Wait," Violet leaned in and tried to clarify. "There was a trash can in there? And she threw up into it? And the pill was still intact when it came out?"

"Aye! Yes. When-when she chuddered it out, it hadn't even had a-a chance to work."

When Violet had found the body, she had not even thought to look around. She had not noticed a trash can or a mug. She had been so shocked that she had gone into a daze. Her tunnel vision had only seen what was right in front of her and what needed to be done, like when it was crunch time in the kitchen.

"What about the vomit?" asked Violet. "What would cause that?"

"Her-her heart, me duck!" Dr. Glenn almost yelled it. "Yes, she may have felt-felt ill because of the old ticker. But that's why she had the pills."

"Do you think that's what killed her?" Violet was curious

now as she threw a glance through the swinging kitchen door at Laurel and Paul who hugged demurely in the corner of the gallery.

"No, no, that's rubbish. Er, uh. H-how do you mean, my dear?" Dr Glenn took a deep breath, looked around the room, and tried to speak very slowly and clearly so everyone would understand him. "She-she would have taken her normal pill this-this morning, so taking a second pill if she was feeling more-more symptoms would have just made her more comfortable, as it were. They are very low-low dose. The only way her death could be the pills' fault, you understand, was if she-she did not take any of them, or, uh or, if she had taken far too many of them." He looked around the room and nodded a little before continuing. "But then-then she would have had to have taken them earlier than she did if it was-was an overdose. And it would have had to be quite on purpose, you-you know."

"You don't think it was an accident," Greta gasped. "You think it was suicide?"

"No." Doctor Glenn shakily pounded his cane on the floor. "I mean to say that it-it was plainly not an accident, but she was not-not the sort of person to off herself either. It was quite simply her anatomy finally giv-giving out."

Everyone in the kitchen seemed to relax back into a form of grief after all that threat of intrigue had dissipated. Greta looked down. Katy crossed herself in prayer. Robert and Barbara hugged. Violet stared at the wall. Unlike everyone else, she was not convinced that the explanation would be so simple. What had really happened?

I took those saved bits and tried to use them to point to the caterer girl, if anyone even bothered to look. I put them in place at the last minute, right in the middle of everyone. No one noticed. No one ever notices what's happening right in front of them.

Chapter Five

How Was She?

Minutes later, all the party guests and staff were spread over every available piece of furniture. Katy had the most comfortable chair because Jake had made sure of it, Pastor Schmidt was still planted in the same corner, and everyone else either sat slumped and drunk or meandered aimlessly through the room. After the elevator dinged, Detective Sean 'Don' Donnelly took lumbering strides into the main room where everyone waited for him. His balding dark hair had been combed in a hurry, but it was barely noticeable because he was even taller than his friend, Jake. His shoulders sloped down under his new olive suit coat making him look perpetually relaxed and his kind, sleepy eyes elicited trust.

As everyone in the room turned with hope to the newly arrived detective, Jake rushed over to greet him first with Violet right on his heels.

"Hey man, thanks for coming." Jake shook Don's hand firmly and leaned in.

"Hey, no problem. Sorry about the circumstances, but I am actually glad I get to work with you on my first case as detective." Don smiled a little as he said this, but he kept his voice low so the rest of the room wouldn't hear their conversation.

Don was probably Jake's best friend, although neither one of them was the type of guy to put it that way out loud. He had just recently made detective with the Austin Police Department after paying his dues for them as an officer and as an Army MP with Jake for several years.

"Hi, Don," Violet said over their handshake. "I-I found the body."

"I know, dispatch told me that a friend of the mayor's with a heart condition died during a party. How are you holding up? This is your first body?" Don asked as he knit his eyebrows together to show his concern. His eyes had a sleepy shape but were keener and more piercing than they usually looked when they were hanging out on a Friday night.

Violet and Jake gave the detective a quick rundown of the party as some uniformed officers slipped into the room, as if on cue.

"Thanks for telling me the situation, but you will still have to get this all down on paper. Like, in a statement, either with me or an officer." Don patted Violet's arm gently and turned to the rest of the room and said, "Thank you for your patience everyone!"

The detective spoke smoothly to feign more consideration than he was feeling. "We will try to get you out of here as quickly as we can, but we will need brief statements and contact info from all of you. We just need to know where everyone was during the party, if you saw anything, and your opinion of how..."

Don flipped open a small notepad that was still crisp and new. "Of how Francesca LeBaron was feeling and acting tonight. Then, hopefully, we can let you go and maybe contact you in the next few days. From the looks of things, that is all we will need from you, though."

A barely audible groan came from the crowd as officers spread out and gathered the people into separate groups.

"Violet." Don turned. "Is there a place where I can interview people away from the crowd?"

"The only spare room is where Mrs. LeBaron died," Violet said with a grimace. "Would you like to use the kitchen? Can I keep cleaning up behind you while you interview?"

"This is really just a formality, so sure. As long as you feel up to that and if you make yourself scarce."

"Okay, thanks." Jake started gently rubbing her back while Violet spoke. "I think what I need now is some cathartic cleaning."

"Before you start, I'd like to ask you questions first seeing as how you found her." Don said this as he gestured her towards the kitchen.

Although the catering crew had been cleaning a bit during the party, the once immaculate kitchen was still a disaster. Plates were piled next to the sink after the sink had filled with large bowls and things from the prep work, the chafing dish was extinguished, but still had food sitting in it, undoubtedly near room temperature by now, and the tablecloths that were dotted and ringed with red wine and espresso had not even made it into the room yet. Violet couldn't stand it. She faced the other direction but could not escape the smell of cold meatballs and warm smoked salmon. The sooner she got these questions over with, the sooner she could clean.

Don turned in his seat to match Violet and opened his rigid notebook. "Okay, so how was Mrs. LeBaron acting during the party? How was she?"

"Well, it was hard to tell, I don't really know her and apparently she was always very curt and rude."

"Did she seem agitated or worried about anything?"

"Yeah, I guess so. At the beginning of the party she was very composed, but then she had an argument with Luke, her grandson. They ducked in there. I could hear them arguing, but I couldn't make out any of the words. And I should tell you, Luke was acting very weird. I think he was up to something. And lots of people handled her drinks..."

"Mm-hm. But let's focus on Francesca's movements for now," Don muttered as he took notes, clearly not concerned with Luke's funny business or Violet's suspicions. Maybe it really had been nothing serious after all. People have all kinds of secrets with their doctors that are perfectly legal.

"After their argument, they went back out to the party. She came back in here and then went to go lie down within a few minutes." Violet stared at the wall and unconsciously raised her right eyebrow as she concentrated.

"Okay..." Don paused as he wrote.

"Oh, and she asked for water and took a pill because she was a little short of breath."

"Ah, alright. When was this?" He seemed satisfied as he

continued to scribble.

"It was almost exactly an hour before I found her dead. So, like nine." Violet nodded as she spoke. "Yeah, like five minutes before nine o'clock."

Don looked up a little bit surprised. "How do you know the exact time it was?"

"It's just that she said she didn't want to be disturbed for about an hour, so I looked at the clock. I wanted to start cleaning up at ten and some of my stuff is in there. Oh right, but when she went in the room, we asked if we should get her doctor. She said no and not to fuss."

"This is great," Don said, looking a little relieved as he started writing again. Realizing his eagerness was showing around the corners of his professional mask, he added, "Sorry, this…must be difficult. Take your time."

After a moment of writing, Don looked up very seriously. "Alright. Now I need to know about when you found the deceased."

"Well," Violet started, trying to be as serious as the usually kooky Don was being. "It must have been right at ten o'clock. I had just finished having a conversation with Greta, so she was right behind me when I opened the door. Immediately I smelled vomit, before I even turned on the lights."

"So, you had to turn on the lights? They were off?"

"Yeah." She started to feel queasy again.

"I turned on the switch and found her slumped back on the couch, I'm the one that moved her to the floor."

Violet's heart started to pound.

"I didn't know what to do. I think I panicked, so I started CPR."

Violet started panting.

"It was awful. She was cold. I…"

Don stepped next to her. "Are you alright? Take as much time as you need."

Violet felt light-headed and her lips tingled. As the room started to spin, her heart felt like it would pound out of her chest and she felt like throwing up. Everything went dark just for a second, then she felt herself being lowered gently to the floor. Don's face was there. He said something that Violet couldn't make out over the throbbing rush in her ears, then he left just for a moment before reappearing with Jake and Dr. Glenn.

Dr. Glenn moved deftly for such an old man, feeling her pulse and checking her eyes. As Dr. Glenn spoke, Violet could hear again. She still felt like her heart was beating slow, but hard.

"How was she before she fell?" Dr. Glenn asked Don before noticing that Violet was alert. When he asked her, Violet described all her symptoms to Dr. Glenn as he checked her vitals again.

"Alright, me duck." Dr. Glenn said as he dug through his bag. "You are very lucky. You are going to be fine. I'd like you to take this." He produced a small black pill. "It's only a bit of activated charcoal."

Jake brought over a glass of surprisingly still water.

"I suspect you got a wee bit of Francesca's digoxin when you gave her mouth to mouth."

"How? What is that?" Jake asked, worried.

"Francesca was taking some digitalis for her heart. It's actually the same tall, spiky flower they have in the floral arrangements here, and..." Dr. Glenn was gearing up for another long tale.

"Wait, isn't that poisonous?" Jake was even more worried now.

"Oh, don't get your knickers in a twist." Dr. Glenn was still very British, but actually more understandable now that he was in doctor-mode. "It is used all the time in small doses to treat heart conditions, like Franny's. It's true that digitalis toxicity can stop your heart if you eat it or some such rubbish, but this young lady got a miniscule dose. Just enough to get some heart palpitations. Definitely not enough to kill. You don't even need to pop over to hospital, just drink lots of water, rest, and a dose of activated charcoal should speed things along."

Violet was doubtful. Maybe there was something off about the doctor after all. She resolved to go straight to the hospital if she felt even slightly dizzy again.

"Thanks, but…does that mean I won't get to clean?" Violet asked, genuinely worried. She knew it was silly to want to get back to cleaning, but the mess was definitely not helping reduce her stress level.

"I've got it," Jake said with a crooked smile, knowing that cleaning the kitchen would make Violet more easy than staying by her side.

After bringing a more comfortable chair for Violet into the kitchen from the main gallery, Jake started on the dishes while Violet watched, feeling guilty.

Don continued questioning the guests that had actually spoken with Mrs. LeBaron, while uniformed police officers took names and contact info from everyone still present. Crime scene investigator-types were going in and out of the spare room, while another detective that Violet had not seen come in was talking to Laurel outside the constantly opening kitchen door. Violet listened intently, trying to assuage her suspicions.

"Miss Laurel Moretti," the older detective said in staccato sentences. "Sorry about all this. My name is Detective Taylor. Can you give me a complete list of everyone who was here tonight?"

He was shorter than Don, probably Violet's height at 5'10", but solid and square with a sharply buzzed haircut and a worn, outdated suit. His jawline could cut glass and looked freshly shaved, looking much more like he had been in the military than Don, who had been a military police officer for eight years.

"Of course, I have it here." Laurel sniffed as she brought out her sleek, rose gold phone. "Would you like me to send it to you?"

Detective Taylor looked at the phone with ill-concealed disgust. "No, thank you. Please just write it down." He shoved a small tattered notepad into her hands that was already flipped open.

"Oh, uh, okay." Laurel took the pad and pen that he offered

her in surprise and started transcribing the long list from her phone to the paper as if it was a foreign concept to her.

Violet was still troubled about Laurel. She liked Laurel, admired her even, but how could her strange behavior be explained? Why had she rushed to secretly wash that cup? What had been in it? It had to have been the cup that Paul had asked her to take to his grandmother. The deed that she had then passed off to Katy. Could Katy have put something suspicious into it?

It wasn't possible! Mrs. LeBaron died on her own, and wasn't murdered!

From her comfortable chair, Violet felt like she could see everything and listen even better than Jake who was still picking up and washing dishes. Even if this was routine and not a murder, it was still interesting to Violet. This was people-watching in the extreme. The shock and disgust were wearing off and she got to comfortably listen as Don questioned people.

At the request of Paul's mother, the bride and groom were going to be questioned first so that they could get on their way. Paul was chosen first.

"Thank you for staying late to talk to us. Paul, was it?" Don opened.

"Yes, but uh, if you are going to officially look me up, all my records actually say Paolo. My mom insisted on an Italian name, but I like to just go by Paul." He blushed and wiped his palms down his lap.

"Thank you. Now, let's get right to it, shall we?" Don said, then both men fidgeted in their chairs slightly, then locked eyes.

"You want to know if I killed my grandmother, don't you?" Paul said with a slight frown.

Don was dumbstruck but played it off well. Violet could see his shock, but maybe only because she knew him. "Well, why do you say that?"

"Because I am going to inherit her money and because I have some debt." Paul bowed his head as he said this.

Don let what Paul had said hang in the air for a moment.

"Do you? I actually didn't know that." After another long pause, Don asked very calmly and evenly, "Did you kill your grandmother, Paul?"

"No!" Paul's head shot up to look the detective in the eye with defiance. "She was my granny! It was just her atrial fibrillation. I didn't need to kill her. No one did! She was old and had a heart problem, we knew this day was coming."

"By all accounts she was feisty." Don shrugged. "How had she been the last few years? Maybe you got tired of waiting? Maybe you needed that money now."

After an ominous pause, Paul laughed. "Hah! Why would I? Check my financial records!"

Don scribbled in his notebook to show his nonchalance. "Thank you, we will."

"My debts aren't that bad, and they can wait!" Paul suddenly leaned in, his defiance back, and he started to fiercely whisper. "Besides, I am marrying a literal billionaire. Why would I jeopardize that? And why would I need money?"

Don raised his eyebrows then wrote something in his notebook during another long pause. "Don't worry, Mr. Jorgensen. We just have to ask everyone some basic questions. All I really want to know is how your grandmother was acting at the party." Don leaned back with a triumphant smile. It was the same smile he gave Violet sometimes when teasing her just to amuse himself.

"Oh sure, I think she was normal. But I can't say that I was really paying attention." Paul's face fell and he muttered, "I was distracted."

As if realizing that that sounded suspicious, he added with a nervous smile, "You know, with wedding stuff."

"Anything out of the ordinary?" Don lead, becoming interested. "Anything you can tell us could really help."

Paul almost deflated and wiped sweat off his brow with one hand and scruffed his 5 o'clock shadow with the other hand.

"Uh sorry, what did you want to know again?"

Don smirked.

Next was Dr. Glenn because he was already in the room rechecking Violet's pulse.

Doctor Glenn told the detective everything that he had already spilled before the police had arrived, with several bird-walking narratives that had nothing to do with tonight strewn in.

"So, as I told this lot, it was plainly not an-an accident, but she was not-not the sort of person to off herself either. It was quite simply her anatomy finally giv-giving out. Everything is consistent with her-her heart condition. If the pill had gotten to dissolve before she chuddered it out, it may have helped, but…"

"Wait a minute. The pill didn't dissolve!" Violet piped in, sitting up straight with wide eyes even though she was supposed to be resting and not interfering.

"Yes, my-my dear?" Dr. Glenn asked, clear that Violet was onto something but not grasping what it could be.

Don had not looked up but was still writing, obviously not concerned or maybe trying to hide his annoyance at being interrupted.

"If the pill didn't dissolve, then how did I get some?"

Don's head snapped up and he looked at her with wide eyes. The doctor's hand trembled in front of his mouth, and even Jake turned off the dish water and slowly turned around. There was a long, silent minute that ended with everyone looking at the doctor for an answer.

"Well, I-I supposed there must have been some on her-her mouth from another source. Or did you eat or-or drink anything?" Dr. Glenn was suddenly concerned.

"No." Violet looked at Jake's disapproving face while she said, "I kinda forget to eat when we have a big catering job. Kinda ironic, I know."

"Well this changes everything," Don said with a blank face, then stalked over to the door to confer with his colleagues before turning back. "What else did you see? And how did you say she was just before she went to lie down?"

*Just that nosey caterer. She was too stupid to get framed.
Too stupid and too much in everyone else's business.
My plan was perfect, but she ruined it.*

Chapter Six

How Did It Happen?

Violet had finally gotten to express her suspicions. The mug of herbal tea from Laurel and Paul, the frantic washing of that cup, the handoff between Luke and Dr. Glenn, the way Francesca had switched the espresso cup destined for Mrs. LeBaron nervously between her hands for a while, the stint of time when that espresso lay unattended in the party, Luke handling it, and even the glass of wine from Pierre that Francesca had made distasteful faces about. Don now listened and wrote intensively, then went to confer with Taylor.

When Don came back, he was stoic. He brought a lab tech with him in a white jumpsuit.

"Ok, Vi." Don crouched in front of her looking worried. "This is now a possible murder investigation. We need to swab your mouth to make sure that you do have digitalis toxicity and that you aren't just faint from not eating."

"But I feel better, and Dr. Glenn already gave me activated charcoal."

Don held up a palm. "Even though most of it will be gone, there should still be traces of the poison, or uh, medicine, no, chemical. So we can take the swab to the lab and find out why you fainted and maybe how it happened. We will also test Mrs. LeBaron's lips, vomit, and teacup to find out where it came from, what it is, and how you got it. Even though you said Laurel washed it twice, it might still have some trace if we are very lucky."

Don put his hand on top of her shoulder. "Don't worry though," he said. "No matter why you fainted, you are going to be fine. It was either a tiny dose, or none at all."

Their friend stood up and talked to Jake in hushed tones while the CSI-type rubbed Violets lips with one cotton swab and the inside of her mouth with another.

"Yeah, she'll be fine."

"Thanks, Don." Jake looked relieved.

"I am worried about this investigation though," Don went on, confiding in his friend because he knew Jake had the right kind of background and brain for this sort of thing. "If she got some dig poisoning, that means it was on the old lady's mouth. And if it's on her mouth, then that means she got a dose in the last couple hours at least. Maybe it was on her lips from food, maybe it was in her stomach and ended up on her lips when she puked, but either way it was not from her pills. The pill she takes in the morning for her a-fib would not be in her stomach anymore and the pill she took at the party never dissolved."

They paused and thought for a moment. "Maybe she took a pill right before the party," said Jake. "Just because no one saw her take one doesn't mean that she didn't. Even in the elevator on the way in!"

"Yeah, ok." Don pointed at Jake. "You may have a point. I guess we need the lab guys to analyze the samples and tell us if they match."

"Check that Violet has the same form that was on the deceased, check that the deceased had the same form on her mouth, in her blood, and in her pills, and check that her blood had the right levels. Maybe the dosage of her pills is off. This may still be an accident or suicide," Jake said, giving his friend's back a stiff pat.

"Phew! I hope so. This is the first case they are giving me as detective because they thought it was so straightforward. She's old, she had a heart condition, and she died of apparent heart failure during a nice party. Not exactly a place one wants to commit suicide. What happened should be pretty cut and dry. If it's not, this is going to get crazy! The victim was family friends with Mayor Adler, so the chief wants answers right away. I'll be under constant scrutiny if this escalates," Don confided to Jake.

"How's the partner? He's got your six, right?" Jake asked,

nodding his head toward Detective Taylor who was now rushing in and out of the spare room and main gallery.

"Yeah, he's a good detective, but maybe a little too stiff and 'letter of the law' if you ask me." Don pursed his lips slightly, then glanced down at Violet. "Well, take care of the little woman…"

Violet playfully kicked Don's leg that was barely within reach. Jake and Don turned to smile at her.

Don chuckled. "And I'll definitely call you tomorrow. Whether the lab has found anything or not, and whether I have more questions for you or if I can, hopefully, tell you that this whole business is wrapped up." Don sighed before he continued. "But now I do have to treat this like everyone is a suspect, until we know otherwise."

"Innocent until proven guilty?" joked Jake.

"Overkill and constant vigilance until I know I can relax." Don was attacking his job the same way he played board games with Jake.

"We understand, Don. Thanks." Jake took Violet's hand while Don marched off to meet up with Detective Taylor.

Laurel was next, so that she could go get her beauty sleep, according to her future mother-in-law. When she came in, Laurel asked if Violet was alright. Obviously the whole party knew about Violet fainting, so they probably knew about everything else that had happened that night, too.

"Hello Miss Moretti," Don said, smiling warmly, this time with his partner sitting silently behind him.

"Hi Detective Donnelly. Or should I call you Don?"

The two carried on pleasantries for almost five minutes. Violet couldn't help but notice how differently Don was treating Laurel and how relaxed Laurel was, despite the fact that she must have known that she was there to be interrogated.

"Thank you for staying late to talk to us, and I'm so sorry for your loss." Don danced around the real questions that he wanted to ask.

"Thank you, but I really didn't know her very well." Laurel

tucked one side of her bob behind her ear.

"But I understand this will change the mood of the whole weekend. It may make it more...bittersweet."

"Maybe. But I gather that her passing was not very unexpected, or...unwelcomed," Laurel said with a faint smile and mischievously raised eyebrows. "I don't know if anyone has told you, but she had a heart condition, so everyone knew this day was coming."

"Ah, so the wedding plans are still going forward?" Don asked.

Violet made sure to say nothing, but she hung on every word.

"Yes, of course. I will need to actually be able to talk to Paul and see if he thinks it would be too insensitive to continue, but I don't think anything should get in the way of us getting married on Saturday. Nothing else can get in our way."

"So you have had some obstacles?" Don asked.

"I think every couple has their challenges, but we have gotten past them. We both forgive each other and are determined to get married." Laurel's eyes sharpened as she spoke.

"Aw, that's sweet." Don prodded. "So you wouldn't want the wedding to be delayed? Or cancelled?"

"Absolutely not."

"Do you know anyone else that would want the wedding to be cancelled?"

"No," Laurel said, a little too quickly.

"Not even Mrs. LeBaron herself?"

"No," Laurel fired back.

"Miss Moretti, I am asking because we are now waiting on the lab to tell us whether or not Mrs. LeBaron had any help in her passing tonight. Either from herself or someone else."

Laurel's eyes widened slightly, but she kept her composure.

"So there are some questions that we need to ask. Just to rule out any possible motives."

Laurel squirmed in her seat a little under Don's piercing glare. "Okay, shoot," she said, shaking the other side of her hair out of her face.

"Miss Moretti, did you have any reason to want Mrs. LeBaron gone?"

"Hm, no." Laurel's eyes were still sharp, and she spoke with an edge in her voice.

"Did you know that her will, according to her family, leaves all her assets to Paul and his brother?"

"Yes."

Don leaned in slightly and spoke a little lower. "Did you know that Paul is coming to your marriage with some significant debts?"

"Yes," Laurel answered so coolly that the detective was visibly taken aback.

"You know that he needs money?"

"Well, I wouldn't put it that way. He has some debts that he is still paying off, but he is paying them off and I intend to help him with that."

"So you…don't want Paul to have his own money? You didn't want to…maybe benefit from her will too?"

Laurel glared at Detective Donnelly. "No."

"Or maybe you didn't want to have to pay for his debts."

Laurel folded her arms and finally let loose. "I had nothing to do with her dying and neither did Paul. I have no idea how it happened. Why would I ruin my rehearsal dinner and risk ruining my wedding? I love Paul and we are going to get married, in debt or not. So he is still paying off his credit cards because he chose to pay his student loans off first. So, what? My family has probably given away a million dollars in university scholarships, so how is this any different? I am glad I am blessed enough to be in a position to help him…because I love him."

Laurel was starting to tear up now as she continued. "Besides, my parents insisted on a prenuptial agreement to protect my family's fortune. It says that neither of us has claim to anything that the other person enters the marriage with, only what we 'acquire while married.' If I wanted his grandmother's money for myself, it wouldn't do me any good to kill her before the wedding. Now in a week or so…"

Laurel held her hands out in a shrug before returning to her indignantly folded arms.

"I see your point," Don said, nodding slowly. "I'm sorry to have upset you. We really do have to explore every possibility to find out how it happened. For what it's worth, I believe you are innocent."

Now it was the other Detective's turn to wriggle in his seat.

"But, by the by," Don continued, a little too relaxed to be natural. "Do you know who took Mrs. LeBaron's cup of herbal tea out to the kitchen sink?"

Laurel froze in her chair except for a long breath in. "I did."

"You did?" Don feigned surprise, since he had already been told this fact.

"I did," she said again, with confidence and authority. "I was trying to clean up, but that was before I thought that she might have…had some help."

Laurel and Don glared at each other for a moment.

"I'm sorry if I disrupted your investigation." Laurel's words were an apology, but her tone was defiant and strong.

As soon as Laurel was shown out, Detective Taylor stood up.

"You can't comfort a suspect! And you should not be upsetting such influential people," Detective Taylor barked.

"Taylor, you don't want me to ask her tough questions AND you don't want me to comfort her? You have to pick one. Should I be tough on her or not?" Don was belligerent.

The senior detective drew in a huge breath and was about to lay into his junior detective, when another guest came through the door. Luke was swaggering in like he owned the place, as usual, and came to sit down in front of the two detectives. He smelled of two different kinds of smoke and had bloodshot eyes.

"Well, gentlemen, I heard you wanted to talk to me." Luke combed his hair out of his face momentarily with his fingers before it flopped back down to conceal his left eye.

"Why don't you go take the other guests so we can get these people home faster?" Taylor said to Don through clenched teeth. Violet still sat in the comfortable chair in the kitchen but was afraid, now, to move and remind Detective Taylor that she was there listening to every word.

"Yes, sir," was all Detective Donnelly said before stalking

out of the kitchen.

"Luke Jorgensen," Taylor said upfront. "I can look past all this evidence I am seeing that would interest our narcotics unit, if you can answer my questions and help me understand what happened here tonight." His voice was raspy and low, making him sound more relaxed than he appeared.

Violet remembered what she had witnessed during the party. The secretive handoff between Luke and Dr. Glenn could also be something that the vice unit would be interested to hear about. She had not even been sure what had been exchanged for the money, though. It had been paper, but what was on or in that paper? Information for blackmail? Drugs? Prescription slips? Or could it have been a poison used on Francesca LeBaron?

She considered telling all of this to Detective Taylor right then, but thought better of it. Maybe Don had told him, besides, if she called attention to herself, then he would undoubtedly make her leave. Instead, Violet decided to wait and talk it over with Don more later.

Luke slumped a little more and muttered, "Fine."

"Did you know that you and your brother stand to inherit your grandmother's entire fortune?" Taylor asked.

Luke's affectation slipped as he asked, "Does this mean that it wasn't her heart that killed her? What was it?"

"We don't know yet, so I'll be asking the questions. Now, again, did you know that you and your brother stand to inherit your grandmother's entire fortune?"

"Ch-yeah, I think everybody knows that." Luke was smug and apathetic once again.

"So you and he will benefit a lot from her passing." Detective Taylor was supposed to be asking a question, but it came out sounding more like an accusation.

"Yup."

The silence between them was palpable.

"I didn't kill her. You can't think that." Luke slurred just a tad as he spoke.

"Why not?" Detective Taylor was searching Luke with his gaze. "Why can't I think that?"

"'Cause I didn't! I wouldn't ruin the wedding like that."

"Aw, that's sweet of you," Taylor said, dripping with sarcasm.

"No, well yeah, but not like that. Yeah, I want him to be happy and everything, but I mean...for me." Luke looked down at the table ashamed and scratched at an invisible spot. "I need him to get married so I can start hitting him up for money."

"Ah, but now you don't need that gravy train since you have Granny's money!" Taylor clenched his fist against the table.

"No way, man. Do you know how long it takes to get money from an estate?" Luke's eyes were pleading now. "It can take years. I still need him to get married 'cause I need money now! I have a lot of... undocumented...debts. They are not to a bank, if you know what I mean. As soon as Paul got back from his honeymoon, I was going to ask for $20,000."

Taylor whistled. "That's a lot of money!"

"Not to Laurel! I'll think of something like, I am going to invest it or start a new company or something, but they will give it to me. Why would I want to stop that? Or even risk it? I need this wedding to happen, man."

To Violet, Detective Taylor looked convinced. But he didn't say as much.

Violet was feeling much better, so when Detective Taylor stepped out of the kitchen for a minute, she started prepping some pitchers of water and the leftover bottles of seltzer to serve to the marooned guests.

Katy and Greta came in saying, "Hey, are you feeling okay? How are the interviews going?"

"Oh yeah, thanks. They have made me drink a lot, so I think whatever it was has worked its way out of my system. But now I have to pee!"

"Ah! Go, go!" Greta joked, being used to talking to a toddler.

"Are you still shaky? Do you want us to come with you?" Katy offered.

"I think I'm okay," Violet said shyly. "Maybe send in a search party if I'm not back in five minutes."

They all chortled as Violet walked away.

On her walk, Laurel caught up to her.

"Hey Violet, I know it's short notice, but with all that has happened I don't think we will be having a family luncheon tomorrow. I'm so sorry." Laurel grimaced a little and continued. "I think the rest of the wedding plans are still on, but I am going to go talk it over with Paul right now."

"Of course!" Violet agreed wholeheartedly, despite her fear of the food sitting in her fridge. At least the family luncheon had been a small affair, so Jake and she would be able to eat through the sandwiches and salads before they went bad. "You need to do what's best for your family. And I think everyone could use a chance to sleep in tomorrow."

"Thank you," Laurel said, relieved. "I'll text you about the other plans as soon as I know."

With that, Laurel left with Paul, solemnly gripping hands again.

When Violet came back to the kitchen, Detective Taylor had not returned yet and Katy and Greta had already prepped the water, a few crackers and leftover caprese skewers for the restless crowd.

"Thanks guys!" Violet beamed. "This should hold them until the police are done questioning everyone, right?"

Greta nodded then asked, "Have you heard anything about how much longer they are going to be? It's midnight!"

"Nope. You?" Violet looked at Katy.

"Nope," said Katy and Greta together, exhausted.

"Do they know how it happened?" asked Katy.

"No."

Greta filled the momentary silence. "Well they already interviewed me. It didn't sound good, Vi. I had to tell them about Paul…thinking about me. They know that we dated, that there are still feelings, that I knew exactly what digitalis is and that I have been around it constantly for about two days, and they made it sound like I am jealous of Laurel or something. They said, 'Maybe you wanted to stop the wedding', and 'maybe you wanted Paul to have money of his own so he could marry you!'" Greta let out a sharp sigh, "Can you believe that?"

"Yeah, that's kind of what they have been saying to everyone though." Violet tried to comfort her sister. "Katy, did they ask you stuff like that?"

"Kind of," began Katy. "I really didn't know her or her family, so they didn't ask me very much. But I told them about when I went in that spare room to bring her some herbal tea because Laurel told me to, and they said that will help them narrow down time of death."

All the women got quiet for a long moment. With all the hubbub it was easy to forget why they were all really here. They were here because someone had died right in there, around the corner. While they had been eating and talking, or working and serving, someone's life had been extinguished.

"I also overheard them talking to Antonia. Or should I call her Mrs. Jorgensen? They were trying to accuse her of being mad at her mother for not passing on all that money to her, I mean Antonia." Greta rambled, showing her unease. "But she said that she had known for years about the money skipping her and going to her boys. She said, 'I do wish I had more, who doesn't?' She said she wasn't happy about it, but that it was no reason to ruin a $30,000 wedding!"

"Wow! Thirty thousand?" Violet was shocked. With her as the caterer, there were not too many other places to be spending that much money in her mind. "Mine was only like five thousand."

The ladies giggled like schoolgirls while they picked up the trays and tubs of food, drinks and ice to bring them back out to the main gallery room. At the door, they were stopped by a tubby officer who held up his hand with outstretched fingers.

"Nope, I can't let you do that," he said before Taylor swooped in.

"This is a possible poisoning case." Detective Taylor practically scolded them. "And a crime scene. Get all this back in the kitchen. We need to bag and tag all of it and throw away the rest."

Violet and her friends, dejected, set the newly prepped food on the kitchen counters and walked away, as instructed, before the crime scene investigators swarmed.

When they returned to the main room, they fanned out amongst the guests empty-handed. Violet chose to wait to talk to Don in a corner near where Pierre was just sitting down for his questioning.

"I understand that you had some run-ins with Mrs. LeBaron's mean streak, is that right?" Detective Donnelly was saying once they were settled. "Want to tell me about what happened tonight?"

"Oh that? Mm, that was nuthin'. Just an old bi-uh, grump being stuck in the past." Pierre refrained from cursing and dismissed the question with the wave of a hand.

"So she didn't offend you?" Don prodded. "I think I would have been offended."

"You?!?" Pierre spouted as he looked the detective up and down.

"No, no." Don did have a way of putting his foot in his mouth on occasion. "Uh, I just mean if I was…in your shoes."

"Mm." Pierre agreed "Well it was no glass of Cos Contrada, but I'm used to it."

He paused, but Detective Donnelly merely stared at Pierre to get him to keep talking.

"I'm used to it, okay? If I knocked off everyone that said something mean to me about being gay, I would have been in jail since I was five years old!"

"Alright. What kind of past do you two have? From what I hear, she had gotten you fired. How did that happen?"

"I know that sounds bad," Pierre said dipping his head and waving his hand out. "But it ended up being the best thing for me!"

Don simply, quietly, stared again, which must have made Pierre uneasy.

"I was just Peter, living in a tiny apartment with two other brothers and being the buyer for her snooty club," Pierre reminisced with a sneer. "Okay. I was messed up when I got fired, but if I hadn't been fired, I wouldn't have found this new path! Now I am a quasi-celebrity with a home in Paris for the tourist season! I'm livin' my best life now!"

When everyone had been questioned and all the guests and staff had at least one copy of each detective's business card, they were informed that they were finally released. The crime scene investigators had also just wrapped up with the spare room, taking samples, pictures, confiscating the washed mug, and the body. Since it was close to two o'clock in the morning, Violet and Greta sent home Katy and Jake to get some rest and went to work on the very last of the mess, like the last water glasses and the uneaten half of a tartlet that had still been sitting in the possible 'crime scene'.

"Do you think she was poisoned?" Violet thought again of the herbal tea that had gotten suspiciously cleaned up and the paper that Luke had acquired from Dr. Glenn. She still wanted to ask Don about that paper to see what he thought of it. It could have been nothing. It probably was nothing, but it could be everything.

"No!" Greta exclaimed as she handed Violet the water glass.

Violet poured it down the sink drain and washed it. When Violet turned back to take the plate and leftover tartlet from her sister, Greta grabbed her wrist, making Violet look at her pale, shocked face, then follow her gaze to the plate.

Violet now stared at the plate too, but didn't see anything that would cause the terror that was plain on Greta's face.

"That's not curly dock," said Greta, in a cold, wavering voice.

"What?" asked Violet, not understanding what she was referring to or what the implications were.

Greta picked up the garnish leaf that decorated the top of the holy cannoli tartlet and held it up for Violet to see. "We garnished these tartlets with curly dock, but this is not curly dock. They are really similar, but this is not the same. This is foxglove. People mix them up all the time but...Ugh! how could this have happened?"

When Violet still looked confused, Greta cried, "Digitalis!"

Holy Cannoli Cups

Makes 24 mini-muffin sized cups. If you want to take these cannoli cups up a notch, garnish them with edible flowers. Just make sure you know which leaves and flowers are edible! Like gladiolas, mint, or violas, but not foxglove!

Crusts-
8 Tablespoons or 1 stick (125g) butter, softened
½ cup (100g) white, granulated sugar
1 large egg
1 ½ cups (190g) all-purpose flour
⅛ teaspoon baking powder
½ teaspoon ground cinnamon
¼ teaspoon ground nutmeg

Fillings-
2 cups or 12 ounces (340g) semi-sweet chocolate chips
½ cup chopped or coarsely ground pistachio nuts (65g)
8 ounces (250g) ricotta cheese
Zest of a half an orange
2 Tablespoons honey (21g)
¼ - ½ cup (120mL) heavy whipping cream
½ cup (90g) mini chocolate chips or chocolate sprinkles (optional)

1. Prepare crusts by preheating oven to 350 degrees F (180C) and greasing a mini muffin tin.
2. Cream butter and sugar together until fluffy, then beat in egg.
3. In a separate bowl, whisk together flour, powder, cinnamon and nutmeg.
4. Mix dry ingredients into wet ingredients until no spots of flour remain.

5. Divide dough into 24 equal balls and press each into a mini muffin cup. Try to press the dough up the walls of the cup, even though they will fall and you will have to do it all over again.

6. Bake at 350F (180C) for 9 to 12 minutes, or until the edges are getting golden-brown.

7. Immediately, while they are still hot, squish a hole into the middle of each cup with a cookie scoop or press the warm cookie back onto the walls of the muffin tip with a spoon. Let cool after you shape them.

8. Meanwhile, whip ricotta cheese, honey and orange zest. Once incorporated, slowly add cream while the mixer is running. Keep whipping until filling is thinned, fluffier, and incorporated. Start with ¼ cup of cream, and add more if needed. Cover and set aside.

9. Once crusts have reached room temperature, coat insides of cups with melted chocolate. Microwave chocolate chips for 30 seconds at a time, stir, then microwave for another 30 seconds until chocolate is just barely smooth and glossy. Spoon chocolate into each cup, spread to coat the sides and top edges, then pour out excess.

10. While chocolate is warm, spread pistachio pieces on a small plate and invert the cups onto the pieces to coat the top edges of the cups with pistachio bits. Set aside and let cool.

11. When chocolate has cooled, pipe or carefully spoon filling into each cup until beautifully mounded. Garnish with mini chocolate chips, chocolate sprinkles, orange zest, edible flowers, or anything else.

12. Serve immediately or cover and refrigerate until party time. These can even be frozen a long time before, then thawed out in the fridge for about 12 hours before serving time.

I remember not even considering the fact that it might not work. I had to do it.

Chapter Seven

Was It Her?

Violet's head whirled. Her scalp winced as confusion reigned and questions flooded her mind. Was she responsible for someone's death just because she didn't know any plant identification? Would she have to live with that guilt for her whole life? Would she get sued for wrongful death? She would be finished. No more owning her own business. No more working in the food industry at all! She would be completely unhireable in any other kitchen. No one would want someone guilty of such negligence in their kitchen, in their restaurant, or tied to their reputation. Could she even go to jail? She couldn't even imagine how dirty everything must be in a prison! It was too horrible to think about. She and Greta had agreed that they had to tell Detective Donnelly, but Violet had to get home to talk this over with Jake first.

When she got close, she texted Jake and he met her downstairs in athletic pants and a free t-shirt.

As soon as she saw him she broke down. He walked up to meet her as she parked, then she flung herself from the car into his waiting arms.

"Hey, Missy. Are you still shaken up? Didn't cleaning go well?"

While they walked up and down from their apartment, taking multiple trips to carry in all the equipment, Violet relayed the whole story, even the highlights from the interviews he had missed. As they wrapped up putting the last things in the second fridge, Violet's narrative drew to a close and she started crying again.

"I guess the leaves that Greta and Katy had brought for me

to garnish with must have gotten mixed up! Or maybe a leaf from all the floral arrangements at the shop must have fallen in! Does that make me responsible? What if I am liable? How could I be so stupid?"

"Sh-sh." Jake pulled her over to the couch and lead her to sit on his lap. "First, I don't think that is why she died, and second, I don't think that would be enough to kill someone. Then, even if it was, that is pure accident! You are definitely not criminally responsible."

"Maybe if the person already had a heart condition!" Violet looked at Jake with despair in her eyes. "They might even think that I planned to do it, that it was premeditated!"

Violet broke down the rest of the way into sobs.

"No way," he murmured as he leaned his head back and stroked her hair. "As of now, we don't know what killed her. Even if it was digitalis, I don't think that a bite from one leaf would do it. Plus, you were not the one responsible for ordering the greens or identifying them. This is not your fault. And even if the police think it is for a minute, they will work it out. Don is not so anxious to condemn you. They will realize that you have no motive, not much plant knowledge, and would never risk your livelihood by pulling a stunt like this. They'll figure this out. We'll figure this out."

She continued to cry, but the violent sobs abated. Jake's steady breathing and stroking of her hair was comforting and somewhat mesmerizing.

Violet woke up, leaning on Jake's chest with the early morning light streaming in through the apartment's sliding glass door. She had not even realized that she had fallen asleep, although it had probably been close to 3am. This was a lovely way to wake up, until her neuroses kicked in. She thought of how she had fallen asleep before showering, or even brushing her teeth! She ran her tongue over her teeth and felt the tiny sweaters that they now wore. *Yuck!*

She turned her head as a precursor to getting up off the couch and saw the pans and utensils still cluttering the kitchen. At least she had put all the food away, but how had she left so much undone?!

Oh no! She thought. *I never called Don to tell him what we found!*

Violet shifted her weight to reach into her back pocket and retrieve her phone and continued the movement to haul herself off the couch silently. She didn't want to wake up Jake, but she needed to tell Don what she had found as soon as possible so she didn't look even more guilty.

As her phone's screen lit up, there was already a notification that Don had sent a text. All it said was

Call me when you wake up.

She was already in trouble! Was Don going to tell her that she was now the lead suspect? Was he going to tell her to watch her back, to tell the police everything? Flee the country? It probably would not be that last one.

"Violet." Don's voice was firm but tired. "Thanks for calling me. We need to talk. Can I come over?"

"Uh yeah, I'll make us breakfast. Have you had chilaquiles lately?" Although Violet was almost whispering, and out on the balcony, Jake stirred and sat up as she spoke.

"My favorite!" The detective forgot himself for a moment and then regained his composure. "Yes, that would be fine. I'll be over soon."

As Jake let Detective Donnelly in, Violet had just finished brushing her teeth and pulling her dirty hair up into a quick ponytail. She was now gathering the frying pan, eggs, spatula and butter. Don must have already been close when he called.

"Hey guys," said the detective, loosening his tie. "Me being here isn't exactly a secret, but maybe we shouldn't tell everyone about this, okay?"

"Okay. But I have to tell you something." Violet quickly spilled the information that she had been meaning to tell him earlier.

"Alright." Don had not taken any notes and he sounded hesitant to condemn Violet. "I think you can relax. When you hear what I have to say…"

"What do we know?" Jake cut straight to the chase.

"Well, first of all, no one else has gotten sick. And we have lab results back, but the autopsy is being done as we speak." Don looked at each of them in turn as Jake took over cooking the eggs. "They moved Mrs. LeBaron to the top of the list, so they did some preliminary assessments already."

Violet turned to look at the detective. "Is it my fault? Was it me?"

"Hey!" Don put up his hands in front of him defensively. "I'm convinced that you did not do anything. That's why I know it's okay for me to be here talking to you. It helps that you did, in fact, suffer some slight effects of digoxin poisoning."

"So I did get some of the poison?" Violet asked, rapt.

"Yes, just slightly. But you did pick up some of the poison from Mrs. LeBaron."

He paused, looked concerned, and went on in a business-like tone. "Mrs. LeBaron had very high levels of digoxin in her system. It was present in her stomach and her mouth and lips which suggests that it was not from her pills. Also, her latest pill was thrown up so immediately that it had not dissolved, as you know. We tested it and the others in the bottle, and they were all normal, not tampered with. Anyway, these levels from her blood test are high enough, that we think it was intentional."

"And you don't think it was suicide."

"Now why don't I think it's suicide?" Don asked slyly, analyzing Violet.

"Well, she didn't seem like the type of person to commit suicide at all, but especially not in the back of a party, and ESPECIALLY not in such a gross and undignified way. It wasn't her." Violet thought for a moment, then went on. "And she was a fan of Paul and Laurel getting married, so she wouldn't have wanted to jeopardize that by doing anything at one of the wedding events."

"I agree," said Detective Donnelly. "But it's nice to hear it from someone else, someone that knew her."

"I barely knew her. I didn't even know the name of her

heart condition."

"I'd have to check my notes, too. Turns out almost no one knew the exact nature of her heart condition, but that is really what killed her. If her heart had not been weakened already, then…"

"So she ate the leaves and flowers at the party and that was enough to kill her because of her existing heart condition?" Violet looked puzzled. "Is that why no one else has gotten sick? They ate leaves but they don't have heart conditions?"

"No, no," Don said. "If they had eaten leaves or flowers, they still would have gotten sick. They'd probably be throwing up, just not dead. Because of that, we think that Mrs. LeBaron had the only digitalis leaves. We don't think that any other food was contaminated."

All three thought silently for a moment.

"Wait, even in her case," said Violet, "most, if not all, of the garnish was still on her cannoli cup when we found it, so maybe she had another one earlier in the party. And that one was poisoned, too."

"Okay, so…lab results show other chemicals present, so it was a natural, unrefined form, like the leaves. Her pills only have a dose of digoxin, the one chemical, so again, not her medication. However, the chemicals also were so concentrated that it couldn't have been from eating a leaf or two. There also weren't any leaves in her stomach contents, just maybe two bites of ricotta cheese, water, wine and coffee."

Violet tried to ask a question, but Don went on.

"Guys, it was such a high dose and so concentrated, that it can only mean that someone intentionally made poison." Don paused and looked at both of their reactions. "They collected a bunch of the plant, cooked it down or something, then gave it to her. They planned this thing. She was murdered."

After letting this sink in for a moment, Don went on. "It wasn't a mistake of a few leaves."

Violet first felt relieved, then ashamed for feeling relieved that it was not her food that had killed her. There was still a murdered woman! At least she was not responsible for killing anyone. Her mind then went on to wonder about the type of person who would want to hurt someone, to kill someone. Had a mistake been made in her kitchen or not?

"So it was just an incredible coincidence that she got the tartlet with the misidentified leaves?" Violet scoffed.

"I agree, it's not very likely, but I don't know the whole story yet." Don paused to think, then changed tacks. "Digitalis poisoning works very fast. Given what time she arrived, it is clear that she was given the poison during the rehearsal dinner. We just don't know how. If we figure out the real delivery method, then maybe we can figure out who."

They all stood there in silence for a long time. The only sound was fried eggs sizzling on the stove while the smell of browning butter filled the early morning all around them. Light angled steeply in through the sliding glass doors of the balcony, but most of the apartment was dreary in the early morning light.

This person had plotted and planned, then worked long and hard, all with the goal of murdering someone. That kind of evil was troubling, and the fact that someone like that had been at the party, breathing the same air as Violet and her loved ones, was chilling.

Finally, Violet decided that it would not be insensitive to ask, "Does that mean I am in the clear? If it wasn't the food, then I won't get in any hot water?"

Donnelly hesitated, then looked at her. His sleepy eyes looked even more so with dark circles under them. His bloodshot eyes even looked sad. "Mostly. Everyone at the party is still technically a possibility, but you had no motive. My partner and I are…looking at other suspects."

There was another pause as Jake turned back to the stove and tossed tortilla chips and salsa verde into the eggs with deft flicks of his wrists.

"I know you guys had nothing to do with it, but my partner is not convinced. He thinks you could have wanted the publicity, or that you could have been doing it for your sister."

"That's ridiculous!" cried Violet, as Jake didn't flinch and kept cooking.

"I know. Don't worry." Donnelly held up his hands again.

"That's why I wanted to talk to you guys, but without everyone knowing about it. My partner only cares about the rules and I need to talk to someone who can actually help me work this out. It's my first big case and there is a lot of pressure to nail someone, anyone, to the wall. My captain is even getting pressure from the mayor. It's making my partner just look for someone that he can make a case against, not the truth."

Jake put steaming bowls of chilaquiles in front of each of them as they stayed gathered around the kitchen island.

"What do you need from us?" Violet said before her first bite.

"First, as the caterer, did you see what she ate and drank? Like I said, the stomach contents just show drinks and a tiny bit of that ricotta cup thing of yours. We tested the leftovers of that dessert and it was clean except for the garnish, so what, if anything, did you see her drink?"

"Well, I remember her drinking some tap water in the kitchen with us, but that was only from Greta in a freshly washed glass. And it couldn't have been her. Then Katy took her some herbal tea while she was resting in the back. Obviously it couldn't have been Katy either, but she had gotten that tea bag from Paul and Laurel…"

"Hm, okay." Don swung open his notebook and began to scribble. "Anything else?"

"Yeah, um." Violet dug deep in her memory of the tiny details of the party. "I think I already told you about everything I thought was suspicious, like that herbal tea. I know she had a glass of wine, but it was poured from the same bottle that lots of people had shared. And then there was also that cup of espresso. She had announced that she wanted one, so Antonia took Katy's new cup to give to Francesca. Antonia then stood around with it stalling, then handed it to Paul to hand to his grandmother. I guess that was a good opportunity for either of them to put something in it."

"This is good." Don jotted furiously and seemed about to say something.

Violet interrupted. "Wait! I almost forgot! There's more!"

103

"She had barely sipped that espresso when she put it down to take Luke into the back room for their argument!" Violet grew more animated now. "AND THEN, when they came out, Luke is the one that handed it back to her!"

"So Luke could have put something in it when he handled it."

"Or anyone at the party!" Violet exclaimed with excitement, then grew disappointed when she saw the defeat in Don's face. "When she was in the back arguing with Luke, her espresso was just sitting on the table. I was so distracted by the argument that I didn't watch it. Anyone in that room could have done something to it."

Don's optimism had faded again, and he just sat, tapping his notebook with his pen. "I guess that would have been too easy, huh?"

"Sorry," Violet said although she was not sure what she was sorry for.

"No, no, you've been a big help. All of this is helpful." Don tried to comfort her but the desperation in his voice prevented his words from sinking in. "There is a lot of information to sift through, but I still need it all. That brings me to the other reason for our conversation."

"Ulterior motives?!" Violet joked.

"Well kind of." Don smiled. "I need what you saw, but I also need your brain and even your access."

When Violet looked puzzled, the detective went on. "I need help from both of you. Well, Jake knows how all this goes, and two heads are better than one and all that, but mostly I need you, Violet."

"Me? Why? I don't know anything about investigating a murder!" Violet blushed.

Jake set down his fork and glared at Don.

"And it could be dangerous," Jake said.

"Maybe. But you've got the brain for this." Don leaned in toward Violet. "You figure out every mystery and you always know the solution to the puzzle. And you're observant. Crazy observant."

"Don, this isn't a movie or a puzzle, this is real life! I don't know real crime!" Violet grew nervous as he pushed the point.

"But you know people! And you can notice and even overhear things because you will be right there with them. You also know a lot of these people and can give me background information."

"Oh, you want me to be your spy?" Violet asked, smiling for the first time that morning and trying to push aside her apprehension.

"If that helps you." Don smiled back. "You can also get me into these parties if needed. I am supposed to be treading lightly. There are a lot of big wigs around that I really cannot piss off if I want to make it as a detective."

"Yeah, I was told the mayor might be at the wedding."

"Exactly." Don jabbed the air with his finger. "I have to solve this, and I have to do it discreetly. And if I have your help, I'm sure I can wrap this up faster. But if we can keep the fact that you're helping me quiet, it'll be better for the both of us."

Violet had to think about it. Of course she wanted to help solve this murder, but what help could she be? It's not like she could crack it wide open all on her own! On the other hand, Don was saying he just needed access, tips, and for her to just keep her eyes and ears open as she catered these parties, which she was planning to do anyway. Still, he could get in trouble for talking to her too much about the case, and if this were one of Jake's books, she could make the wrong people mad and she could be in danger. Her help could also be seen as intensely biased and get her in trouble with the law!

Jake spoke, drying his hands on a kitchen towel. "Don. I'm not sure about this. But…I see how it might be necessary."

Jake and Don looked at each other.

"Why don't you tell her who the main suspect is?" Jake said.

Don snapped his head down and grimaced. "Yep, you do know how this works."

"What?" Violet was worried again. "What do you mean? I thought you said that we weren't really in trouble!"

"You're not." Don raised his fatigued eyes to hers again, "But it looks bad for . . . your sister."

105

Violet's sister? Not Greta! There was no way she was guilty! It couldn't have been her! Violet's stomach reeled and the nameless guilt was palpable. Even though she was the little sister, Violet had always been the one to protect Greta. Greta was the impulsive sister, so it was Violet that would always get her out of trouble, defend her, and bail her out. How could she let her sister down now? If being observant really could help, then she had to go to work.

Violet did need to get back to work, to keep her hands busy and cook, or did she? The plans for today's lunch were cancelled, but would tonight's events still happen? She knew there was no family luncheon, which is good because she was completely not ready for it. The blue mango muffins were all that were totally done and ready for the luncheon, and those she could eat, hand out to friends, or even take to church. Her hands needed to get busy, though, so she packed up some of the muffins in a big Ziploc bag while she continued her discussion with Don and Jake.

If the wedding party wanted to cancel everything, that would seriously dampen her chances of propelling her business and of helping clear Greta. There was no way Greta could kill someone! She knew that, and Don knew that. The detective laid out the facts as his partner had done for him, and Violet had to agree that it did look bad.

Greta had a lot of the plant that was the murder weapon, had the plant knowledge, and was in the kitchen helping with the food. She had helped with doling out coffee, had knowledge of the old lady's heart condition, and had even been the one to get her water when Francesca came into the kitchen! Greta had a romantic history with Paul that was not entirely closed, and phone records show that they had talked several times recently. The police were thinking that maybe Paul and Greta had worked together!

It was bad. Anyone could see that. The facts lined up, but it just couldn't have been her.

"Don," Violet said. "It was totally over between Paul and Greta! I wasn't sure myself until I overheard a conversation that I wasn't supposed to…"

"See? You're working for me already!"

"Ok, but Paul was admitting that he needed closure, but Greta convinced him that they did not work when they were together, that he really loved Laurel, and that it was just his cold feet talking."

"Hm, ok. That's good," Donnelly contemplated.

"There has to be someone else who's a better suspect!" Violet exclaimed. "Like, couldn't the killer have dried out a bunch of leaves and brought them to the party, in say, a tea bag?"

"Definitely." Don nodded with enthusiasm. "That's my favorite theory at the moment. I think Paul could have put it together to give to the grandma."

"Yeah, I don't think it would take much plant knowledge. And some people have it in their yards. It didn't take a plant expert surrounded by the flowers, like Greta, it could have been anyone!"

Violet took in a little gasp. "Did they find any chemicals on the mug that had the herbal tea? Have they tested it yet?"

"Yes, and no." Don sighed, deflating again. Then he clarified. "They tested the cup, but it didn't have any detectable trace left. Either it wasn't the murder weapon or Laurel had already washed it too well."

The three of them sat and ate their breakfast for a minute, deep in thought.

"So, you saw Paul hand this tea bag to Laurel?" Don asked to break the silence. "Could they have been in on it together?"

"I guess so. But they wouldn't want to ruin their rehearsal dinner, or even their wedding." Violet found herself scrambling for excuses and reasons it could not have been Laurel. "It could have even been made by someone else and given to Paul for his grandmother."

"Sounds risky, but we can explore that," Don said, humoring her.

"So who had motive to kill her?" Jake wondered.

"First, I think of Paul and his brother Luke so they can inherit," Don mused. "But it could have also been their parents. They could be angry about not inheriting."

107

Violet took the idea and ran with it. "I thought of them, but Francesca LeBaron's will was written like five years ago. Why would they just now decide that they were mad?"

"Well maybe the boys just now decided that they need money. Luke has always been in trouble with the law and seedy characters, and Paul had mentioned that he was in debt," Jake contributed.

"I was up checking financial records pretty much all night, and that wouldn't make sense." Don rubbed his stubble of beard and explained. "Luke is totally flush with cash and Paul's debt isn't that bad. Paul's debt will also all-but-disappear on Saturday."

"Do you mean when he marries Laurel?" Violet clarified. "I know he said that, but they do have that prenup. Maybe he wasn't going to get his debts paid off like he thought. She sounded genuine and generous when you interviewed her, but maybe she is not really in control of her money. It is her parents' money after all."

"I think he was relying on her generosity, but like I said, his debts aren't that bad," Don reiterated.

"And like you told her, I think Laurel is innocent." Violet changed tacks.

"Why do you say that?" Don asked.

"Like she said, the financial motive would only make sense after they are married and I can't think of any other reason for Laurel, or Paul, to kill Mrs. LeBaron."

"Ok, but maybe she just didn't want to have such an unpleasant relation."

"If she was being killed for being unpleasant." Violet raised an eyebrow. "She would have been killed a long time ago. And everyone had that motive!"

"I guess so," Donnelly admitted. "Just during the party she pissed off the sommelier, the little floral assistant, Luke, and her own daughter."

"But remember that this was planned," Violet interrupted. "This wouldn't have been a case of someone snapping because of something that happened at the party. This was some old grudge, or for some kind of goal. So that rules out Katy, but I guess not Pierre."

Don countered. "Okay, but he is better off than he was before she got him fired, so I don't see a motive."

"Yeah," Violet conceded. "But anger doesn't always make sense. Even if it was a good thing after a while, he still had time for that grudge to fester. Maybe he never forgave her."

"Maybe." It was Don's turn to concede." But he's not anywhere near the top of my list."

Don sighed then went on down the list of people at the party. "What about the photographer? Did they know each other?"

"I don't think so," Violet said around a bite of breakfast nacho.

"Pastor Schmidt used to get big donations from Mrs. LeBaron, but lately they have stopped," Detective Donnelly said with a shrug.

"Yeah, I get the idea that going to church was her husband's idea. So, when he died, Mrs. LeBaron stopped participating." Violet wiped her mouth with a paper towel.

"Okay, I don't see that being a motive though." Don remembered his breakfast and crammed a whole chip in his mouth.

"Me neither," Violet admitted.

"Oh! Dr. Glenn!" Don sounded like he had just found the murderer. "Last night I discovered that he has been the family doctor forever."

"Yeah . . ." Violet did not see the significance, and she had already known that.

"Even before old Mr. and Mrs. LeBaron were married," Don explained. "Some people even thought that she would marry Dr. Glenn."

"Really?" Violet was surprised. Sure, they were both old, but their personalities were so opposite that she couldn't picture Mrs. LeBaron and Dr. Glenn as a couple.

Seeming to read her puzzled expression, Don added, "I guess they both changed a lot as they got older."

Jake laughed out loud at this despite being silent for so long, which made them all snicker.

Violet was ready to break down. She had been determined to wait for news from the wedding party about whether the bachelor party, bachelorette party, and wedding were still happening, so she had distracted herself with cleaning the kitchen. Now she was done wiping out the oven and she couldn't wait any longer. Don had left with his bag of muffins and it was time for everyone to get back to work. The bachelor party and bachelorette party were tonight! True, most of the parties would be liquor, but Violet still needed to make the finger foods. She checked in with her to-do list.

Bachelor Party - mostly manned by Jake

Marinated Steak Skewers - m. rare steak, carne asada marinade, avocado, tomatoes

Mexican Street Corn - baby corn on toothpicks, butter, crema, q. fresco, chili p., cilantro, lime

Fry cups with 3 sauces. Sweet potato and regular fries from Noon Mediterranean

Bleu cheese with bacon - artisanal bacon, bleu cheese bechamel

Nacho cheese with green chiles - sharp cheddar bechamel, sautéed hatch chiles

Garlic aioli with truffle oil - parmesan, white truffle oil, garlic aioli, green onions

Plus ketchup, tabasco, sriracha, and fry sauce on a lazy susan

Booze ala Pierre with Pierre serving

Bachelorette Party - manned by me

Champagne selection from Pierre with club staff and Greta serving

Three kinds of Texas-themed Macarons

Grapefruit macs with grapefruit buttercream filling (yellow and pink)

Peach macs with peach jam filling (coral and orange)

Cayenne macs with molasses buttercream filling (red)

Chocolate Strawberry Tort with Cream Cheese Whipped Cream

Lemon Rosemary Ricotta Mini Cupcakes

A lot of that had been prepped. Bacon was baked, green chiles sautéed, and buttercreams whipped. The mini cupcakes had been baked and sealed up in huge Tupperware and the steak was marinating, but there was so much more that needed to be prepped right now. Violet had to know. She had just resolved to call Laurel when her phone started to vibrate on the couch's end table. Of course, it was her mother, she always called at the worst times.

"Oh Violet! Honey!" Barbara sounded frantic and like she was talking through her car's sound system.

"Is something wrong?" Violet plugged one ear and closed her eyes to concentrate on listening to her mother's garbled voice.

"Greta! She's been arrested!" her mother wailed.

Chilaquiles Verdes

For 1 person, just double the recipe and use a bigger frying pan for more people.

You can make this more of a meal with shredded chicken, but I like to keep it simple for a quick breakfast.

½ cup (130g) your favorite green salsa or salsa verde
1 large egg
½ cup (100g) shredded Mexican cheese, I use a blend, but use whatever you have on hand
2 big handfuls corn tortilla chips
2 Tablespoons crema or sour cream
A wedge of lime
Cilantro, chopped
Chives or green onions, chopped
Avocado slices, optional

1. In a small frying pan, pour in salsa and a tablespoon of water. Heat over medium until salsa is simmering.
2. Gently crack your egg into the middle of the simmering salsa, turn heat down to medium-low, and cook gently for about 5 minutes. You are basically poaching your egg in salsa.
3. When the white of your egg is cooked but the yolk is still runny, sprinkle cheese to cover the top of the egg and the salsa.
4. When cheese is melted, add tortilla chips and toss to coat. It's okay if the yolk breaks here, it's all part of the delicious sauce.
5. Transfer all the contents of your pan to a shallow bowl then garnish with crema, lime, cilantro, green onion and avocado. Serve immediately before it gets soggy.

Didn't she deserve it? Yes. Absolutely. I was defending people against a tyrant! No one wanted her around and the world would be done a favor by anyone that helped her leave it.

Chapter Eight

Who Done It?

"What?" Violet's stomach turned over on itself like an omelette.

"Your sister has been arrested! They think she murdered Mrs. LeBaron! Oh Honey, it's such a mess. Luckily, Lindy was already at preschool, but I was called to come get her."

Violet could already tell where this was going, but she went on listening to her mother. She felt her pulse quicken.

"So I've got Lindy right here, but I am out all day. I am going to sit on that police department until I can bail Greta out. Are you home? Can I bring Lindy to you?"

Violet knew that Barbara and Lindy would already be on their way. Although Violet was busy, too, and not sure how she felt about an anxious kid who was in a tough emotional spot, she knew that she was in a better position to have Lindy. She could just hang out and color or watch TV while Violet cooked.

"Uh, sure," Violet admitted. "I don't have anything fun to do. Oh, and I need you to come get her tonight so I can go to Laurel's bachelorette party. It will be tasteful, but...I still don't think they would appreciate me bringing a child."

"Yes, of course. See you in a minute!" Barbara blurted it out and hung up abruptly.

So she really was already on her way. Lindy wasn't that destructive toddler anymore, so the house was ready for her, but Violet wasn't sure that she was. Violet could be fun with Lindy at their house, and with Greta as their buffer, but here? Jake wasn't even here at the moment, and he was usually the fun one.

Violet needed to cook. And clean! Kids were so messy! And sticky! Maybe Violet really could have Lindy watch TV all day. Violet was still worried about the mess but knowing that

Jake would be home soon and knowing how much Lindy would be mesmerized by the TV, now she could get back to worrying about Greta.

Arrested? Don had said that Greta was a suspect, but didn't they have anyone better? Like Laurel and Paul? There were a lot of people with much more motive than Greta. She didn't even have any motive! Was Detective Taylor that blindly ambitious? Violet had to call Don before she could concentrate on anything else.

"I'm so sorry," Detective Donnelly said through the phone. "My partner went over there faster than I expected. He really thinks that the evidence all points to Greta."

"But you know that she didn't do it!" Violet was trying not to cry.

"I'm sorry," he said again. "I'm not sure my partner cares about that. He doesn't care what I say and I'm not even sure that he cares about the truth. He just cares that he can make a case against your sister. When I try to say anything, he -- he just gets mad."

"But the conversation that I overheard…between her and Paul…and the herbal tea!"

"Yes, that is some good evidence in her favor. For me that takes away any chance of motive. I'm driving over there now to straighten that out, but she still had the best means and opportunity. I think she'll be released, but she won't be in the clear."

"Okay," Violet sniffled. The tears started now that the immediate stress was abating. "My mother is coming down there to get Greta, so, you know, you might be in for an earful."

"I don't know that it will be right away. It could be hours. We still have to get her out of booking, I'm going to try to get the charges dropped,"

"She doesn't care. She'll wait," Violet interrupted.

"Okay," Don sighed. "Just tell her not to piss off Taylor, okay? He's friends with the chief and is getting a lot of pressure to close this case, too. He's a good detective, but a stickler and I don't think he should know about how much I have told you. Neither of us wants to get on his bad side."

Ten minutes later, Katy had confirmed over the phone that she had things well in-hand at the flower shop and Jake had returned and promised to make garlic aioli and cream cheese whipped cream far away from each other to avoid flavor contamination. Everything was ready when Barbara's signature knock resounded. Before Violet could walk over to let them in, she looked up to see the saddest little person that she had ever seen in real life.

Lindy stood with an oversized lunch box dangling from one finger and her pink backpack showing around all sides of her. Her posture was wilted, and her head had lulled slightly to one side where her little side-ponytail dangled limp and tangled. Her t-shirt that said 'Dreams come true' betrayed how ecstatic she usually was and just accentuated the stark contrast now.

Violet's heart unexpectedly broke at the sight and she automatically dropped to one knee and held her arms out as far as she could. Lindy met her in the middle and they threw their arms around each other and just stayed there. Lindy's hands were cold on the back of Violet's thin button-up shirt, so Violet felt a little more keenly and squeezed a little tighter.

"She hasn't eaten lunch, so she brought it with her to eat here." Violet's mother's anxiety was in the way of her seeing anyone else's grief. "I'm going to get Greta and I'll make sure that I'm back before six tonight."

When they didn't answer, Barbara melted a little and came to stroke Lindy's hair. "It will be alright, Honey. I'll go get your mom and bring her back."

After Violet and Lindy finally released each other, they bid good luck to their mother and grandmother and sat on the couch. Lindy said that she wasn't hungry, but Violet surprised herself by insisting that Lindy needed to eat something. Violet's anxiety was at an eleven with a kid eating lunch on her upholstery and her sister sitting in jail, but it felt good to be taking care of someone that needed her.

This little person craved Violet so much. She was shocked to realize that it felt fulfilling.

"How are you, Sweetie? Are you okay?" Violet leaned in, realizing that this must be even harder on a child than it had

116

been for herself.

"Fine." Lindy didn't even look up from her pb&j. "Grandma said Mommy will be back for dinner."

"Um, I think so." Violet hesitated. "But, you know, even if she misses dinner tonight, you will still have fun eating dinner at Grandma's house. I think you get to sleep over!"

"Yeah." Now Lindy looked up, pawing her flyaways out of her face with a flat, sticky hand. "Grandma said that she'll make my favorite dinner. Pancakes!"

"Ooh! Grandma makes the best pancakes!" Violet was having trouble holding up her end of the conversation and keeping a brave face.

This innocent little ray of sunshine next to her could not have her mother taken away from her. Violet could not have her sister taken away from her. Even a little while in jail could mean the collapse of her sister's business, then Greta would have nothing to come back to but Lindy, and no way to take care of her. Then, Violet realized that Greta could have Lindy taken away from her, too. Then, would Violet have to take Lindy in?

She was not ready to be a mom, was she? Violet imagined crying tantrums and smudging hands. Crayons and cookies smeared into the couch. No more funny business with her new husband ever again. They didn't even have a wall between their bedroom and the rest of the apartment! Jake was right that kids were great, but all the time? Violet's heart grew three sizes anytime Lindy was around, but today it felt like her chest would explode. Was that anxiety or love? Violet concluded that it was probably a mix of the two. Love and apprehension for the girl next to her and the girl sitting far away in jail.

If this Detective Taylor and the rest of the police department were so antsy to find anyone to pin this murder on, then Violet would do as Detective Donnelly had asked. Violet would watch, listen, and spy. She would look deep into the real suspects and solve this puzzle. Violet decided there on her couch that she was done crying and that she was going to find the real killer. No matter what.

While Lindy finished her lunch and watched 'Pinkalicious', Violet could make macarons and think. She mindlessly gathered ingredients and sifted powdered sugar and almond flour while she made a list in her mind and occasionally took notes in her tiny book. Who could have done it? Who were all the possible suspects?

Everyone at the party

Violet had to narrow that down, so who would have had access to that back room? She listed the people that she had known had gone in that room before the murder.

Me
Greta
Jake
Katy
Michael
Pierre

But wait. Couldn't anyone have gone in that room? It wasn't locked and everyone was too busy to watch that door the whole time. Since it was off a little hallway and not directly off the main room or kitchen, there were probably times when no one could see the door. Anyone could have slipped in there, especially during a crowded party. Besides, Violet didn't think that she was poisoned in that room. Francesca had gone in there after she had already started feeling sick. She had probably been discretely poisoned before that, but not necessarily. It had to have been while she was in the main room, right? She was poisoned in the rehearsal dinner. Narrowing the poisoning down by who had the opportunity wouldn't do any good. It could have been anyone there that night.

In books, it was usually someone that no one would notice like a mailman or a waiter, so Violet searched her memory. There was no one there like that. No representatives from the gallery were there, no waiters were used, no repairmen, no mailmen, there wasn't even a bathroom or elevator attendant. No one could have come in except guests and Violet's staff.

As she separated eggs, Violet resolved to think about motive. Dozens of people had motive to hate Francesca LeBaron, but who had motive to actually kill her? And what kind of motive? Just for being unpleasant during the party?

Pierre
Katy
Laurel
Paul
Greta
Me
Anyone at the party

However, this person had to have motive to kill her long before last night so that they could cook up or dry out the stuff. She exed out that last list and started over.

Motive usually boiled down to money or love. Or love's twin, hate.

Would it have been for money? Or about spite over money?

Antonia, Paul's mother
Henning, Paul's father
Paul
Laurel, but not really
Greta, but not really
Pastor Schmidt
Luke
Pierre?

119

Not Pierre, because he was making more money now than he did before.

Or love? Or rather, being bitter over lost love?

Dr. Glenn? A million years later?

Or some other reason entirely?

Michael
Pierre
Anyone at the party
Luke?

Violet's mind and stand mixer set on high to whip egg whites and wonder about Luke. He had been acting strangely and particularly livid with Francesca last night. What had they argued about? Money?

Violet knew that Luke was in debt or some kind of money trouble, despite his clean financial records, because his whole family knew about it. He had asked them all for money! And she had overheard his interview with Don. Luke had debts to people other than banks. Loan sharks? Bookies? The mob? Some other kind of seedy character? Could he owe enough money that he needed his grandmother's fortune and couldn't wait?

Being family, he would definitely know about his grandmother's heart condition and could have easily slipped something into his grandmother's coffee, tea, water, or wine during the party. He was definitely self-centered enough to kill for money and then let someone else go to prison for it. Violet had no idea if Luke knew about plants, but he knew drugs. Besides, anyone was one internet search away from knowing all about digitalis and foxglove.

Violet decided that Luke needed a closer look. He was going to be at the bachelor party early tonight, being the best man, so she would try to ask him some discrete questions then.

"Aunt Violet?" Lindy surprised Violet out of her reflections. "Can I help?"

"Oh…" Violet had images of the kitchen covered in powdered sugar and ruined macarons, but she didn't want to say no. "Ok, but these cookies are very difficult and you have to do exactly as I say. And be very careful!"

Lindy nodded emphatically and smiled for the first time since arriving.

Violet finished whipping the egg whites and had Lindy dump in the dry ingredients. Violet couldn't just stand by and watch, so she wrapped her arms onto both sides and helped the tiny hands pour slowly and carefully. Violet could tell that Lindy was concentrating and taking her task seriously, which made Violet's heart lilt a little. She smelled Lindy's strawberry-shampoo hair and automatically kissed the back of her head as they finished pouring.

"Wow! Great job!" Violet chirped. "You didn't spill even a tiny bit!"

As they finished and piped the macaron shells, Lindy stood on a flour bucket to watch. Then Lindy got to carefully bang the pans on the counter. After every loud *SMACK!* Lindy would giggle and look to Violet for approval. When they finished and set the pans aside to rest before their stint in the oven, Lindy leapt from her flour bucket and into Violet's arms. They whirled around together as Jake emerged from his writing and answered the unheeded knock at the door.

When they stopped spinning, with Violet a little breathless, Jake, Greta, and Barbara stood beaming at them from the front doorway.

"Mommy!" Lindy yelled and ran to Greta as they enfolded in each other's arms.

"Mommy!" Violet joked in the same tone as she gently hugged Barbara. "How did it go?"

"Oh, well…fine." Barbara was still preoccupied, but less than before as she continued. "Greta just has to make her court appearance and can't travel outside the county."

Greta stood and turned to face her mother and sister, with a glance at Jake, saying, "Thank you all so much."

No one knew what to say, so all the girls shared a group hug for a long moment. Jake had left them to it and was staring at his cooking assignments on the dining table when he said, "Sorry, ladies...uh, Violet, do we know if the parties are happening tonight?"

"Ah sh-shoot!" Violet changed her exclamation as she realized Lindy was in earshot. "I'll call Laurel right now."

Violet was on the balcony with Jake working hard in the apartment behind her as she dialed Laurel.

"Violet!" Laurel burst out as soon as she picked up the phone. "I'm so sorry I never called you! Is it too late to tell you that we are still having the bachelor and bachelorette parties?"

"Oh good! I've been working on the food like they are, so I'm relieved."

"Yes, our older relations might think it's a little inappropriate, just on principle, but Paul and I are agreed. Convention be damned! Nothing else is keeping us apart! We are getting married no matter what!"

"Good," Violet said out loud, but wondered at Laurel's phrasing in her mind. Continuing their wedding plans didn't exactly support her theory that they were innocent of the murder.

"Will you please join the party tonight? Everyone there is going to be a relative and I believe I'll be bored stiff. But you...you seem like you could be the life of the party if someone got you good and drunk!" Laurel's party girl side peeked its head out for a moment.

"Me? Oh no. I hate getting drunk! Too sloppy!" Violet twittered.

"Ah yeah. Paul told me that you are a neat freak." Laurel's teasing smile showed through in her voice.

"I don't know about freak, but..." Violet tried not to be offended.

"Don't worry. I mean it in the best possible way! In fact, we have to get together. I need some of that to rub off on me!"

"Ok, I'll hang around tonight. Whenever I am not being the caterer then I'll stand by to make sure you don't get too drunk and embarrass yourself in front of your whole family!"

Both girls guffawed and signed off, finding that they were

now more excited about the approaching evening.

As Violet re-entered the apartment and slid the balcony door closed behind her, she found Greta and Lindy tangled up together on her couch. They were both asleep with just a whiff of a smile on their lips. Then for just a moment, Violet found herself with a stirring. A yearning.

Jake broke the spell as he approached her with little notebook open in his hand. "Does this mean you are investigating?"

Violet pulled Jake back onto the balcony for privacy as she snatched her book out of his hand.

"Don't read that! But yes, I am," Violet snapped. "And you are, too!"

"Vi, this could be dangerous!" Jake was bordering on frantic. "I can't let you get hurt!"

"You won't," Violet said as her tone softened, and she pecked him on the nose. "We're investigating on the downlow. No one will even know about it."

Jake cracked a reluctant smile. "Ok, just promise me that you won't do anything dangerous."

"Cross my heart," Violet said as she pulled him in for a long, torrid kiss.

Violet and Jake arrived early at the bachelor party to find Katy arranging floral greenery by itself in antique beer steins on each of the tables in the Zilker Park Clubhouse.

"Hi-ee!" Katy chirped, sounding even more bubbly than usual. "I've almost got it! I just have that table left, then I can help you set up food if y'all want."

"Thanks, but you should put your feet up!" Violet protested. "Aren't you worn out?"

"I feel great! This is all so excitin'!"

The rustic stone walls, heavy, aged wagon wheel chandeliers, and roaring fireplace made it look every bit the classic man cave. With someone's collection of German beer steins on the tables and wood print tablecloths, Violet had to admit that it was indeed the perfect bachelor party.

Jake pulled up a cushioned chair behind Katy as Violet

brought in another load and Katy finished the last decorative stein. After Katy reluctantly accepted the seat and Jake had gone out to retrieve more party supplies, the ladies were able to talk about him.

"That's a good man you got there," Katy panted up at Violet as she squirmed to get comfortable. "I hope you know how lucky you are."

Violet didn't know what to say as Katy settled, rubbed her belly and looked tired.

"Are you okay?" Violet asked with a head tilt.

"Oh yeah. I just get winded, that's all."

Violet was at a loss for words again. She had not meant to ask if Katy was okay right here and now. Violet worried about Katy in the long run. She was far from her family, alone, and having her first baby.

Just then, Pierre came in with a dolly loaded with crates. His dark, willowy arms still looked graceful even when he was hauling whiskey and rum. Tonight he wore a dusty rose-colored button-up shirt with tailored gray slacks.

"Hey girl!" Pierre also seemed extra chipper as he asked, "Where should I do my thing? What do you ladies have planned?"

Violet and Katy helped Pierre set up in the prominent front corner next to the drinking fountains while Jake happily left to go make bechamel sauces for the fries.

"I'm glad they didn't cancel, that would have been rough on all of our businesses." Violet tried to get the conversation onto an idea that they could all share, wedding work.

"Girl, liquor doesn't go bad. I could have just saved it for the next party. I think they shouldn't cancel cuz you can't let people like that old lady win. If she's going to get dead in the back room just for some attention, then you still gotta do you!"

"Oh, haven't you guys heard? They found out that it was murder!" Violet said as she looked between their shocked open mouths, realizing that maybe she wasn't supposed to say that.

"I know they thought maybe, but..." began Katy.

"How do they know?" interrupted Pierre.

"I think it's partially because I got some of the poison when

I gave her mouth-to-mouth. That means it was on her mouth even though her latest pill hadn't dissolved."

"Mm, so it was that? I hope you learned not to do CPR on dead bodies again!" Pierre crooned.

"Yeah, it's not worth the risk, especially if they've been dead for a while like her," Katy added.

"I guess you guys are right. It was pretty stupid. She was even cold, but...I panicked! I don't even think I did it right. I guess I need to brush up on my CPR."

They said nothing, but Pierre swept at Violet's hair and Katy rubbed Violet's other arm when Violet started to tear up.

"Ok, back to work! We need to finish here so that we can get over to the bachelorette party." Violet shook off her train of thought, wiping her eyes.

"I already dropped off the champagnes, so you good over there," Pierre said.

"Don't you need to head over there even sooner than me?" Violet asked Katy.

"Oh I will. But I have more to do here first," Katy said as she looked around the room.

Katy helped put the fries in the oven to stay warm with a pan on the table for Jake to keep refilling during the party, then put out the tiny chafing dishes as Jake filled them with the sauces he had made for the fries. As Violet joined them with the newly grilled and coated skewers of mini Mexican street corn, the venue's coordinator appeared from the back. She looked tall, blonde, and efficient as she checked in with everyone. The only thing to break up her sleek silhouette was a protruding belly that made her look like she was carrying a basketball under her skirt suit.

Another pregnant woman. The universe was definitely trying to rub Violet's face in the subject.

Bachelors started to pour in the door. When Paul came in wearing his 'Taken' t-shirt with paint smears in his hair, he looked utterly surprised and almost scared to see them all standing together.

"Sorry!" Violet apologized by reflex "Aren't you guys early?" she asked.

"Yeah, uh, we finished paintballing a little earlier than we expected. I hope that's okay," Paul said in a daze.

"Of course!" Violet said. "We are almost done, but Pierre is ready for you!"

Pierre lifted his arms with a bottle of Smirnoff in one hand and a shot glass in the other and successfully elicited a happy roar from the crowd. They all gathered over by the fire and liquor table, handing out shots while Violet, Jake and Katy finished setting out all the food and the quiet event coordinator disappeared into the back again.

Violet watched Luke. He was so happy to be handing out cigars to the party. Could he have killed his grandmother? Or could Paul? Could either of them really compartmentalize that well?

Luke noticed her staring and followed her into the kitchen when she went to get more supplies.

"Hey Vi." Luke sighed in her face as he backed her against a counter. His breath reeked of liquor and his hair was sweaty and stringy. Violet was using all her energy not to freak out that he might drip perspiration on her.

"Ok, you're drunk. Got too much of a head start on the party, did ya?" Violet sneered.

"No such thing! The party never stops!" Luke leaned in even closer to purr, too wasted to read Violet's face. "You wanna party, too?"

Violet was too disgusted to hold back. Her skin crawled and her scalp winced as she freaked out and pushed him off of her.

"Was it a party when you killed your own grandmother? THAT party was ruined!"

Luke stumbled back but still didn't lose his cool. "What? I didn't kill her." Luke's usually suave smile was a little too crooked and sloppy to be charming now. "You think I killed her?"

"You need the money, right? Or did she find out about your little secret and you had to keep her quiet?" Violet was swinging in the dark, hoping to hit on something that would get Luke to talk. She had no idea what she was doing or what his secret was, but was willing to try anything to get him to make a mistake, especially now while he was not thinking clearly.

Luke suddenly sprang forward and grabbed Violet by the collars of her white button-up shirt. Violet was so surprised and cornered that she had nowhere to go. Her hands went instinctively to his clenched forearms, but they were slippery and nauseating.

"How do you know about that? Did she tell you? Or did you talk to him?"

Violet's eyes grew wide and a lump rose in her throat. Her scalp tried to crawl up as she groped the counter behind her for something to use to defend herself.

It was Luke's turn to sneer now as he looked her up and down and released her. "You got nothin'. Yer just a little…"

A grabbing hand on Luke's shoulder turned him quickly, then FLUMP! A dull thud echoed through the kitchen as Luke doubled over Jake's fist.

"Stay away from my wife," Jake said, calmly and evenly, still clenched and staring at him with wild eyes.

Violet sighed as Luke stumbled out of the room. Then Jake relaxed and swept her up in his arms.

"Are you okay?" Jake asked with concern in his eyes now. "You should really get out of here."

"I will, thank you!" Violet wrapped her arms around his neck and tears pricked her eyes despite her best effort. "I'm fine, really. He's just drunk."

Violet quickly filled Jake in on what happened and her suspicions of Luke.

"Ok. I can also be your eyes and ears here, as well as your hands." Jake swept Violet's hair behind her ear with hands as tender as scallops. "Don't worry. We'll figure out who did this."

Grandma's Fluffy Pancakes

Makes about 16 - 4" pancakes

2 cups + 2 Tablespoons (about 270g) all-purpose flour
2 Tablespoons (25g) sugar
1/2 Tablespoon or 1 1/2 teaspoons baking powder
1 teaspoon baking soda
1/2 teaspoon salt
2 cups (500mL) whole milk (2% works too, but whole is best)
1/2 cup (125g) whole plain yogurt, (low fat is okay, too)
2 whole eggs
1 teaspoon vanilla extract
4 Tablespoons or ½ stick (about 60g) butter, melted before you start

1. In a medium-sized mixing bowl, combine flour, sugar, baking powder, baking soda, and salt. In a separate, larger bowl whisk together milk, yogurt, eggs, and vanilla. While whisking milk mixture, drizzle in melted and slightly cooled butter.
2. Now pour dry ingredients into wet ingredients. Mix together until just incorporated, but not too much!
3. When no dry pockets remain, cook on griddle or in non-stick pan over medium-low heat until golden brown on both sides. Don't know when to flip? When the opaque, puffy doneness starts to crawl up around the edges, flip the pancakes. If they get too brown, turn down the heat!
4. This recipe is great doubled for a big crowd or if you want leftovers to carry your through the rest of the week!

Mini Mexican Street Corn

This variation on the street food classic is with skewered baby corn so that it is cleaner and more manageable at a party. The corn skewers can be roasted, broiled or grilled before getting all dressed up. Use Polar baby corn or another brand that you know doesn't smell like a barnyard, or even fresh or frozen if you can get it!

1 can (15 ounces or 250g) whole baby corn, drained, rinsed twice, and dried on a towel
About 7 skewers
¼ cup butter (57g), melted
¼ cup (25g) finely shredded cojita cheese, or parmesan if you are in a bind
5 limes ready to be squeezed for juice, or about ⅔ cup lime juice (about 160ml)
½ Tablespoon chili powder
¼ cup (50g) sour cream or Mexican crema
¼ cup cilantro, finely chopped

5. If using canned corn, add rinsed and dried corn to a small bowl with ½ cup (120mL) lime juice and ½ cup (120mL) water. Soak it for about an hour (or more) to leach out that canned-corn-smell. At the end of that hour, remove from lime-water and drain on a towel. If using fresh or frozen corn, boil it for 5 minutes, then drain and dry.
6. Set out melted butter, squeezable lime, sour cream, chili powder, shredded cheese, and cilantro all in bowls ahead of time so it's easier to assemble your masterpieces when they are done cooking.
7. Skewer 3 or 5 baby corn on each skewer, fairly near the pointed end. Grill skewers of corn until grill marks appear. Canned corn is already cooked, so just get it to have some lovely browned spots. I use a George Foreman grill and it takes about 7 minutes.
8. Hold skewer over butter bowl and dribble butter over the cobs in a way to let the excess fall back into the butter bowl. Then set skewer on a work surface and heavily sprinkle cheese, then lime, then chili powder. Next spread or dribble sour cream, then sprinkle cilantro. This layering promotes the most topping stickage.
9. Garnish with lime and/or cilantro and serve immediately or chilled later.

I had to help everyone get out from under her thumb and there was only one way to do that.
To the whole family, everyone, it would be a blessing.

Chapter Nine

Can You Keep A Secret?

After setting up Jake and the bachelor party, Violet arrived at the Westwood Country Club at the same time as Katy to set up for the bachelorette party. Luckily, Laurel's party had started at the nail salon with manis and pedis, so Violet and Katy had plenty of time to set up, even if Greta didn't show up.

"Do you know if Greta is coming?" Katy asked. "I don't think I need her, but I haven't gotten to ask if she is okay and just check in with her."

"I think she is okay. She told me that she was coming tonight but might be late."

"Oh, ok." Katy wilted as she spoke

Violet said. "Don't worry! I'm here to help and we have plenty of time."

"Thanks." Katy sighed. "And Greta made all these arrangements early." She signalled to the dozens of pale pink rose bouquets over her shoulder. "So I don't have to worry about her approval."

Violet knew what she meant. Greta could get positively manic about getting everything exactly as she wanted them for an event, to the point where she would make more mistakes than normal. Hopefully, with all that had happened and with all the preparation they had put in, Greta would be able to let go and let them handle this.

After arranging and spritzing all the globes of blushing roses in tall, clear vases, they turned their attention to the food. Thanks to meticulous planning, nothing needed to be made or served warm, just beautifully displayed. Only Pierre's champagne needed to be put on ice, so the bottles were delved into crushed ice in beautiful galvanized tubs.

As the two were putting the last tub of ice onto the drink table, Greta swept in looking rejuvenated.

"You made it! And you look great!" Katy exclaimed.

Greta responded. "I feel great! But sorry I am late."

Violet broke in, hot on the tail of Greta's apology. "How is that possible? You were in jail this morning!"

"A great nap and a snuggle with my girl can do wonders! Plus, I have every reason to be optimistic!" Greta sighed.

"Maybe you don't know, but you are the lead suspect, and this is now a murder investigation!" Violet was dumbfounded.

"Don't try to bring me down!" Greta argued, speaking over the top of Katy's head to Violet. She was now dampened and irritable. "Don't be so negative!"

"I'm sorry, I-I just want to be realistic about the situation," Violet defended herself.

"I am being realistic! I didn't kill her, the justice system really does work, and you are going to find out who really did it!" Greta guessed through her anger and plead maniacally into Violet's face again.

"Me? I-I'm trying...but..." Violet stammered, surprised by another person that thought she could solve a mystery. Violet was now determined to find out who had committed the murder, but she was not about to start going around telling people that. She wanted to be discrete and work from the shadows, despite how she had handled the situation with Luke at the bachelor party.

"Okay, I am trying, but you guys! Don't tell anyone!" Violet stage-whispered. "I don't want the killer to know! I have to do it without the bad guy or the police catching on. I think the main thing I have going for me is invisibility as the caterer, so please, keep it a secret!"

"I won't tell," Katy said, as Greta made the motion of locking her mouth closed.

Surprisingly muted bachelorette party guests were already milling around the overstuffed velvet couches and tall glass vases of flowers when Violet brought out the last footed cake plate.

"OOoooo! Is that chocolate?" Laurel's sister asked.

"And fresh strawberries?" Laurel's mother, Carina, added. "You don't get to see many fresh strawberries in baked goods. Don't they release too much moisture or something?"

"Well yeah. But this recipe is specially designed for it." Violet blushed.

Carina was impressed as she called everyone over, welcomed them, briefly prayed over the food, and invited everyone to enjoy the spread. She didn't mind that Violet had not actually said that she was ready.

Laurel was radiant again in a dusty rose tulle skirt and white button-up shirt that looked three times as expensive as Violet's. She greeted all the guests and then came over to Violet.

"Thanks so much for staying, and sorry about the short notice! Do you have time to sit down now?"

"I'll be out in just a minute." Violet stalled going into the party.

She wasn't sure she wanted to be in the center of the attention. She needed to watch and listen for anything suspicious and do her actual job of replenishing dishes as they got low. Even if she had felt like she fit in with this crowd and knew that it wouldn't put off Laurel's mother, she still just liked to stay invisible. She wanted to fade into the background. Luckily, after returning with the cream cheese whipped cream, Laurel seemed occupied with her guests. Violet could stay behind and observe.

As no obvious suspicious behavior arose, wild accusations started to float through Violet's mind. Outrageous theories surfaced, then flowed away just as quickly. Could Laurel have wanted Paul to have his own money? Could Laurel's mother have wanted Paul to have his own money? Did her family object against the marriage after all? Could Laurel's sister be jealous and want to get the wedding cancelled? Could Luke be jealous and want to marry Laurel himself? The possibilities were endless! How could she ever find the killer without more information? Probably the only people that would know everything about what was happening were Francesca,

133

hopefully Paul and maybe Laurel.

It had to involve their wedding, right? Anyone at the rehearsal dinner could have gotten to Mrs. LeBaron at any time. They were her friends and family. The only reason for her to be killed at a wedding-related event would be to involve the wedding, or the people there, wouldn't it? Perhaps the murder carried a message with it. Violet needed to understand what was really going on. She needed to talk to Laurel.

In her interview with Detective Donnelly, Laurel had definitely lied. There was no way she had just been trying to help clean up. She had snuck away and cleaned up that herbal tea before anyone else had even know that they were dealing with a murder. Even when they were not talking about the mug, it had felt like Laurel was keeping a secret. She had held something back. Maybe it wasn't important, but maybe she knew who had killed. And why. Violet needed to find out.

As the party slowed down and all the food had been replenished, Laurel came to implore Violet again.

"Please come out into the party! I've been pleasant to everyone, my mother has gone home, and I'm bored out of my mind!"

Violet giggled. "Sorry. You mean polite conversation and delicate food isn't your idea of a good time?"

"Hey, the food is amazing. But my mother did not exactly plan a 'bachelorette party.' This isn't very me, is it?" Laurel gave an epic eye roll which reminded Violet of Laurel's mother.

The structured champagne tasting went off without a hitch and everyone seemed to enjoy the Texas-themed French macarons and other desserts. Violet had guessed that there would be extra 'BBQ macarons' left over, being the weirdest flavor they had served, and it was looking like she would be right. As the older guests left the bachelorette party, the younger ladies got progressively more inebriated. Laurel's sister was in the corner dancing with their cousin, another cousin was passed out on the couch, and Laurel's work acquaintances were at the door flirting with the club's handsome event coordinator who had come to check on the party.

Laurel came over to another one of the tufted pink couches to talk to Violet specifically.

"Thanks so much for your help. This was fun, in its own way." Laurel was kind even when she was tipsy.

"Sorry that you didn't get the kind of bachelorette party you wanted, though." Violet felt the need to apologize to Laurel's dismal face. Laurel was usually so vibrant and full of life, but now she seemed weighed down and bitter.

"No, it's alright. I had one with my sister and cousins, had one friend fly in, like a week ago. We crawled down 6th Street. It was great."

"Then what's wrong? Are you nervous about tomorrow? Or the murder?"

"No, no. Nothing else is going to get in the way of me marrying Paul tomorrow. Don't worry about me, I just tend to be a sad drunk. I really don't know why I keep doing it, being wasted is no fun for me. I have the most fun when I have no chemical help getting there."

Violet tried to see through Laurel. Finally, Violet decided that this was her opening. Laurel was tipsy, chatty, and close to the subject of her marriage and people that might want to stop it or send the wedding party a message. Violet also believed that they were starting to become friends. Violet could do what Don wanted and what Greta needed - get some answers.

"Speaking of chemical help…we have to figure out this murder." Violet jumped in with both feet.

Laurel looked back at Violet, sad and wistful. "I heard they arrested your sister. I'm so sorry."

"I know that she didn't do this. There's just no way!" Violet stared at Laurel. "Do you have any ideas?"

Although Violet had tried to keep the question vague, Laurel zeroed in on her meaning and narrowed her eyes at Violet. "So you did see me wash that cup."

Dark Chocolate Strawberry Tort

This recipe is fantastically easy, but elegant. It is also a rare chance to add berries straight on top!

1 cup (200g) granulated sugar, plus 1 Tablespoon for sprinkling
¼ cup, or ½ stick, (about 60g) butter, softened
½ cup or 3 ounces (85g) semi-sweet chocolate chips, melted
2 large eggs
½ teaspoon vanilla extract
½ teaspoon other extract, like almond, chocolate, strawberry, or orange
1 cup (120g) all-purpose flour
¼ cup (25g) Dutch-processed cocoa powder
1 tsp baking powder
Dash of salt
1 pint strawberries, halved, or other berry (about 300g)

1. Grease a 9-inch springform pan and preheat oven to 350 degrees F (180C).
2. Cream butter and sugar together until it resembles wet sand, then cream in melted chocolate, scraping the sides of the bowl.
3. Mix in eggs, one at a time, then extracts.
4. In a separate bowl, whisk together flour, cocoa, baking powder and salt.
5. Beat dry ingredients into wet ingredients, then spread in an even layer on the bottom of the pan.
6. Staying about a half-inch away from the sides, cover surface of the batter with strawberries, or whatever fruit you choose to use. Keep fruit really close together, and even touching, in order to fit it all on.
7. Pat the berries lightly to flatten and nestle them into the batter a little, then sprinkle with 1 Tablespoon of sugar. Bake for 50 - 60 minutes, or until an inserted toothpick comes out clean.
8. Let cool for 5-10 minutes in the pan, then run a knife

around the edge of the pan and remove from pan.

9. Serve with Cream Cheese Whipped Cream, ice cream, or just a sprinkling of confectioners sugar.

10. This freezes well, so make it ahead, wrap it in cling film and freeze it indefinitely. When ready to serve, thaw in the fridge overnight, unwrap, then warm in a 300 degree F (150C) oven for 10 minutes.

Cream Cheese Whipped Cream

This upgraded whipped cream is soft and velvety, and has a lovely tang! It is also more stable, so you can make it the day before and use in any recipe in place of whipped cream. If you like your whipped cream sweeter or if trying to please kids, use the optional powdered sugar.

1 - 8 ounce package of cream cheese or neufchatel, softened or room temp (or 225g of soft cheese, like Philadelphia)
1 Tablespoon honey, or more to taste (or 21g)
1/2 Tablespoon lemon juice (or ¼ of a lemon)
1 cup heavy whipping cream, chilled (about 250 mL)
1/2 teaspoon vanilla extract
Optional - 2 Tablespoons powdered sugar

1. Place cream cheese, honey and lemon in large bowl and whip until completely smooth.

2. Whip ¼ cup of the cream into the cream cheese mixture until completely smooth. Scrape down the sides of the bowl. Repeat 3 more times for a total of 4 additions (1 cup.) Mixture will first get more loose, then more fluffy with each addition.

3. Chill mixture after it is smooth, either 10 minutes in the freezer or 20 minutes in the fridge.

4. Retrieve and whip mixture on high speed one more time and beat in vanilla. Use immediately or store in airtight container in refrigerator to firm up a bit. It will last in the refrigerator about 3 days.

Chapter Ten

Can Anyone Help Her?

Laurel and Violet inspected each other for a moment. The tension started to mount, and Violet grew anxious. Had she ruined her chance to grow close with this innocent, engaging friend? Or had she enraged a dangerous murderer? Laurel was too wilted to be able to read. Violet's nameless dread grew until Laurel hiccupped and giggled.

"I realize that looked bad. I told the police that I was just cleaning up, but I don't think they bought that for a second. Well, I admit it." Laurel let out a long sigh.

Violet was suffering during every moment of that drawn out breath. Had Laurel just admitted to killing Mrs. LeBaron? Would she admit it to the police? Had she just succeeded in clearing Greta?

"I cleaned up that mug because I thought it might be murder. It sounds so silly now, but I thought that maybe Paul had killed her." Laurel let out a laugh that obviously sounded more ironic than it was supposed to.

Violet didn't laugh. "So you don't think so anymore?"

Laurel tried to laugh again, but hiccupped. "Of course not. I talked it out with Paul, and he made me see."

Violet was still dubious, and it must have shown on her face.

"Ok, let me explain," Laurel began. "When she died, I thought it very well could have been murder. I thought that it might have been this herbal tea that Paul had given me to give to his grandmother at the party. I got so mad at him! He had it change hands, then I had it change hands! It could have gone to anyone! If it was poisoned, he could have killed someone else! He killed have killed me!"

Laurel stopped ranting and went back to looking distended to Violet. "I was talking to Paul about how I had tried to help cover his tracks by washing that cup when he calmed me down and explained it all.

"He hadn't poisoned his grandmother! That cup wasn't poisoned! The grocery store by his house, his H.E.B., just has this herbal tea that she likes a lot. It's also one that is safe for her to drink with her medication. Her neighborhood doesn't have it, so he brings it anytime he is going to be around her."

"Laurel…" Violet tried to find a way to say it gently.

"No." Laurel waved a limp hand. "I thought that he still could have added something to it too, until he pointed out that the timing was all wrong for that! She also hadn't drunken any of that herbal tea! It had to have been earlier in the party! It couldn't have been Paul's tea! Do you see?"

Laurel now leaned forward with urgency as Violet considered it all.

"I do see. The herbal tea was too late, she was already violently ill by that time. Hm…" Violet thought about this for a long moment then leaned in. "You need to tell the police."

"Tell them I lied?" Laurel reeled. "Why would I do that? They aren't suspecting me. There is no evidence against me or Paul! It wouldn't help clear your sister, so why do you care?"

"You're right that it doesn't help Greta, but it does help you!" After a pause, Violet warned, "You haven't been arrested, but you are on the detectives' short list. The fact that you tried to hide something that wasn't evidence in the first place actually proves your innocence! You thought the mug was significant, even though it wasn't, because you had nothing to do with it!"

The two women exchanged relieved smiles as Laurel sat up a little straighter and said, "I will tell them, then nothing can get in our way!"

Why did she keep saying things like that? Why did she speak as though the whole world was trying to keep her from marrying Paul?

"What do you mean?" Violet tiptoed. "Have you and Paul

had a lot of obstacles?"

"Oh yeah. Ha! We've been through it all and we are still determined to get married!"

Violet knew about some of their trouble. When Paul had made a pass at Greta, had he told Laurel about it? Had he confessed to his mental lack of devotion?

Violet led a little further away from the subject of Greta. "Like what? Has your family been against the match? I know Paul's family loves you."

"Nah." Laurel flopped an arm onto the upholstery. "Our families have been great, helped us even, except for insisting on a prenup. No, it's been all our own faults. Mostly me though. No one can help you escape your own stupid mistakes."

Laurel slouched down again with one of the biggest sighs Violet had ever heard.

"I broke us up right before Thanksgiving, around my birthday," Laurel began to explain. "I was shallow. I was dwelling on how frivolous he was with money, but his generosity was the first thing that attracted me to him!"

Violet didn't see how this could have anything to do with the murder, but she listened as Laurel now seemed like she needed to get it out.

Laurel seemed to lose herself to the memory of that day.

"How could I fault him for being too generous? It was how we had met after all.

"I had been dragged to our golf club by my long-time boyfriend. He said that it was important to socialize with 'the right kind of people.' He therefore needed to mingle with Austin's social elite at the 'best golf club with his best girl.' He would say that no one could help him but me. I knew that he also just loved to golf. Even if it was going to rain as the forecast had said, there was a chance that he could fit in his 3pm tee-time. So, we were doing what he wanted to do. We always did what he wanted to do. How had I never seen that until that day?

"He had always convinced me by saying that it was what he needed to do. His career, his political goals, his angling. It always came first. I had gone along because it was his career. It was important. More and more I had been longing for fun, though. I had fun with my girlfriends from college, but the last one was about to move away. How would I have fun then? Maybe Donald could have fun with me, like a boyfriend should, but I was starting to see that he never would. He would never do what I wanted to do. I had started to resent him for it that day.

"It started when I didn't want to go golfing, but was reaching a breaking point as we sat on the covered terrace outside so he could smoke a cigar. It was unexpectedly cold, and I sat there shivering, watching him with my short-sleeved cardigan pulled as far around me as I could stretch it. Did he even care that he was making me sit out in the frigid wind? He had made sure that we were out of the rain, but wasn't that just as much for himself? Did he ever really do things to help me?"

Laurel's story started to get heated, but then she took a long pause, playing with the hem of her skirt, and went on.

"He rolled his cigar slightly between his thumb and index finger, trying to look relaxed and sophisticated, but he really looked like a kid that was trying too hard. His eyes darted around, seeing and being seen by all these pitiful 'right kind of people'. He, like all of them, had overly white teeth and perfectly manicured nails. You know the kind. His parted blonde hair was dark with gel and had not moved all afternoon, despite the blustery fall wind. I had been taken in by his height and handsome, sharp features, but I could finally see past them now. He would be a good politician, but not with me on his arm.

"I knew then that he would not help me and that no one could help me. I had to get out from under him all by myself. I impulsively got up and swept around my chair in one grand, furious gesture. I was going to give him a piece of my mind right there in front of all his beloved 'right kind of people', but instead I had stepped in front of someone. He had been hurrying out the door, planning to go past me and into the rain, when my grand gesture bumped into him and made him lose his stride."

Laurel now looked down with a smile and went on with an impressive impersonation of Paul's distinct way of talking.

"'I'm sorry! Are you alright?' Paul's first nugget of kindness to me was more than I had received that all day." Laurel's story went on.

"'Entirely my fault,' I said, or something like that. I realized later that I must have had my eyebrows up and been speaking as if in a dream.

"'No, you're not alright. You're freezing! Let me help you.' Paul then swept off his argyle cardigan and wrapped it around me so fast that I couldn't protest.

"I glanced back, but Donald was still in conversation with the table next to him. He hadn't even noticed this stranger who was chatting up his girl right in front of him!

"'But you'll be cold now!' I cried.

"A smile spread across Paul's face. Now as I remember it, it was as if in slow motion. As it started, I noticed his perfect lips pull tight, then reveal charmingly imperfect teeth that were still well cared for. Then it grew to inhabit his whole face, crinkling his cheeks and shining out through his dark blue eyes.

"'It will just get soaked and keep me cold where I am going.' He pulled it a little tighter around me with just the right amount of power to make it sexy. 'Looks good. You keep it. My mother made me wear it, but I never liked that sweater anyway. You're actually doing me a favor.'

"With one more smile he said, "Sorry, gotta go!" then darted out into the drenching rain before I could say another word.

"I stood transfixed, watching his athletic run out onto the golf course. He even ran handsome. I found out later that he had dashed out to help his mother. She had dropped her phone somewhere out in the rain."

Laurel blushed a little, but hiccupped and went on.

"'Wow!' I had whispered to myself before I became conscious that my boyfriend might have heard. But when I turned back, Donald was still rolling his stump of a cigar and benignly smiling with the man at the next table."

Laurel seemed to recall herself and snapped out of her memory. "And the rest is history, as they say."

"Wait." Violet steered the conversation since Laurel seemed to be too intoxicated to remember why she had been telling the story. "So, you didn't like that he was too frivolous, and you ended it?"

"Oh, yes." Laurel became sad and dreamy again. "He had lent money to friends and had three investments all fail at the same time. He didn't ask for money or anything like that, but when he hadn't gotten me a present for my birthday. Well, it came up. Even now he has some credit card debt! He says it's because he chose to pay off his student loans first, but he should have been more careful!"

Violet became silently judgemental, then remembered that she had some debt herself.

"It wasn't about the birthday present, or even the money itself," Laurel defended, reading Violet's expression. "I just got worried about putting my parents' legacy into his hands. Would he misuse it? Or blow it all on his friends that wanted to start...mushroom farms?"

The wheels in Violet's head started turning. Did this mean that Paul was in more debt than anyone had believed? Could he have needed his grandmother's money after all?

"We broke up, went our separate ways...and dated other people." Laurel sneered.

"He dated someone else?" Violet was surprised that he had moved on so quickly and conveyed the outrage that she thought Laurel wanted to hear.

"Well that part is okay. I was already serious with someone else, but it was when I found out that he was dating again that I realized I had to get him back." Laurel was gazing into the middle distance, no doubt replaying the scenes in her head.

"It had been a couple months, and when we talked it all out, he said that his new girlfriend wasn't very serious. Not even really a girlfriend." Laurel then waxed sentimental and put her hand on her heart. "He said that he was thinking of me all the time and didn't know how else to move on."

Violet tried to smile and look approving and encouraging

but stayed silent as Laurel was on a roll.

"I also understood that he views fortune the way I do, as a way to help people and make the world a better place." Laurel gave Violet a sly look and went on. "He also agreed to reign it in a bit, so we didn't end up poor. You know, we still want to have something to leave to our…children."

As Laurel mentioned children, she seemed to remember something and grow sour, but tried to shake it off. Violet wondered if Paul and Laurel were having the same disagreement about having kids as she was having with Jake.

Then Violet was struck with a new possible lead. "Laurel, how did your exes deal with the news that you were getting back together? Like, did they take it well?"

"Well Paul's little blonde was fine, but I had moved on with that jerk that I was dating before Paul." Laurel grimaced. "He did not appreciate getting dumped for Paul a second time."

"Whoa! I can imagine." Violet screwed up her face.

"Yeah, he told me to not come crawling back when things don't work out with Paul. See? He's a jerk!" Laurel offered another signature eye roll. "Paul and I are ready to stay together forever now. We have poured our hearts out to each other, committed, and we are ready to do the work to stay married for the rest of our lives. Divorce and separation have ruined too many people we know. It takes work, but we are ready and devoted. I know it and he knows it."

Violet thought of the baby argument that she guessed the couple was having, plus Paul's quest for closure with Greta. "No matter what?"

"No matter what."

Laurel and Violet gave each other forced, comforting smiles then moved in for a hug.

Violet was loading the boxes into the car and leaving the country club cleaner than she had found it when she noticed a string of texts from Jake.

"Got everything done here at the clubhouse. Don't worry, it's clean."

Another said, "Full disclosure. There was a stripper, but no,

I didn't watch. You can show me your appreciation later."

Then, "Returned the rental van and going to bed."

Violet smiled and sent a text back.

Just loading up. Be home in 45 min.

Jake and Laurel had both offered to help her pack up, but she had reassured them both that no one needed to help her. Jake had to get to bed since he was always more productive in the morning and Laurel was obliged to sleep off the champagne before her big day tomorrow. Besides, this is what they were paying her for! But the offer had cemented the idea in her mind that she and Laurel were now friends.

Both had lost most of their girl friends after everyone else had moved away after school. She suspected that they were both open to finding some local friends now that they had found the loves of their lives. Violet would have to keep her number and call Laurel after the honeymoon was over.

This was what Violet was daydreaming about on her drive home and as she pulled into her parking garage and got out to start unloading. She was so busy planning girls' nights out and double dates that she barely noticed a dark figure skulking up behind her. A reflection slid along the car and paused a few inches from her back but what she noticed first was the smell of whiskey and trashy women's perfume.

When Violet's mind registered his breath on her neck, she whipped around with a gasp. Her hands flew to her heart as she recognized him, and true fear wormed its way into her mind. In this moment, Violet had no doubt that she knew who the murderer was. He was wasted beyond where any inhibitions could touch him, and he looked furious. He held nothing, but his bare hands were clenched into fists and looked as though they were itching to swing. There was no one else in the parking garage that could help Violet, no one to even hear her scream. She didn't want to give him that satisfaction or to succumb to the terror. She was alone with him and would have to keep her head if she wanted to survive.

Texas-themed macarons

First, Basic Macarons. About 30 small sandwich cookies. This
is the 'plain' French macaron. Think of it as a blank canvas.
You can add a bit of gel food coloring and make it any color.
You can add a filling or an extract and make it any flavor. You
can "paint" the tops, add zest or gold leaf, anything! This is the
recipe to start with and get right before you move on to more
complicated details There is a lot that can go wrong, but just
follow the instructions and you will be fine. As always, read
all the directions before you start because you will need to
know what you are in for. Yes, you should have a healthy fear
before you start to make these. And I give myself a long time
window - these can take 2-3 hours!

For the macarons -
2 cups or 240g powdered sugar
1 cup or 112g almond flour
Pinch of salt
3 large egg whites, at room temperature (no hints of yolks!)
¼ cup or 50g white sugar
¼ teaspoon cream of tartar

For the filling -
½ stick or 2 oz. or about 57g butter, room temperature or
softened
¾ cup powdered sugar, or about 75g
½ teaspoon almond extract, or other extract like vanilla

Assemble your ingredients. Get ready like you are on a
cooking show because things will progress quickly as soon as
you actually start whipping your egg whites.

**Sift together the powdered sugar, almond flour, and salt
into a medium bowl.** Usually I don't bother sifting, but it is

important here so your batter is smooth. Force lumps through the sifter with a rubber spatula until only big bits of almond remain. You can have up to a tablespoon of bigger pieces after this step. Throw them away or eat them and be happy that they will not be in your batter, popping bubbles and making the tops of the macarons lumpy. Set aside your sifted dry ingredients while you prepare everything else.

Whip egg whites in large bowl. When starting to get foamy and white, add sugar and cream of tartar. These ingredients stabilize your egg whites, so don't add them too early or too late. Add them when your egg whites are still wet enough to dissolve the sugar, but are already frothy. If you want to add food coloring (up to ten drops of liquid, or even better, up to ⅛ teaspoon of gel, depending on how bright you want the color,) I find that this is the best time.

Continue to whip until egg whites reach "stiff peaks." This means that when you take out the mixer, the egg whites stay exactly where you left them. If they move a little, that is "soft peaks"and they need more mixing. The best way to test is by looking at the end of the beater. Pull the beater out and flip over to point it at the ceiling. If peak folds over like a chocolate chip, that's soft peaks and it needs more whipping. If it stands up like a mohawk, that's stiff peaks and it's perfect. If it is separated and clumpy, that is over-whipped and you have to start over.

Fold half of your dry ingredients into your egg whites, then the other half. Fully incorporate the first half of your dry ingredients into your egg whites with a rubber spatula, then add your other half. This should be a gentle folding lifting/ mixing method so that you don't squish all the lovely bubbles that you just created. If you want to add an extract, (about ½ teaspoon) I find that this is the best time. As soon as there are no dry pockets, you need to start watching the consistency.

Fold until batter flows a little, but doesn't run. This is the hardest part. Batter that is under mixed will just flop back into the bowl in globs when you lift it up. Overmixed will be runny and dribble back in a solid stream. You want it to be in the middle where the batter starts to flow in longer masses, but still feels light. Some people describe it as hot lava consistency, but that doesn't help me as I have never mixed lava. Just not dolloping egg whites and not running cake batter.

Load into piping bag with no tip or a ½ inch circle tip and pipe out into little 1 ½ inch circles on parchment paper or silicone lined baking sheets. With practice, you will find that piping them smoothly from the side and ending with a swirl around the outside edge helps the tops stay perfectly smooth. These will spread a little as you pipe, so leave about an inch between your circles. I use a piping bag with no tip for this part. I have fit the cookies on two big cookie sheets, but depending on how far you space them, you might need three or four.

As you finish each cookie sheet, bang them on the counter. Despite all your efforts to keep those precious air bubbles, you want to get rid of the big ones. As you finish piping each baking sheet, hit the pan on the counter or table 4-8 times to ensure that the tops of your macarons will be smooth. Hit them hard enough that it's pretty loud, but not so hard that you have stuff flying around the room.

When you have piped and whacked all the baking sheets, heat your oven to 300 degrees F (150 C) and wait. The key to getting the "feet" or bubbly, crusty bottom part on each cookie is letting them sit out at least 30 minutes before baking. This makes the tops dry out and forces them to expand up instead of out. During this time the oven can preheat, you can clean up, or make the filling.

Bake at 300°F (150 C) for 20 minutes. Bake one sheet at a time on the middle rack of your oven. Do not underbake! The macarons should not get browned at all, but they can't be underdone or they will stick to the pan liner and break. If they are done you will be able to pull one off the parchment paper or silicone liner. You can test doneness by prying one up or just trust your timer if you know your oven temperature is accurate. When they come out of the oven, I let them sit on the cookie sheet for about two minutes just to make sure that they won't stick.

When fully cooled, fill and sandwich two same-size shells together. Gently flip shells on their backs and pipe one side with filling then top with the other side. The amount of filling that you use is up to you, but make sure the cookies are cooled so the filling won't just melt out. If you are going to have to transport these but you still want them to look perfect, I wait and fill them on site. Otherwise, fill and seal them in an airtight container. Some people say these cookies are better the next day, so if you have an event you can make them ahead. Freezing them also works well, so you can fill them with ice cream and put them in the freezer!

Filling -
You can use ice cream, frosting, ganache, jam, lemon curd, anything to fill these shells. Since you can't mess too much with the shell recipe, just an extract, this is going to be where the flavor really lies.

Basic Buttercream -
First, whip ½ stick (about 50g) of butter until light and airy. Next, add powdered sugar ¼ cup (25g) at a time, mixing slowly at first each time. When all ¾ cups (75g) are fully incorporated, scrape down the sides of your bowl and add your extract. Finally, whip frosting on high speed one more time to make it light and fluffy. Load into piping bag and distribute on the flat side of half of your macaron shells before sandwiching and serving.

Peach macarons -
From a brewery supply store, or online, purchase peach extract to use ½ teaspoon in your macaron shell and make a peach buttercream with peach jam

Grapefruit macarons -
From a brewery supply store, or online, purchase grapefruit extract to use ½ teaspoon in baking your shells and make a grapefruit buttercream with a little bit of grapefruit juice and a lot of grapefruit zest

BBQ macarons -
Add ½ teaspoon smoked paprika and ¼ teaspoon cayenne chile powder to your macaron recipe and whip up some buttercream with ¼ cup molasses and 1 Tablespoon of ketchup

Chapter Eleven

Was It Him?

"What are you doing here?" Violet asked with a trembling voice, trying to hide her panic and backing slowly away from him as she slid her phone out of her pocket.

"I'll ask uh queshionz!" Luke's voice cracked as he spit out the words into a slurred yell.

Laurel may be sad and chatty when she had had a few, but Luke was an irrational drunk, and she suspected, an alcoholic. His eyes seemed to be everywhere and nowhere while he swayed and shook with rage. He looked mad enough to kill, and probably already had. These were the kind of people that scared Violet away from drinking. He was so disheveled that it looked like he had crawled there. He edged closer to her, wreaking and wobbling, looking frighteningly unpredictable. What would he do to her? How could she get away? If she could get past him, she could run to the stairs and to Jake.

Luke grabbed Violet by her wrists, making her phone clatter to the ground far under the car. Her arms coiled up in front of her chest in defense as he held her there. He shook her hard, throwing himself off balance more than he had planned. His grip was slippery, and he almost lost her arms while his feet stumbled. Violet had a brief moment of clarity after mourning the loss of her phone and realized this unsteadiness might prove useful.

"Yer gonna tell me wha you know. Cuz I can't have you goin' around tellin' people stuff 'bout me!" Luke leaned in like he had earlier that evening. His eyes were huge, and his forehead shone with sweat. "Who dih you talk to?"

"I-uh-," Violet's mind raced to think of a good lie, but

realized that in his state she could talk circles around him, and he probably wouldn't even remember this tomorrow. She felt some of her strength return and decided to get some answers. She pushed through her fear and threw her arms down to her sides, easily escaping his grip. "I know all about what you and your grandma argued about that night. How did that go again?"

"She zaid she waz gonna rat me out!" Luke was confused and distracted now, and sounded offended as he went on, "She s--said tha she woo make sure tha I wen to prizon this time! Then I say that I'd say it was all Glenn's fault, and she zaid that she and he would get their stories stray and say that he didn't have a choize."

"Right! She found out about the illegal thing that you and Doctor Glenn were up to!" Violet pretended to know it all, she was still terrified, but all the pieces were finally coming together in her mind. Violet had virtually forgotten the handoff that she had witnessed during the rehearsal dinner. Immediate events had pushed that suspicion to the back burner, but now she needed more. Was it him? Had Luke killed his own grandmother for what she had seen? Or what she had said to him?

"You DO know about ih!" Luke was surprised and irate again. He pulled up his hands and wrapped them loosely around Violet's stretched neck.

Only then did Violet realize how terrible of an idea this all was. As her fingers scrambled at his hands and arms, she knew she would have to get her answers another way. This was too perilous of a position to be in. She had known that she was afraid, but she suddenly realized that she had not been terrified enough. Her back was pressed against a concrete pillar and her head leaned back against it. Luke now had his hands under her chin and his body held hers in place. Her heart hammered the inside of her rib cage as she realized that she might die right here and now.

"Wait, wait, I won't tell anyone!" Violet eked out the words as Luke began to slowly tighten his grip, "We're friends! Why would I tell anyone? You know, sometimes I think that we could be more than friends."

His hands loosened slightly, and she wrapped her fingers over his to pull them down. "Yeah." She went on in the best seductive voice she could muster in the moment. She moved slowly and prudently, like dealing with a wild animal. She had a plan, but she needed him to not kill her first. "I don't think now would be a good time, though. Do you? My husband is coming down to help me unload, the wedding is in less than 18 hours, and…"

Violet rambled on steadily as she held his gaze and slowly leaned farther and farther to one side. He followed her in a daze. Finally, when all his weight was leaning precariously on one inebriated leg, she stuck out her own foot and tipped him over it. His vague attempt to stop his fall was crippled by her jutting leg and he fell, sprawling on the pavement.

Violet scrambled under the van for her phone, but it lay just beyond her reach. Quickly she twisted her body around and kicked the phone, making it skitter out the other side.

Her other leg was seized as Luke turned her over and pulled her towards him. He was kneeling now and leaned forward until Violet brought a knee up and kicked him backwards with a thud.

With that Violet scurried to her feet and took off running in the opposite direction. She didn't pay attention to where she was going and, in her panic, she slipped on a spot of oil. She tripped into another concrete pillar, then whirled to see where Luke was and met with his fist. His wild, swinging punch landed on her outer cheekbone and made her turn and double over in pain and shock. His second blow had been right behind his first in a quick combination, but his reflexes had not been as fast. His right fist plowed into the concrete pillar behind where Violet's nose had been.

Violet's attacker was doubled over cradling his bloody hands together with his stomach, so she pulled herself up and gave him a stiff kick to the groin to make sure he wouldn't follow her this time. His legs and elbows pinched together on impact and trapped her leg, making them both fall.

After a long string of expletives, Luke threatened, "Oh, I'll geh you fer thiz!"

Violet pried her ankle free, clasped her phone, and escaped to the ascending stairs. Violet didn't stop running until she collided with Jake's arms as he came out of their front door.

"Hey! Forty-five minutes exactl-wait, what's wrong?"

As Violet offered a lightning fast explanation, Jake lead her gently to the edge of the bed.

"And-and I just ran! I don't know where he is…or if he's coming…or waiting…"

"Stay here. Call Don!" Jake commanded as he unlocked the finger safe and retrieved a boxy Glock from the closet.

"No! Don't! Stay here with me! Don't go looking for trouble! I'm here. I'm-I'm safe now." Violet's eyes watered as she tried to convince herself as much as Jake. She forced herself to take a shuddering breath as he squeezed her hand and let his wild, ice blue eyes bore into hers.

"You won't feel safe. I promise I'm not looking for trouble or revenge. We just need to know that he's gone." Jake pressed again. "Stay here. Call Don!"

"No!" Violet tried to protest again, but Jake had already torn out the door, locking it behind him.

Violet was haunted by imaginings of Jake shooting Luke, or someone that looked like him that happened to be in the parking garage. He was too furious to make good decisions and should have just stayed inside!

Then Violet remembered his training. He had learned as a Military Police investigator all that he needed for situations like this. Luke wouldn't be able to get the drop on him, or get his gun away from him, right? Jake could keep his cool better than anyone Violet had ever met. Jake wasn't frantically chasing someone; he was just clearing the garage and the area around the building because he loved her and wanted her to feel safe and comfortable.

She took a moment and a deep breath. Her skipping breaths slowed and her pulse left the realm of "hummingbird." Jake would be fine, and she was safe now, but a lot had just happened. Violet now knew what had happened to Francesca LeBaron. It was him. Mrs. LeBaron had to be silenced because she had known too much. Instead of getting caught and going to jail, Luke had killed his own grandmother!

As she assessed her oily hands that gripped her phone with white knuckles, she just now noticed that her shoe must have come off in the struggle. Violet related to the woman's last moments of life. That kind of fear was terrible. Worse, she believed, than the death itself. Had she known that it was her own grandson and heir that had killed her? She couldn't imagine that kind of disappointment and distress. All those years and worries invested, just to end up with a grandson that was cold and heartless. Granted, not every child grows up to be a murderer, but how could you know what kind of people your children and grandchildren would grow up to be? Was there any hope for any of us? He had grown up with every advantage and still ended up a sleazy, grimy, murdering good-for-nothing. Why did anyone have children? Why was it worth the risk?

If kids could do this to the people that loved them, then did family ties mean nothing? Violet wondered but as soon as she thought the words, the answer started to come to her.

The Jorgensens were not exactly the model family. It was actually a wonder that Paul had ended up as well-adjusted as he was. Mom was selfish, Dad was removed, and neither one of them had been any kind of parent to either of their boys. Family ties had not exactly been on their priority list. Perhaps their advantages had been, at least part of, their downfall.

Now she thought of Luke with a pang of pity, but still mingled with the abhorrence and revulsion left over from their 'conversation'.

She replayed it in her mind as she instinctively washed her hands over and over. What was the illegal thing that Francesca had caught them doing? And how long had Francesca known about this and not told anyone? If she had been determined to turn Luke in to the police, why hadn't she done it yet? Or had something changed? Or had she just found out that night? If she had just found out that night, then Luke would not have had time to make the poison. Unless he carried it around with him for just such circumstances? If so, the police would find bottles of poison, ready for the next potential informant. Jake was right, she needed to call Don.

Violet dried her hands and dialed, trying to gather her thoughts, but when the detective answered the phone it all came spilling out, jumbled and unintelligible. The immediate danger, Jake, the handoff, the attack. All of it came pouring out.

"Wait," Don interrupted. "Ok, I've got some uniformed officers going to Luke's apartment, his parents' house, your place, and his brother's apartment to look for Luke and something that might match your description of these papers from Dr. Glenn. But what are you saying just happened?"

Violet's voice still shook. "Luke attacked me. He was going to silence me just like he silenced his grandmother! He hit me and was going to strangle me! Jake is out there, making sure that he is gone."

"Ok." Detective Donnelly sounded urgent, but cool and professional now. "I'm on my way over to you to make this official. But are you okay? I think you should get checked out at a hospital."

"No, no." Violet's cheek hurt, but not that much. Her head, neck, and teeth felt fine, but mostly she did not have time for all that. She knew it was OCD of her, but she needed to shower and get back to cooking. She didn't need to be in an emergency room with no real injuries while the clock was counting down to the wedding. At least she could stop thinking about her sister's looming indictment. "I'm fine, but I do want to press charges or whatever. He came after me, and I think he is our murderer."

"It definitely sounds like it. Okay, I'll see you soon. Keep the door locked until I get there."

When Detective Donnelly arrived, he brought a familiar shoe and a distraught Jake with him to find Violet nursing her wound.

"I hadn't even realized," Violet explained, pointing to the shoe, then her injury. "I guess Luke's ring must have cut me a little bit."

Up her cheekbone and halfway to her ear was a small

jagged tear that had bled enough to cause a small rivulet of blood to reach her neck and catch her attention once she had calmed down.

"Well, the slight upside is that it will be good for proving what happened." The detective softened as he looked at their disheartened faces and said, "I've got lab techs downstairs taking samples of blood they found on a cement pilon, which should match Luke Jorgensen, and I just got a call that they picked him up outside his apartment. Don't worry. We got him. And I'll tell them to look for traces of blood on his ring."

"Yeah, uh, left hand. Luckily he didn't get me with his right. That hit the pillar."

"Okay, then they can also check for lacerations and contusions on his right hand. It sounds like he will need to sleep off the party in a cell. But could you come down early in the morning when I question him?"

Violet looked to Jake who nodded. "Yeah, like eight?"

"Perfect, thanks. I'm so sorry that this happened, but don't worry. With all your help we are going to nail this guy to the wall!"

"In court, of course," added Jake with a coy smile. "Thanks for finding me before anyone else did. That would have looked really bad to anyone but you."

"You mean you don't think you should be found by police officers while you are on a man hunt and wandering around with a gun and crazy eyes just after your wife has been attacked?" Don said in mock disbelief.

Jake looked down and chuckled, but when Don displayed his sarcastic side, it didn't look good on him. At least not to Violet.

The two men shook hands, then they hugged briefly before saying their goodbyes. The detective then left the couple embracing each other alone in the dark apartment.

When Violet's alarm went off a few hours later, Jake was already in the kitchen.

"I couldn't sleep," was the only explanation that he offered.

As Violet looked around, it appeared as though Jake had

157

been baking, slicing and dicing, and even shopping, all night.

"You bought choux pastries, and frozen puff pastry?"

"I know you like to make them," Jake said while washing radishes. "But we have really run out of time for this gig. Especially since we have to go down to the station in a couple hours."

"Ok," she conceded. "You're right. And it won't break the bank."

Silently, they hulled strawberries, baked frico wafers, and skewered deconstructed salads all before the sun made its debut for the day.

Violet stood in the dark cavity behind the mirror watching Luke wring his hands together under the table. She had signed her statement and he had spent last night in a cell, but this was far from over. Detective Taylor stood resolutely beside Violet with folded arms, watching her but trying to look like he was not watching her. Detective Donnelly, fully professional and stoic, circled Luke slowly. The interrogator watched every twitch as he asked his captor all about what had happened in the parking garage.

Luke sat composed, all traces of being sloppy drunk gone except for his disheveled clothes. He hadn't asked for a lawyer yet, which proved that he thought he could talk his way out of the charges altogether. He had slick answers for everything, but he continually side-stepped the question of why.

"I was plastered, okay?" Luke shrugged, "Isn't that reason enough? I make bad choices when I've had too many. Just the fact that I drove there wasted should tell you that I wasn't in my right mind!"

"Why come after Violet at all? You must have had a reason, right?" Don asked as he circumvented Luke's chair.

Luke clawed his hair back on one side. "Maybe I thought she was into me. She did hit on me while we were in the parking structure."

Violet stood with Jake's arm around her. At this she felt his arm tense almost imperceptibly.

"It was a strategy to get out of there alive!" she whispered.

He didn't answer because they had been instructed to stay quiet, but Violet knew that Jake felt better when his arm relaxed and squeezed her a little tighter.

"That can't be the only reason," the detective coaxed. "What did you two talk about last night?"

"She talked a bit about getting together some other time. We also talked about the wedding, her husband, and I said that I would be back another time."

"You didn't just say that you would come back. You threatened her, didn't you? You had a reason to come after her last night, and when that didn't work you threatened to come back and finish the job!"

"Nope." Luke was staying way too relaxed, like he had done this before and knew that he could get away with anything. "Vi and I talked about getting together another time and she said that last night was bad timing. I just said that I would be back another time. If she heard it as a threat then I'm sorry, but I meant it as a friend."

"Bastard!" Violet finally lost it as she realized that the threat charge might not stick. He could still be charged with assault since there was proof of that, but attempted murder charges might not work either. Violet's neck had not bruised, so there was no proof that he was about to strangle her. Even the bruise and cut on her cheek were not severe and luckily they were small enough to be covered by her hair. They didn't have enough to hold him. Her blood had washed off his ring by the time they had swabbed it for evidence, so the only evidence that he had been there at all was his blood on a concrete pillar. He could downplay him hitting Violet and walk away with a good lawyer.

They had to get him for murdering his grandmother. He was guilty of silencing her and they knew it. Don seemed to be on the same wavelength.

"So what about your grandmother? We know that you tried to kill Miss Violet Whitehouse. Did you kill your grandma too?"

Don stared straight into Luke's eyes as his face turned sallow and surprised.

"What? Oh, no!" Luke seemed genuinely aghast.

"Was it for the money or because she was going to tell the police about you?" Don knew that he had Luke on the run now.

"Whoa, look." Luke had slid down in his chair, but he sat up straight now. "I didn't kill anybody! It wasn't me!"

The detective just stared at Luke.

"I wasn't going to kill Vi, I was just trying to scare her! So…I just punched the pillar thing. But I definitely didn't kill my Granny Franny!" Luke was starting to sweat and shake as he went on. "The only time I went near her was when she…"

"If you want to avoid the murder charge, then you better tell us everything." Don stood up tall and victorious. "It's the only way I can help you, Mr. Jorgensen."

When Luke still looked reticent, Don whispered, "I'm a homicide detective, I don't have any interest in drug charges."

Luke's head snapped up in surprise. "Ok, I-We have a little understanding, Dr. Glenn and I."

Luke paused, dragging his long brown hair back, away from his bloodshot eyes, with both hands. "I sell his prescription slips. And…use some of them too."

Luke looked broken now as Violet watched and Don pulled up his pants. "Is business good?"

"Yeah, or it-it was while I was staying in our neighborhood. I hadn't had any problems…un-until a week ago. When I sold at this club downtown, I-I had a run in with…someone else… saying I was selling in their…uh, territory. It cost me a lot of money to get out of there. I-I gotta make a bunch of money before the end of the week to pay it back to…certain people. A loan shark, I guess."

"Who?" Don asked with excitement behind his voice.

"I barely know him. He's a friend of a friend."

"What's his name?" Don persisted.

"I don't know! I've just heard people call him 'King'." Luke seemed like an obstinate child now with his arms folded and his back slumped in his chair once again.

Don pushed. "Is that his last name?"

"I swear, I-I don't know, okay?" Luke looked ashamed as

he went on. "I was looking for a way to borrow money fast and...and my bookie led me to him."

"How do we get in touch with him? Give us his number."

"I don't have it! I'm telling you all I know, okay? I just get in touch with him through my bookie." Luke whined.

"Okay. We'll come back to that." Don offered one of his signature heavy pauses. "What happened with Francesca LeBaron?" Don urged, barely above a whisper.

After slowly leaning forward onto the stark metal table, Luke acquiesced. "I bought a bunch of prescriptions from Dr. Glenn at the party. I could sell 'em easy to get the money I need. Well, Granny Franny, er, my grandmother, saw us make the deal that night and started yelling at me. She said that she was going to turn me in and make sure I went to prison this time. She wouldn't pay for that badass lawyer anymore and I would rot in jail for corrupting an innocent old man."

Luke clawed his hair back again with quivering hands. "She was right. I-I was mad, but more mad at myself. I avoided her the rest of the night and was talking up the bridesmaid to...uh, for something that always makes me feel better."

Luke paused, staring at his hands as they picked at each other, then went on. "Dr. Glenn is the nicest old guy! And I can't think of a way out! I have to make this money by next Friday or they'll kill me...or whatever!"

"Alright." Donnelly let out a stern sigh as his keen eyes bored into Luke. "You keep helping us and we'll see what we can do."

"Sorry, Violet," Detective Donnelly said as he came into the room with Violet and Jake. "I believe him. I don't think he killed her."

"But he's so..." Violet struggled for words as she pointed at Luke through the mirror. "Ugh, you're right. I agree," Violet sounded defeated. "It wasn't him. His motive was too new, and he wouldn't have had time to cook up the poison."

"And I don't think he'd do it for the money. There is no way he'd get the inheritance money in a week and he had another plan. One that would actually get him the cash in time," Don added.

"He also seemed to really love his grandmother. I think he still thought of her as his 'Granny Franny'," said Jake.

"Eh…love doesn't stop people from murdering each other as much as you would think. But poison also isn't Luke's usual weapon of choice." Don pointed briefly to Violet's neck. "When Luke Jorgensen gets mad, he strangles."

Violet's hands flew to her neck, still shaken. "That's true."

"We'll still get him on assault." Don touched her elbow gently. "The other charges, maybe not, but his blood was on that cement pilon. We'll get him."

Detective Taylor stepped forward and interjected. "What about this 'King' guy? How do you want to track him down?"

"Why do you need to?" asked Violet.

Taylor sighed and turned to her as if pacifying a child. "Because, young lady, maybe it was him. If he owes this guy money, then he would definitely want Luke to inherit a large amount of money."

"Does he know what the Jorgensens stand to inherit? I don't see how unless they knew each other. And doesn't everyone know that it takes a long time to get inheritance money?"

"Well, maybe he'd be willing to wait longer if he knew what was coming. He could be trying to get even more out of Luke later instead of however-much he owes him now." Don was trying to smooth things out between Taylor and his friends. "Luke might have even mentioned that inheritance to make the guy wait longer to collect. Or the booky friend? If he's friends with this booky, maybe he knows the situation and clued in the loan shark. There are lots of possible angles."

"Yeah, we'll get to checking him out." Detective Taylor stuck a finger in Violet's face. "You can go back to cookin', and leave this to the professionals. We'll find out if it was him."

Strawberry, Radish and Arugula Salad

For the dressing -
3 Tablespoons (30mL) balsamic vinegar
2 Tablespoons (42g) local honey
¼ cup (60mL) extra-virgin olive oil
1 shallot or 2 Tablespoons red or sweet onion, grated or diced super fine
1 teaspoon salt
1/2 teaspoon black pepper, or to taste
For the salad-
1/2 bunch of radishes, about 5-6 radishes
4 ounces or about ⅓ or ¼ package (about 110g) thick-cut bacon, diced
5 ounces arugula, (120-140g rocket) twice washed and dried on a towel
1 lb. fresh strawberries (400-450g), washed and dried on a towel
3 ounces (75g) goat cheese or feta cheese

1. For the salad dressing, combine all ingredients in a jar and shake vigorously, if you don't have one, put it all in a bowl or mini food processor and stir or pulse.
2. Finely slice radishes into neat discs and place in a small bowl. Pour salad dressing over radishes and toss to combine. Set aside to prepare other ingredients.
3. Cook diced bacon in a small skillet over medium heat until cooked with crispy edges, then move to a paper towel-lined plate to cool and wait for your other ingredients.
4. After arugula has been washed and dried, fluff and place in large serving bowl.
5. Hull and quarter strawberries and arrange artfully on your bed of arugula.
6. With half of your cheese, Pinch soft goat cheese or finely crumble feta cheese onto the top of your salad, reserving the rest of the cheese for the final layer at the end.
7. Crumble bacon over your bed of strawberries and cheesed arugula, then add your marinated radish slices, including all

the salad dressing.

8. Now add the rest of your cheese artfully around the top of your tasty mound of salad.

9. Serve immediately. If you arranged it beautifully, toss the salad after bringing it to the table. If it's not pretty, toss it now. Either way, it will be deliciously fresh and flavorful.

Chapter Twelve

Did We Get Him?

Jake and Violet appeared to do what Detective Taylor said. They were back in the swing of cooking and even ahead of schedule when Violet approached the subject of 'King'.

"I don't think Don is going after the right person," Violet began.

All Jake said in answer was an exhausted chuckle.

"Do you know any bookies or loan shark types?" Violet asked.

"Not anymore. But I think I knew a couple guys while I was in the army. Why?" Jake knew what was coming.

"It seems to me like they would be pretty smart about money," Violet speculated.

"I think you're right. They, or at least the good ones, don't get caught because they are good."

"They would know laws well enough to sidestep around them and avoid getting caught."

"Hm. Agreed," Jake said.

"Do they operate on return customers like other businesses?"

"I...don't know."

"Well, imagine. If you were a loan shark and you had a client who was going to be rich soon, wouldn't you be awfully nice to them?" Violet mused.

Jake said nothing.

"If it were me," Violet went on, "I would want to hold on to that customer. Especially if he were prepared with a tidy way to pay his current debt on time. He would pay his debt, have a good experience, and be a return customer, right?"

"I think you might be relying on loan sharks being too benevolent and reasonable." Jake smiled.

"Okay," Violet conceded. "But if you were thinking self-interestedly, isn't that what you would do?"

Jake countered. "You are also assuming that they are patient. With foresight and long-term goals. That is not how I imagine them. The guys I have known that have loaned money, granted they were small time, were more worried about quick returns and their next hit."

"Alright," Violet said, switching tacks. "In either case, I don't see them acting the way the detectives are thinking. Either they have long term goals and want Luke to pay his debt the easy way, on time, and have a good experience and be a repeat debtor...OR they want a quick return on their money and are not willing to wait for the inheritance to trickle down to them."

"So you don't see this loan shark threatening Luke and killing the grandmother at the same time because those... conflict with each other?" Jake asked.

"Yeah. I mean, does that make sense to you? If they knew that he was inheriting, then they would be nice to him. If they are threatening him, then I think that proves that they did not kill his grandmother." Violet reasoned. "Plus Luke's debt was too new and the failure of his plan to pay them was too recent for them to be exploring creative avenues to get their money back."

"Hm. So what if they killed the grandmother not because she was the cash cow, but because she was the narc? It was her that was going to prevent Luke from selling the prescription slips, to get the money, to pay them back. Right?" Jake checked.

Violet considered this. "I guess so. But they didn't know that! Luke had just had that conversation with his grandmother behind a locked door. I was just outside and no one else was standing there with me. And even if they were, I couldn't hear the words they were saying, just loud angry noises."

Jake countered. "He could have told them."

"But then they would have to be at the party!" Violet

argued, then considered it. "If he had called them and told them over the phone, they couldn't have gotten to Mrs. LeBaron fast enough for the way and timing in which she died. For the person to find out and kill his grandmother, they would have had to be already in the party to get the news. I just don't see it. I also believe him that it's someone that Luke doesn't know. He knew just about everyone at that party."

"Just about," Jake agreed.

"And he is supposed to have never met this person," said Violet.

Jake was out of dissensions. "You're right. So she wouldn't have been killed for the inheritance or for getting Luke busted, at least by the loan shark."

Violet vented. "I think Don is barking up the wrong tree."

"Well he was right about one thing…" Jake gave Violet a sideways glance. "You do have a brain for this."

Violet had decided that it was time to check in with Greta again. Greta had been arrested the day before and Violet had let her have a morning all to herself with Lindy to recoup and recharge. Now, with the wedding hours away and the food well in-hand thanks to Jake's purchased shortcuts, Violet needed to make sure that Greta and Katy had the flowers ready.

As Violet swept into the giant floral refrigerator, a forest of pinks loomed over and around her. Touches of purple and green heuchera filled the spaces between white and baby pink peonies and the cursed foxglove creating spikes of magenta and violet.

Katy found her first. "Oh hey, I thought I heard someone come in." She brought a box with a boutonniere in each hand.

"Yeah, hey!" Violet never was sure what to say to Katy. "How are you guys doing? Do you need help?"

Katy turned to let Greta answer as she came in with clear boxes of her own. "I think we just finished. Thanks though. We had our other orders for tomorrow cancel, so we are especially prompt!"

Greta sounded upbeat, which Violet knew meant that she

was upset despite her tone. Violet looked inquiringly at Katy.

"We've had four cancellations today. That's way above coincidence." Katy pursed her lips.

"It'll be fine!" Greta argued. "People might be scared because I got arrested, because they think I'm a murderer, but it'll get cleared up soon. After all, my sister's on the case!"

"Shhhhh!" Violet hushed them.

Greta just laughed. "What? No one's here! It's just the three of us and Windsor! We already know that you're investigating, and Windsor is always so distracted that he probably wouldn't hear us if he were standing right here."

"Ok, but, come on!" Violet whined.

"Actually, I think he is outside anyway," Katy corrected. "He was meeting a friend in the back parking lot, like…ten minutes ago?"

Greta grunted. "Ugh, I have told him a million times to stop doing that! Let's go get him!"

As Greta marched out, Violet and Katy instinctively followed her to stand behind her. They rushed forward when the view of the back parking lot hit them.

At least four patrol cars were fanned out around the back of the building plus Don's unmarked police car. Detective Taylor stood cuffing Windsor's arms roughly behind his back and reciting his Miranda rights. Windsor's greasy locks grazed the hood of Don's car as he was bent over, struggling slightly. Don stood with Luke on the other side of the loading dock, speaking sternly in his face.

Red and blue lights winked as Detective Taylor said with smug satisfaction, "Windsor Noble, you are under arrest for the murder of Francesca LeBaron."

"What is going on here?" Greta yelled to the police throng in general as a short, uniformed woman stepped up to speak to her.

"Ma'am, we need you to step back inside right now."

"This is my property and I have a right to know what is happening. And that's my delivery man!"

"We are making an arrest so please step inside and the detectives will be in to speak with you shortly."

"Alright," Detective Donnelly began. Greta had come in and calmed down, Windsor had been hauled away, and they all sat on some stools gathered in the back of Greta's warehouse space. "So Windsor Noble was your employee, is that correct?"

"Yes, he makes, or made, all our deliveries." Greta sighed, leaning forward so her elbows rested on the counter-height metal table.

"Did you ever notice any suspicious behavior? Not being where he's supposed to be?"

"Sure," Greta shrugged. "He wasn't getting employee of the month or anything, but I never thought he was a murder!"

"I mean small stuff, meetings, missing work unexpectedly," the detective persisted.

"Yup. I was always trying to get him to stop having friends drop by here. They stopped coming in, but he was still always meeting people in the parking lot. I just figured they were... meeting for some herbal refreshment."

"Hm, okay." Don's grunt was halfway between a laugh and a scold. "Does the name 'King' mean anything to you?"

Greta slowly shook her head, but Katy grimaced.

"Have you heard that before?" Don zeroed in on Katy now.

Katy wiggled on her perch and innocently looked into both sisters faces before answering. "We dated for a little while and-and someone once called him that in front of me. Then Windsor got really mad, told him never to say that in front of people, Windsor even punched the guy! That was the first time I saw him...get violent."

"Were there more times after that?"

"Um, yeah." Katy went on in a coy voice, twisting her long hair around one finger. "He even threatened to poison someone once."

"Ok, this is great." Don seemed a little too enthusiastic for the situation. "Did any of you have any indications that he was meeting people to lend or collect money?"

"No," the three women answered in staggered succession.

"Did he carry large amounts of cash? Disappear often?"

"Oh, he would go missing for a few hours at a time. I guess

this isn't very important, but about three months ago I had to crack down on him about driving around in the delivery truck," said Greta. "His deliveries were taking way longer and using much more gas than they should have, so I lowjacked the van...oh, and the truck."

Don leaned forward. "So you have a record of everywhere the truck went on the day of the rehearsal dinner?"

"Sure."

"Could you please print that out for me?" Don sounded excited.

"I'll do it." Katy started waddling towards the office. "Anything to get off this stool and go sit in a real chair!"

When Katy brought back the paper a few minutes later, Detective Donnelly had only a few more questions as he examined the time stamps on the record.

"Was Mr. Noble supposed to be at the rehearsal dinner?" Don asked as his eyes ran over the paper.

"No. Well he dropped off a bunch of stuff when we all drove over together early, but then he left and had the rest of the evening off." Greta sounded grave to Violet.

Detective Donnelly frowned at the list, then began to smile. "According to this he came back and was there, parked outside, for the entire duration of the party. Did you know that?"

"No," all three girls muttered.

"That's very interesting." Don's eyes seemed to regain a keen edge as he said, "You have all been a big help. I think we've got something thanks to you, ladies." Don got up and moved towards the door. "Good luck tonight."

Violet followed him to the door to talk to him alone. "You're not coming to the wedding anymore?" she asked.

"Nope. I don't need to." Don lifted the lowjack record and his notes. "We got him!"

Jake and Violet packed up some catering supplies to move them over to the wedding venue. Violet knew that she should have felt relieved, but somehow the conclusion of this case wasn't satisfying. Was it because someone she actually knew was the murderer? Was it the fact that Detective Taylor had been right despite not listening to her? Or was it the facts?

The detectives got Windsor for loan sharking, but the murder charge didn't sit well. The theory that the detectives were sticking to was that Windsor, a.k.a. King, had lent Luke a large amount of money to get out of some trouble created by a turf war. Sure, Violet could accept that. She knew that Windsor's parents had money, so even though he didn't look like it, he could have access to some cash and be a money lender.

It was the next steps in their logic that Violet did not follow. Windsor was supposed to somehow know all about Luke and his situation, even though they had never formally met. Windsor was supposed to be under the idea that Luke was only going to be able to pay if his grandmother died, or that he would be able to pay back more in the eventuality that Mrs. LeBaron died and left Luke half of her money. This was one of the parts that didn't feel right to Violet. Inheritance laws, human nature, the fact that the two guys didn't know each other, and the chain of events didn't seem to add up. It was vaguely possible if Windsor had been at the party, which apparently he was even though they had never seen him. How had he gotten in to poison Francesca? Air vents? In real life, air vents weren't actually big enough to fit a person. A window? The only windows were in the main gallery and none were in the secluded room.

Maybe the police were assuming that Windsor and Luke had worked together? Windsor had the means with access to the plant, they both kind of had motive, and Luke had the opportunity to slip it into her drink. This still didn't sit well with Violet. This means that they would have had to plan this far in advance while their admittedly weak motive to kill her only appeared that evening at the party. Windsor could have planned it ahead of time to get more money out of Luke, but that just didn't feel right. All of it was possible, but wasn't pacifying Violet's suspicions.

"Relax!" Jake read her mind. "They got the guy. The rest of the wedding can go off without a hitch and you can concentrate on food again."

"I guess so."

"Don's good," Jake said pulling Violet in for a hug." He wouldn't be building a case against Windsor if he didn't really believe that he was guilty of the murder."

"I think that's what I'm afraid of," Violet reflected.

As the pomegranate honey pastry cream was being removed from the refrigerator to fill the cream puffs, Violet's phone vibrated in her back pocket, then rang out with the strains of Pitch Perfect 3.

"Hello?" Violet had to inquire again when all she heard were sniffles coming through the phone.

"Violet, I-I need to talk to someone." Laurel sounded more contrite and sadder than her usual demeanor. "I have to keep getting ready, but I must talk to someone besides my mom and sisters."

"Ok. I was going to run out to pick up some supplies anyway," Violet lied. "So should I drop by your house."

Violet was worried that Laurel had heard about her run-ins with Luke and his arrest. Would Luke miss the wedding because of Violet's insistence on pressing charges? Or had she heard about Paul's advances towards Greta?

"It's about Paul. He...well, maybe we should take a walk when you get here. There are bridesmaids everywhere!" Laurel whispered with a touch of her usual joie de vie.

As Violet and Laurel rounded a corner in Mueller Lake Park just across the street from Laurel's immaculate craftsman-style home, Laurel spilled her guts. "Paul lied to me, I think. Oh, I don't know. And about something big. Ugh. It's all so messed up!"

"So how did you find out?" Violet was now convinced that they were talking about Paul and his residual feelings for Greta, but she knew that when a girl needed to talk, she didn't want to be rushed.

"He told me. Early this morning, on our wedding day!"

Violet said nothing, knowing that was the best way to get Laurel to say more. She braced herself to hear things about her own sister that she might not want to hear.

"He told me that he just found out, but it's not very believable." Laurel sighed. "He could have just been keeping it from me until it's too late to cancel the wedding. He knows that I am, that we both are, determined to go through with getting married. But now I don't know if I can trust him! I've got him, but I don't know what to do with him!"

Laurel seemed too scattered, so Violet nudged. "Did he cheat or something?"

"No." Laurel's softness for Paul showed through behind her tears. "He has never done that. I guess his mom cheated on his dad a few times, so he knows how it tears families apart."

Yeah, right! Violet thought Paul's determination to get married and his devotion to Laurel left something to be desired in her mind. At least there was reason to believe that he would not stray once he and Laurel were married.

Violet understood Laurel's feelings, however. Jake's father had left him and his mother when he was young for another woman. It had caused Jake to have strong feelings about fidelity. It was one way that Violet knew that she could completely trust her husband.

"It's that…his old girlfriend…" Laurel hesitated. "I didn't tell you everything that happened when he and I broke up."

Violet was somewhat confused now. They couldn't be talking about Greta, could they?

Laurel looked down and a tear fell from each eye. "Right after we got back together and he ditched that blonde bi-…girl, she kept trying to get him back. She called him, left messages, stalked him online, and even waited for him outside his apartment! He had to change his locks, get a different phone number, all that."

Violet was shocked but hid it well. Paul had been having trouble with two past girlfriends? One had been making overtures to him WHILE he was practically propositioning Greta?

Laurel went on. "When she left a message that she was pregnant, we thought it was just another angle that she was trying to work. She was weird like that. She lied and cheated, tried to make him jealous by telling him that she was dating someone new, everything! We thought she was faking a pregnancy, but things got real when she went to Paul's doctor. Doctor Glenn confirmed it. I guess she hadn't seen a doctor until then, but he even did an ultrasound. The pregnancy was still in the first few weeks, so we…"

Laurel cringed and struggled to go on, "God help us, we asked her to…get an abortion."

Laurel shook with a tiny sob, then continued. "She tried to refuse and to say that this meant that Paul had to come and do right by her, so we, ugh…offered to pay her. She didn't even care about the baby! She was just using it as a bargaining chip to get Paul! Or get back at him, I don't know. I think we felt worse about her getting an abortion than she did! We paid her $20,000 to leave us alone and get an abortion from Dr. Glenn. We never heard from her after that. I guessed what she really cared about was the money."

Violet again said nothing but rubbed her friend's back with one hand and silently judged Paul.

"So everything was fine! She was gone! I never met her, so it was like she didn't even seem real." Laurel's cheeks were now streaked with constant tears. "She wasn't going to get any more money out of us, she had given up the baby, and Paul and I assuaged our guilt by recommitting to each other and agreeing to have children right away after the wedding. We would give that little spirit a good home instead of being used as a pawn in her game.

"But now, Paul says she has NOT gotten the abortion! She's still pregnant and tried to get him back again! And said that they can be together now!"

"What does that mean?" Violet asked.

"I don't know. Paul said he doesn't either." Laurel sobbed again. "But now he will be under her thumb forever if she has his child! She's crazy! She could ruin him, and me and my whole family if we get married! Ugh! How could he not have told me? There is no way that she actually left him alone for months! There is no way that he didn't know about that baby! She's been bugging him for our whole engagement and he just

174

didn't tell me!"

Laurel began pacing the grass just off the path. She twirled her hair around her finger while her low eyebrows knit together.

"You can't be sure of that." Violet tried to be comforting, leaving out her own sour feelings about Paul. "Maybe he has been honest with you about this. I mean he did come out and tell you the truth now."

"When it's too late!" Laurel grumbled. "He tells me the morning of our wedding, when all the guests have already flown in and all the plans have been made. He waited to tell me until he knew that I wouldn't cancel, but he's still trying to get credit for telling me before the wedding! Ooh it makes me want to call the whole thing off just to spite him!"

Violet couldn't help but think of the catering. Right now, Jake was loading up piles of food to take to Laguna Gloria, the wedding venue. If Laurel cancelled, especially to spite Paul, just to work out their problems and get married another day, food for 150 people would be wasted. Rotting and stinking, thrown out and growing putrid with…

"Violet." Laurel interrupted Violet's self-centered and neurotic train of thought. "What do you think I should do?"

Violet sighed and collected her thoughts before answering. Paul may be flighty, but she had never known him to lie. "You might get mad at me, but I don't think Paul lied to you. And I don't think you really think so either."

Laurel sat up straight on a nearby bench but stayed silent for a long time.

"You know, I-I think you're right." Laurel mused and went on. "I do believe his story, I just…I think I just wish it weren't true."

"I'm sorry." Violet sat down next to her and admired how quickly Laurel could dig down and unearth her true feelings on a subject. "It is an impossibly hard situation. And a hard decision, but it doesn't have to be."

"With family money every decision is hard." Laurel sighed, then hissed. "I think I am really afraid of losing any of my family's fortune to that gold-digging little hussy!"

175

"Do you love Paul?" Violet brought them back to the real subject.

Laurel was taken aback. "You know I do," she said with some irritation.

"And why did you break up?"

"I was worried that he was too frivolous with money. I have my family's legacy to maintain!"

"Then why did you get back together?" Violet finally came to the real question.

Laurel sighed again and watched the ducks swimming on the pond before them. "Because money doesn't really matter. He is generous to a fault but has promised to cut back a bit. He has made me realize that money is just a way to do a lot of good in the world. He is so amazing."

"Well, with your common sense and a good lawyer, I think you two can do that child a lot of good without hurting your parents and siblings. You may have to pay child support or whatever, but she probably can't touch your family with the prenup you two have. I think it will all work out. He will weather the storm better with you by his side and as you say, money doesn't really matter. Money doesn't buy happiness. Love and commitment to stay in love is what matters. If marrying Paul will make you happy, I say go for it," Violet said as she slapped her lap.

Neither of them spoke for a long moment while Laurel's breathing slowed and she wiped her eyes and cheeks. Laurel's characteristic command had returned by the time Violet ventured to ask more questions.

Violet had a faint idea. "Hey, did this girl...ever get... violent?"

"No." Laurel looked at Violet questioningly.

"And...was Paul always...clear that he would not be leaving you...no matter what?"

"Of course!"

"Well, what was her name?"

"The slut? Trina." Laurel said with disgust.

"One more, sorry. Do you know...is this Trina having a boy or a girl?"

"Girl, I think. Yeah, she said that in a psycho rant once. Why?" Laurel asked.

Violet gave up. "I just thought I was on to something, but I guess not. Nevermind."

Chapter Thirteen

Was It You?

Violet had to speak to Paul, but she did have one idea first. While Laurel had been talking, Violet had tried to imagine Trina. Blonde, probably pretty, probably Scandinavian. The one 'Trina' that Violet had known was a tall, round-faced, blonde girl, straight out of Sweden. Violet had seen one girl like that in the past few days, so she made a call.

"Hi. I was the caterer for the Bachelor Party at your clubhouse last night. May I please speak to your event coordinator?"

"Who?" The voice on the other end of the line asked.

For a moment, Violet's heart raced. She was on to something! Maybe the girl last night had been a fake event coordinator! She had been walking around freely but looking like she belonged because of professional clothes and a clipboard! Was it Trina?

"So Trina isn't your event coordinator?" Violet pressed, reigning in her excitement.

"Oh Trish? With park service?" The woman piped up in a friendly Southern drawl.

"Uh, yes. Would she have been the one that was there last night, checking in on our event?" Violet's heart was starting to sink, although she told herself that her original thought might still be correct.

"Lemme check the schedule, mm-kay? Hold on a minute, hon."

So the pregnant blonde there last night was probably not a fake employee. Violet had gotten way too excited about that possibility in that half-second of confusion.

"Yes, she is probably the one you talked to!" The woman was overjoyed. "It was Trish!"

"Oh thanks!" Violet tried not to sound disappointed. "Can I please have their number over there?"

"I can do you one better. I'll just transfer you. Hold on, sweetie," the Southern belle said.

As Violet waited, she wondered. When Paul had walked into the bachelor party and looked so shocked, was it Trish that had surprised him? Was it her that had been his old girlfriend? Had Trish faced him, confronted him, and broken the news to him last night? Could Trish also be Trina?

"Hello?" A young woman's voice said over the phone.

"Hi, is this…Trish?" Violet ventured.

When she answered in the affirmative, Violet realized that she had not planned what she would say when she finally found Trina, or Trish. Violet opened with, "I was the caterer at the bachelor party in the Zilker Clubhouse last night…"

"Oh, hello!" The woman's voice rang with recognition, but Violet wanted to be sure and also buy more time.

"Did we meet last night? Was it you?"

"Yes, that was me!" The woman sounded confident and cultured, with a soft French accent.

"Oh good!" Violet vamped. "I was wondering if you… found a chaffing dish there…after we cleaned up last night…"

"I'm sorry, I didn't see anything. But I also did not stay the whole time. Would you like me to keep an eye open for it the next time I am there? I am due to check in again in about an hour."

"Oh, that would be great!" Violet tried to get Trish to keep talking. "So you don't have to stay the whole time while an event is happening?"

"No, fortunately! I was on my way to another event when the stripper came out."

"Ha!" Violet was able to genuinely laugh. "Yeah, no thanks! So you and the mister had a date?"

Even Violet could tell that it was a weird question, but Trish took the bait. "Yes, my husband and I were going on one last date before the baby is born next week."

"Oh congratulations! Good luck! Is this your first?" Violet was finally getting to the information that might tell her something.

"No, my third. Do you have children?" Trish politely enquired.

Violet kindly signed off as quickly as she could by pretending someone was on the other line. Why did the universe want her to think about kids so desperately? Besides, Violet had found out everything that she had needed to know.

Trish could not be Trina. Trish's pregnancy was about three months farther along. She seemed to be happily married, and she already had two kids. Any one of those things wouldn't have definitely taken Trish off of Violet's list, but when put together, Violet decided she was done.

The only other possibility for finding this Trina was to talk with Paul.

Violet had been trying to think of how to make it happen organically, but there was no way. She had to speak to Paul anyway. Violet had a wisp of a lead and needed to follow it through. The only person that knew everything about what had happened with Trina was Paul, and only he could rule her out or confirm her a suspect in Violet's mind.

Her phone still in her hand, she dialed Don to update him.

"Is that you? Let it go, Violet," Don said over the phone. "Windsor killed Luke's grandmother, probably with his help, and you know it. He was released on bail, but we are keeping an eye on him. He's just sitting in his apartment. Nothing else is going to happen."

"I don't know it, and neither do you!"

Detective Donnelly only offered silence.

"Is your partner pushing this? Is he hanging Windsor no matter what human nature would say?"

"Look," he drawled after another pause. "The case is really strong against Windsor and we are under constant pressure to close this case. Your sister is cleared! Don't worry!"

"I am looking for the truth and you should be too! I'm going to talk to Paul."

Violet was so annoyed that she hung up on Don. She was

pulling into the parking lot of the wedding venue anyway. The golf club across the street had an almost full parking lot, but in front of Laguna Gloria she saw only five cars. Paul's Volvo, Luke's beamer, Pierre unloading boxes of wine from a white van, Greta unloading flowers onto a wheely cart from the box truck, and a hatchback she didn't recognize with a sticker that said 'Professional Photographers of America'. Mike must be here before everyone else to take photos. Violet smiled slightly thinking about how annoyed Mike must be about having to wait for the bride to arrive.

The afternoon was warm and smelled of freshly mown grass. Cicadas chirped in the distance and despite the forecasted rain, there was not one cloud over head. It was as if the rich could put in an order for immaculate weather. The looming metal sculpture in front of Laguna Gloria seemed to agree as he stared up in astonishment. Fluffy white dollops all along the horizon signalled that the evening might cool off though.

Violet barely registered any of this. She was set on a mission to find Paul. First, she checked the side and back patios where the chairs and tables were set up, but he was not there. She finally found him coming out of the bathroom. He was flushed and distraught, but alone.

"What's wrong?" Violet instinctively asked when she saw the look on his face.

"Nothing. Wait, my brother was arrested! It's lucky for you that he still made it here to the wedding!" Paul had obviously changed gears.

"I don't think he is responsible!" Violet interrupted.

"Then why would you press charges?"

"Oh, well he definitely hit me," Violet clarified. "But I don't think he had a part in killing your grandmother!"

Paul took a moment to process this. "He hit you?"

"Yes," Violet said evenly while lifting her hair to show her bruise and tiny cut high on the side of her face. "He was waiting for me when I got home. He even tried to strangle me, but I got away and that part can't be proved."

Violet thought Paul looked confused and pitiful. "I'm... sorry. I'm so sorry. Luke has faced a lot of made up charges in the past…but I should have known that you wouldn't do that."

Violet thought, *Made up! Yeah right! I bet they were all true!* Though aloud she said, "I'm kind of sorry that I'm pressing charges against your brother. Although he is dangerous, I know it's bad timing. I wouldn't want to do anything to hurt you and Laurel."

Paul looked down and nodded slightly in resigned gratitude at the black and white tiled floor.

"Is there anyone that would want to hurt you and Laurel?" Violet probed.

"What?" Paul deflected, glaring at Violet now. "What do you have to do with it?"

"I don't think Luke or his loan shark killed your grandma," Violet insisted. "And I know that Greta didn't."

"It's not possible," Paul agreed, but kept his eyes averted as he brought a shaky hand to tug at his collar.

"Exactly, but…" Violet ventured further. "The police think that this money lender and Luke did, and they were looking at Greta for the murder before that."

Paul turned away slowly. "And you're just trying to clear them."

"Yes," pleaded Violet. "Is there anyone that would want to hurt you and Laurel? Want to stop the wedding? And hurt your grandmother? I think it would have to be all those to try anything during the rehearsal dinner."

"No. I mean…" Paul trailed off.

After a long silence, Violet decided to confront Paul now, while they were alone. "I know all about Trina. Was it you who told Laurel, or did she find out?"

Paul's face turned pale as he whipped it up to face hers. "So what?"

"Could she have done this?" Violet stepped in to whisper.

"No way!" he roared. "She has nothing to do with any of this! She's nowhere near, well, anyway she couldn't! It wasn't her. It's my fault that this all got so out of hand!"

He punched the wooden molding, luckily not hard enough to cost him his deposit, and marched out the back door and down the stairs that led to the lagoon below.

Violet imagined an eerily beautiful blonde, far away with her twenty thousand dollars and a burgeoning belly. She could be sending him emails with pictures and ultrasounds to prove that she was still pregnant. Maybe her nagging suspicion about this girl had been totally wrong. Paul said that she was nowhere nearby, but he had also said that it was all his fault.

Could that mean Francesca LeBaron's murder was all his fault? Was it him? He considered it his fault, but could that mean that he had killed her after all? The police had originally looked at Paul for the murder, but why had they stopped?

Violet rushed out to the top of the steps. The wind now coaxed her dark strands into her face as she watched him pacing under a colorful pergola at the edge of the water below. The police had discounted Paul as a suspect because they had waved aside his motive. He was in debt but wouldn't be soon. He would have money, or access to money, after he got married. He didn't need his grandmother's money, but since when did murder motives have to be so logical?

Violet stared at him far away at the bottom of the stairs that crawled down the hill. *Was it you?* She wondered to herself.

She imagined avarice, willful independence, and cocky masculinity. Although Paul had never been like that before, greed can consume a person. Violet understood now. Paul had wanted his own money, not to be controlled by his wife and her tight purse strings. He had grown rapacious and wanted, even if not needed, his inheritance now. He must know how to identify some wild plants from his time on the ranch, so he could have made the poison. He was right there in the party with his grandmother the whole time. It hadn't been the obvious herbal tea, but maybe that was just to throw everyone off?

Even if he had been the center of attention, it would have been easy enough to slip something discreetly into a coffee cup that was on its way to his grandmother. Could he be so unfeeling as to kill his own grandmother? He had always been 'her favorite', but she was incessantly unpleasant and controlling.

Violet couldn't believe that she had never seen it before. Violet felt blind! Was that why Laurel had been so sad? What if that was the real reason Violet's friend had questioned if she could trust him? Laurel had known! She had known that Paul was the murderer and Laurel still loved him anyway. Violet had told Laurel to trust him and marry him anyway. Now, Violet realized what a horrible mistake that had been. Trying to forget the wasted pastry cream and strawberries and pushing past the thought of slimy arugula and radishes, she had to talk to Laurel again.

Violet took one faltering step, then froze.

If Laurel knew the situation and was still choosing to marry Paul, then why should Violet stand in the way of her friend being happy? He probably wouldn't kill her too. Laurel had let slip that the prenuptial agreement they had made specified that all Laurel's family money would go back to her siblings or her children in the event of her death. Paul couldn't get Laurel's money through divorce or death, just by keeping her happy throughout a long life.

Violet softened like room temperature butter. Paul would make Laurel happy. Paul knew that he had to, Laurel knew that he would, and now Violet was convinced. Did the police really have to know? Did the wedding really have to be ruined? Violet tried to persuade herself that her motivations were selfless, but couldn't they be both? Laurel and Paul could get married, escape to their cabana or whatever abroad somewhere, then the truth could come out. The police and Trina wouldn't be able to touch them. Paul's family already owned the home abroad where they were planning to go for their honeymoon, and they could build a new life there. He would then have his own money to send to Trina's baby girl voluntarily. Violet's friends would be happy, the wedding would have been a success, and the case would get closed. Greta and Luke would no longer be murder suspects, Luke would still be put away for being abusive, Don could have his proof, and Greta and Violet's businesses would have some shiny new contacts.

Violet gazed down at Paul once more prowling at the water's edge, then slowly turned around to return to the wedding preparations.

Chapter Fourteen

What Should I Do?

Violet was especially quiet as she piled skewers, arranged platters, and warmed the pink tacos at the last minute. Lighting the candles was difficult, but Violet still appreciated the breeze that was scented with herbs, flowers, food, and the water of the lagoon. Dusk fell and the guests arranged themselves between the manicured shrubs and the weathered stone statues on the side of the Italianate-style villa. All the appetizers were perfectly on schedule when Jake asked if Violet would like to go watch the ceremony.

"I have everything covered here, and Laurel's your friend," Jake cajoled. "Go enjoy yourself, plus, I think you need a break."

"Should I?" It was true, Violet needed a break. This weekend would have been long enough without the added complications of a murder and the ensuing investigation. It was all so exhausting, but Violet had to admit, exhilarating.

Violet looked out over the scene to assuage her inner clean freak before she could walk away. Fluttery, pink ruffled and petaled tablecloths were on each table, each with candles and a flower arrangement made ominous by the presence of foxglove. The cake table had long been ready, with the bakers from Simon Lee Bakery arriving hours ago. They had delivered their ombre pink cake before Violet had even arrived.

Greta wandered, straightening flowers unnecessarily as she walked from candle to candle, using her body to block the wind as she used a long Zippo lighter on each. Katy sat perched on one of the gold ladder-backed chairs by the drinks table that she would run with Pierre. She had Pierre and a Perrier. She looked comfortable and ready as he stood next to her, animatedly talking her ear off.

Inside the long, dramatic dining room, banquet tables sat artistically mounded with the catering. As the only direction they had received was to make everything as pink as possible, it was lovely and soft with food seeming to spill out of baskets. Only the Radicchio Caesar Salad and Pink Pork Tacos were missing, but that was intentional and being seen to by Jake.

The strings of lights that were suspended overhead were glowing and swaying in the increasing evening breeze. Violet breathed a sigh of relief and closed her eyes into the clean-smelling gust. Things were finally starting to settle down. Lights were lit, cuisine was in a steady holding pattern, drinks were chilled, and Violet knew who was responsible for the murder. The sounds of trickling fountains and the distant string quartet floated in as the sun went down over the lagoon, casting the now cloudy sky in pink light to match the wedding party. Everything was perfect and ready for her to step away for a moment.

The ceremony was perfect too. The flowers that Violet had thought were large weeping bridesmaids' bouquets now lay in a seven - or eight-foot circle at the front, behind Pastor Schmidt and his self-satisfied stance. The bridesmaids instead held small tasteful bundles of magenta foxglove and deep purple heuchera, with blush peonies all around. The groom and groomsmen similarly had on the pink boutonnieres that Violet had seen Greta and Katy finishing.

Framing the lawn of chairs were plexiglass pillars with huge floral arrangements that seemed to float in the air. The guests themselves seemed to understand the mood of the scene and spoke in hushed tones before the bride arrived and the proceedings began.

After Laurels' sisters walked down the aisle and exchanged amorous glances with Luke, Laurel graced the end of the passage and made all heads turn. Her white, lacey gown was long at the hem, but had half sleeves of the same lace, but in black. The same black lace lined the end of her trailing veil.

Violet smiled to herself. The dress was perfect. Laurel couldn't stand to be too conventional and appease her mother entirely. This little twist of black was probably appalling to her older relations, but it fit Laurel like a glove. It set off her edgy personality, her dark hair, and her subtly smokey eyes.

The gasps that followed her appearance were mingled awe of her audacity and her beauty. Every eye was transfixed as she glided past on the arm of her father.

But especially Paul's.

The way Paul and Laurel looked at each other let Violet know that she had made the right decision. Violet was doing what she should by keeping quiet until tomorrow. Laurel and Paul welled up and held each other's' hands with almost white knuckled determination as Laurel's lacy gown and veil danced ethereally around them in the growing wind. Flowers, guests, and Pastor Glenn all beamed on the couple as they couldn't pry their eyes off of each other. When they kissed at the end, it was clearly a kiss of beginnings.

Violet sighed and felt comforted that their goal had finally been reached. They were married and no one could stand in the way of that now. Their love was a strange beast, but it was theirs. It was beautiful in that moment, but only Violet knew that it could also be terrible at times. It was lasting love, but it was also a vicious beast to anyone in its way. As long as it made them happy, then Violet had to be content with the delight that showed on their faces.

But how could that be enough? Being in love didn't justify any other actions that Paul had taken. It wasn't love that made him kill his grandmother. It had been greed. What was the right thing to do? Call Don and ruin the wedding? Keep quiet until tomorrow?

The spell over the scene broke as guests clapped and started to rise. Violet hurried away to do her job before any of the guests could reach the food and before she could second guess her own decisions anymore. She also sped to the back before Laurel's mother could catch her swooning or brooding on the job, which Violet seemed to be alternating between.

187

As Violet emerged through the wrought iron gates to the ornately tiled dining room, nine beautiful appetizers spread over two tables were ready and being captured on Mike's DSLR. After the guests descended, mingled, dispersed, and second platters had been laid out, Violet made a small plate for Laurel and Paul.

The elated couple stood just outside the row of huge glass doors on the patio, being congratulated by guests. Just as Violet and Jake had been at their wedding, they were too busy to get themselves some sustenance. Violet snuck up behind them on the flagstone patio and offered them her wares, still wrestling with her resolve to let the information rest until morning.

Paul had the same goofy smile that he had worn at the rehearsal dinner, which now looked almost sinister to Violet since she had learned the truth.

"Thank you so much! That's so thoughtful of you!" Laurel gushed, glowing and taking the plate, but handing it to Paul.

Laurel and Violet smiled at each other a moment before Violet's grin faltered. "Are you happy?" Violet inquired with concern.

"Of course!" Laurel answered with curiosity behind her voice, then she seemed to comprehend and whispered, "Thanks for your advice earlier."

Violet forced a smile and hugged her friend. Even with her face in the white veil of this new bride, Violet worried about Laurel. Would she stay happy? Was the black lace trim on her gown's sleeves just a little too foretelling? To Violet it seemed like a dark lining on a white cloud, instead of the silver lining on the dark clouds that now hung overhead. Violet pushed these thoughts aside, turned, and buried herself in her catering work again.

She didn't have to understand or approve. Their love only had to work for them and no one else. All Violet had to do was keep quiet until tomorrow, but was it what she should do? It was proving more challenging than she had anticipated.

***

The knife reflected the points of lights overhead as Paul drew it to himself. Cameras flashed and people stared as Laurel stepped to the tall, elaborate cake. The ruffled pink work of art seemed to be wrapped in layers of lace, but the chef's knife glided through with no resistance. After the couple fed each other cake without incident, Violet stepped up to cut cake for the guests. People swarmed and cake plates disappeared in droves as Violet's mind dwelled on keeping quiet.

Midnight loomed near and the party had started to breakup before the rain finally started. First, it patted the fluttering tablecloths and made the leaves of the tree shudder. When it started to polka dot the flagstone patio and the concrete walkways, then guests started to migrate, and the wedding crew quickly brought the remnants of cake inside the dining room. The first half hour of drizzles drove the wedding party inside and half of the guests to their cars. Then, people rushed everywhere to get the bride and groom out the front door before the rest of the guests left or the rain gained momentum.

Violet wanted to start cleaning up. The most perishable foods should go first, but plenty of guests were still milling about, so they needed to stay where they were. The bride's mother was nowhere to be found in the swarm of guests, but Paul's mother insisted that the party was continuing and should not be moved. Violet selected the two barest trays and decided to appease her neuroses by cleaning up these first. She consolidated the food that was left and swung the tray around and headed to the small makeshift caterers' kitchen. She dodged people trying to gather others in order to throw flower petals at the departing couple, family members looking for the happy newlyweds, aunts trying to pack some food for their journey, and finally pushed through the swinging doors. Just entering the small galley kitchen, the door at the other end swung wildly, making it appear as if someone had just run out of it.

Paul stood facing the other door with his head down. His posture looked despondent as he swayed back and forth, and a quiet sob escaped him.

"Oh, Paul!" Violet said as she lay the trays on the counter. "Your family is looking for you and Laurel to make your grand escape."

Violet made it sound like a joke, but she meant what she said. The couple could make their escape and live happily ever after, far away. When Paul didn't respond, Violet grew nervous. Why wouldn't he turn around? What should she do? Why did he look so…what did his posture say? Forlorn? Furious? Foreboding?

Her joke hung in the air and grew stale. Did he know that she had figured out his secret? Why would he want to be alone with her in this tiny room with all its knives and noticeable lack of windows? Violet's scalp winced and she became frightened of this man that she considered an old family friend. He wouldn't do anything to her, would he?

Suddenly he faltered backwards, and Violet was tempted to run out of the door that she had just entered. Paul somehow seemed less threatening now. Violet was puzzled as Paul spilled, tripping on his own feet, onto the counter next to them. The Formica resounded as Paul's head slammed against it, bounced off, and came to rest at Violet's feet. He lay on the floor with stab wounds littering his chest. Crimson red seeped through his shirt, blotches slowly growing and joining each other.

"No!" Violet heard herself shout as she scrambled to apply pressure to his wounds. Confusion and neuroses got pushed aside as urgent need outranked them. She wasn't sure what to do, so she grabbed dish towels off of counters, flung her apron off, anything to get more fabric in contact with the gashes that seemed to be everywhere.

"Don't. You shouldn't-" Paul gurgled. As Violet tried to shush him, he went on with insistence, "Don't hurt him! I couldn't hurt him…"

Although Paul seemed to have more to say, he lost consciousness as his head lolled to the side. Violet called for help, not sure that anyone could hear her pleas with the noise of the party.

What should I do? She implored her mind, but she doubted

her own judgment and abilities too much. Violet had made all the wrong decisions when she had found Mrs. LeBaron, and now she couldn't make any decision at all. The pulse throbbing visibly in his neck and the continued flow of blood told Violet that he was still alive. For now.

Pink Hybrid Tortillas

These tortillas are the best of both worlds, corn and flour. They are soft, hot pink, and have a lovely, satisfying texture.

1 big handful of crunchy dried beet chips
1 ¾ cups (265g) cornmeal (masa harina is better if you keep it around, I don't)
3 ¼ cups (415g) all purpose flour, plus more for rolling out
1 teaspoon salt
1 teaspoon baking powder
2 cups (500mL) water
⅔ cups (140g) lard, or shortening

1. In a food processor, grind together the beet and cornmeal. You are trying to get them fully incorporated, so it may take a minute. Then pulse in 3 cups (380g) of your flour, your salt and baking powder.
2. In a large liquid measuring cup, measure out your 2 cups (500mL)of water, then add lard until the water level reads 2 ⅔ cups when you hold the lard all the way under the water. Or measure it out by weight using the grams. Microwave that until everything is hot and melted.
3. With your food processor or mixer running, slowly pour in your wet ingredients until you have formed a wet dough with all your ingredients. Cover and let the dough rest and fully hydrate for about 45 minutes.
4. Preheat a dry cast iron pan over medium heat.
5. Flour your counter or a big bowl with ¼ cup (30g) of flour and turn dough out onto it. Knead in your flour until your

ball is smooth and not so sticky. Then divide into 16 balls for regular tacos/burritos, or 32 balls for mini tacos for a party.

6. Now that your pan is fully preheated, you are ready to start rolling. You can use a tortilla press, but I don't keep one around.

7. Working with one ball at a time, roll out very thin tortillas to be as round as possible between a floured counter and a floured rolling pin. Cook each tortilla in a dry cast iron pan until they turn lighter and get brown spots, or for about 45 seconds per side, while you roll out your next tortilla.

8. Serve immediately or store in a resealable bag in your refrigerator for up to a week. When going back to use them, heat them a little in a dry pan or the microwave to resoften them.

Pickled Red Onion with Lime

Prep Time - 5 minutes
Total time including chill - 1 hour 5 minutes

1 large red onion
½ cup (about 120mL) white vinegar
¼ cup (about 60 mL) lime juice
½ teaspoon sea salt
¼ teaspoon black pepper
¼ teaspoon ground coriander
¼ teaspoon garlic powder (or a couple slices of fresh garlic)
1 teaspoon sugar
½ teaspoon crushed red pepper (optional)

1. Boil 2 ½ cups (750mL) water while you slice the red onion super thinly into crescents. Try to keep the slices uniform for best results.

2. Pile red onion into a heatproof bowl, then pour boiling water over onion slices and let sit for about 30 seconds. I

push the onions down to make sure they are submerged so that they all soften evenly. Next, strain onion out of hot water and set aside the onion while you prepare the brine.

3. In a separate, small bowl, combine all other ingredients to make a pickling brine for the red onion.

4. Pack your red onion into a nonreactive container, I use a mason jar, and push down to pack the onion as tightly as possible.

5. Pour your brine over your packed red onion. If possible, weigh down your red onion so that it stays submerged. I use a glass weight, but you can use a little sauce dish, a shot glass, anything!

6. Refrigerate the mixture for at least an hour, but preferably 24 hours. These pickled red onions will keep in your fridge indefinitely and only get better with time!

Chapter Fifteen

What Will Happen?

Greta came in behind Violet and the pitcher that had been in her hand smashed to the floor, spraying droplets of water and shards of glass. Through tears and rushing adrenaline one sister frantically applied pressure to the wounds and the other desperately called emergency services. Instantly, Detective Donnelly came in with a large first aid kit and started deftly moving around Paul's chest. He ripped tiny pieces of gauze and stuffed them almost inside each incision, stopping the flow and raising their spirits.

The three of them were starting to feel better, and Greta asked, "What will happen to him?"

The answer never came as the door behind Violet swung open again. In the doorway, they heard Laurel start to whimper. She stumbled backwards in an impossibly white satin mini going-away dress, covering her mouth and not succeeding in stifling her own ear-piercing screams.

"Hold him up a little, like this." Detective Donnelly gave the sisters soft direction, then rushed out to tend to the grieving bride's shock.

Violet and Greta stared down at Paul, silently cradling his head and listening to his ragged, shallow breathing. He couldn't die here. He had to fly away with Laurel, get a terrific tan, and die leathery and grey with her on a beach somewhere. Not like this. Not from violence. Not on a kitchen floor hours after his wedding. Not on the other side of a door from the most beautiful wedding and bride that Violet had ever seen.

Sirens could be heard outside before Violet realized that this was actually a development in the case. This changed everything. Not for Paul's escape or for Laurel's life, but for the murder case that held them all wrapped. Why would someone have stabbed him if he was the murderer? No one knew that Paul was the killer. Even if they did, no one in the world felt strongly enough about Francesca LeBaron to kill for her. Revenge killing? Violet doubted it.

Francesca's husband was dead and the only person still alive that had ever been in love with her was Dr. Glenn. He couldn't be a murderer. He was too kind, scattered and frail. He could barely lift a knife, let alone stab someone repeatedly. It was rumored that Francesca and he had been in love, but that was decades ago, and they had clearly been different people then, if the rumors were even true.

Could this mean that Paul had not been the murderer? Then who would have benefited from all of this? Violet had to find the answers to these questions before she could know what was going to happen next.

Paul was taken from them by EMT's and loaded onto a stretcher. He was fed into the back of an ambulance with his father and the EMTs. Laurel stumbled along just behind the procession, sobbing, with her parents steadying her by the elbows and easing her into their car to follow the ambulance. Paul's mother and brother, both with wild eyes and quick feet, hurried to a car to follow as well. Jake held Violet wrapped up in his arms again as they watched the scene.

Police officers swirled around, trying to account for who was there and who the possible pool of suspects could be, but it was impossible. Cars left the parking lot even as they tried to control the crowd and vehicles had been pulling out consistently since the rain started a half hour before. There were no cameras, no witnesses, and the first people on the scene had been too engrossed in first aid to give any kind of chase. Only a handful of people couldn't have done it, but everyone else was a possible suspect in Violet's mind.

Violet hugged Jake a little tighter as she thought how close she had come to seeing the killer. It was a chilling thought that she had come so close, but now was so far from a solution. She had stayed with Paul. Everyone that came in the door had stayed with Paul. By the time he was stable enough to think about anything else, his attacker could have run away, driven away, changed their clothes, anything! They couldn't just look for someone with blood on their clothes who was on the scene! These thoughts were just getting Violet frustrated. Then, as she pulled away from Jake, the speckles of cranberry red on his shirt bewildered her.

Seeming to read her thoughts, Jake raised his eyebrows and indicated Violet's shirt with a glance and a nod. Violet looked down to see her immaculate catering blouse smeared with blood that was now turning rusty brown at the edges. She had not even noticed in the heat of the moment that Paul's blood had gotten all over her, but now it made her skin contract and try to crawl up and away from the button-up shirt.

Even her hands and arms were streaked and smeared. Maroon hid in the cracks around her nails and on her knuckles and stayed imbedded in the crevasses in her wedding ring. The terrifying constellation on Jake's shirt had transferred to him from her own body as they had hugged.

"Let's get your back-up shirt and wash your hands," Jake reassured Violet as he started to lead her to their rental van.

"Wait!" Don had appeared behind them "I'm going to need to keep that shirt as evidence."

"Oh right," Violet muttered. In a moment the full gravity of the situation and the case came back to Violet and her mind felt whisked up into a frenzy. "And I think we need to talk."

After the changing and bagging of shirts, Violet, Jake, and Detective Donnelly walked back towards Laguna Gloria. Their threesome was nothing out of the ordinary, usually accompanied by a rotating date on a weekend night, but their usual flow of conversation was stunted by the current circumstances. As they got close to the main entrance where the din of other voices included crying and low reassurances, their group peeled off to the left and down a hill to be alone.

Finally they sat in a deserted amphitheater overlooking the lagoon. The lit mermaid bronze at the front held their attention as they felt small and alone in this cavernous space.

"This looks bad for me, doesn't it? What is going to

happen?" Violet's words implied a question, but she said it as more of a statement.

"Yes, it does," Detective Donnelly answered.

They all sighed in turn as Violet ticked off. "I was found over the body, it was in a kitchen full of my knives, I was in both parties and I help my sister with the flowers. So, I had all the opportunity and means, but at least I don't have a motive."

"And at least your shirt won't have any blood spatter on it, just blood from contact after the wounds were made." Jake was trying to comfort her, but Violet's mind was elsewhere.

Violet was haunted as her own idea sunk in. "It was probably my knife that he used! I bring them catering with me and I don't think a place like this would have any good knives just laying around."

The sky had cleared momentarily, but puddles on the ground around them shook with the wind that promised more rain was imminent.

"What happened, Violet?" Don asked after a few minutes of silence.

Violet spilled. The flood gates opened, and she told the detective and her husband everything. She explained her doubts about Windsor's guilt, she recounted her conversations with Laurel and with Paul, and she described her suspicions about Paul's greed. Violet went so far as to try to justify not telling Don all she knew earlier and why she had guessed so wrongly with her assumptions. At last, she reached what she had seen and heard in the kitchen with Paul.

"Paul only got to say, 'Don't hurt him, I couldn't hurt him', before he went unconscious. But how did you get there so fast?"

"When I heard the call come over the radio, I was just pulling up outside. I just grabbed the first aid kit and ran in. But about what you learned…"

The detective spoke with a determination that prompted them all to stay silent for a moment while he thought.

"Him," was all that Detective Donnelly said, zeroing in on the pertinent information that they had to deal with now.

"On and off I have been suspecting this other woman, Trina,

of being in on it somehow, ever since Laurel told me," Violet confessed. "But I can't see how that's possible now."

"I agree." Don was stoic.

"Well, I suppose Luke was at the wedding, but Windsor wasn't?" Violet asked.

"Windsor has been under surveillance all afternoon and evening." Don cut down her question with a stern, staccato voice.

"And I don't see why Luke would want to hurt Paul, that doesn't help him at all," Violet went on.

"Mm." Don and Jake made small noises of ascent.

"Do we think that this attack was done by the same person? Did the same person stab Paul and poison Francesca?" Jake tried to dissect the problem at hand.

"Although the two modes of attack were practically opposites," said Donnelly, "I do think that they were either the same person, or two people working together. It's too great of a coincidence to not be related."

"Stuff like that doesn't happen in real life," added Jake in his pedestrian tone.

"Okay, so who benefits from killing both of them?" Violet was stumped.

"Luke," Don said with conviction

"But the murders are in the wrong order!" Violet interjected.

"Paul's not dead," Don interrupted, then relayed the information. "EMTs say that they are almost sure he will pull through. They aren't sure what will happen with his treatment, that is up to the doctor. He may take a while to regain consciousness because he lost a lot of blood and hit his head on the way down, but he should be fine in a few weeks."

Violet and Jake sighed out of relief.

"Do you think it was attempted murder though? Should we be assuming that the attacker meant to kill him?" Jake knew the right questions to ask.

"I'm not sure." Don rolled the question around and went on. "When I was applying the gauze, those stab wounds were not all that deep. We'll have to wait for word from the surgeons and doctors, but I think they weren't deep enough to do real damage."

"Ugh." Violet reeled a bit from the memory of his wounds. She had butchered animals in culinary school but never been in contact with a seriously wounded person. The stab wounds had seemed huge and impossibly numerous at the time, but now that Violet thought back, she realized that Don was right.

Jake side-hugged her tight and asked, "Is it possible that they were self-inflicted? Could Violet have been right about her suspicion of Paul?"

"Hm, again we'll have to wait for the surgeons, but I don't think so." Don sounded official again as he continued, "They can tell us the trajectory of the wounds, which will help a lot. But it is also a lot harder to stab a person than you think. Especially yourself. If he had done it himself then he probably wouldn't have been able to do it so many times. It was probably someone weak or inexperienced. There was also no weapon at the scene. Whoever did it, fled with the knife."

"Oh no!" Violet moaned.

"What are you thinking?" Don asked with excitement.

"I know that's supposed to be good news for me, because that means I couldn't have done it but...my knife!" Violet thought of her lost friend that went everywhere with her rolled up in a bundle. "They used my knife and ran off with it!"

She felt ashamed, but Violet was mourning the loss of her trusty Henckels knife now that she knew that Paul was going to be okay.

"I'll check into that," Don said, deflated again. "But why don't we think that Luke did this?"

"If it were me, er, if I were Luke," said Violet, "I would have gotten my brother out of the way before he inherited half the money. Or at least before the wedding. As it is, half of Francesca's money went to Paul and half went to Luke. If Paul died after the grandmother and after being married, then Paul's money goes to Laurel."

"But you said that Laurel's money goes back to Laurel's family if anything happens to Laurel," Jake argued.

"Yes, but it was a lopsided prenup." Don elaborated from

what he had read. "When I was checking their financials, Laurel's money goes to Laurel's siblings if anything happens to her, but Paul's money could go to Paul's wife if anything happens to him. It's not totally clear, so I guess that's for the lawyers to work out."

"They didn't care about what the prenup said," Violet clarified. "They were committed to staying married. They just signed it after Laurel's family put whatever they wanted in it."

The three friends thought, silently contemplating for a minute, as they heard people slowly leaving the party after offering their statements and contact information to the uniformed police officers on the scene.

"Are we sure about Laurel's…financial and mental stability?" Jake ventured.

"Yes!" Violet sounded offended by the suggestion.

"Yes," Don concluded.

"Alright, alright!" Jake retreated.

"Besides, we are looking for a man!" Violet reminded them.

"Him," Jake repeated.

"Yeah," Don agreed.

"A 'him' that would want to kill Francesca, then kill Paul, and ruin a wedding. Someone that knows poisons and would use a knife but doesn't have much experience in being violent with one," Violet said. "A man, or boy I guess, that would have an old grudge or long term reason to want Mrs. LeBaron dead, but have a new reason to hate Paul and grab whatever weapon is nearby to attack him with in a crime of passion. Someone who might be weak."

Violet trailed off as she fell into deep thought. "Well, we can whittle the suspect list down a bit further."

"How's that?" Don wondered.

"Someone who is weak." Violet turned to the two men with shining eyes in the dark of the amphitheater. "Someone who went to both the rehearsal dinner and the wedding, and I don't think we are talking about a big, strong guy. That only leaves Pierre, who is obviously very feminine, Dr. Glenn, who is ancient. Is there anyone else?"

"Pastor Schmidt?" Jake volunteered. "He's a man of God,

200

wouldn't that make him gentle?"

"Maybe." Don was doubtful.

"I don't think he's that kind of pastor," opined Violet. "He's more 'hellfire and damnation' and showmanship. Besides, he's huge, so he wouldn't have to try very hard to exert a lot of force."

"Mm." Don grunted in agreement.

"Luke if he was high?" Violet guessed.

"Nah," Jake grumbled. "I want it to be him, but he wasn't that high. Just a little, maybe."

"I want it to be Mike," complained Violet.

"The photographer?" Don asked.

"He's just a jerk," Jake said. "They went to high school together."

"Yeah, but I don't see how it could be," Violet complained. "He is short though."

"Hey, take your personal feelings out of it," Don advised with knit eyebrows. "The only way I am allowed to work with you, or that you can be helpful to the case, is if we stay objective. Don't think about who you want it to be. You have to look at the facts!"

"For me, that means Pierre or the doctor," Jake surmised.

"Maybe," Don agreed. "They were both at both parties, had access to Francesca's drinks and Violet's knives, and don't have a history of being violent or particularly tough. The difficulty of stabbing someone would be a surprise, but maybe not to a doctor. And a doctor would know poisons, but would a sommelier? Neither had access to the floral arrangements ahead of time, but I guess Google searches and other sources could account for a lot. We just don't know their motives yet! Both of them have old motives that just don't hang together for me! Could they have some other reason to want Francesca LeBaron dead?"

Violet stood up. "And what will happen when the killer finds out that Paul's not dead?"

The detective groaned as he rose slowly to his feet. "I guess we better find out!"

Chapter Sixteen

Then Who?

Violet crept in the hospital room with Don right behind her, hovering by the door. It smelled of bathroom disinfectant and hand sanitizer as they had just used a pump each. These were some of Violet's favorite smells. Although hospitals had gained a bad reputation lately for germs, Violet loved them. They felt and smelled supremely clean, and therefore comfortable.

Violet had felt guilty leaving Jake, Greta and Katy to clean up after the party, but Don had needed her again. She had to give her statement and she was needed as Laurel's friend. Violet could get in close and find things out in a way that would have made a police detective look insensitive. It would be totally natural for Laurel's new friend to come check on her and ask how Paul was doing. As Don had called ahead and found out that the family physician, Dr. Glenn, would be there, this was exactly where they needed to be to figure out this case.

Violet was needed to get people to talk, but Detective Donnelly was needed to get them into the hospital room. It was well past midnight now and the hospital was running on a lighter staff. Outside, the lights were lowered, and the palm trees swayed in humid gusts of wind. Guests would have been turned away, but the police detective that was working on the case could gain access to Paul's room.

Inside Paul's mint green room, the fluorescent lights were low and the whole wing was in a quieter part of the hospital. Violet and Don had arrived after the bright lights and rush of the emergency room. Paul lay on a hospital bed with his torso tilted up slightly, his mouth full of tubes and his eyes closed. He still looked pale, but the beep of the machines and the absence of nurses seemed to be a good sign. His torso bandages and Laurel's sheath dress seemed impossibly white in the few spots of light that hung in the middle of the room. The angelic scene was only broken up by the discomposed Dr. Glenn asleep in the corner. His neck had accordioned to one side and his cane was propped against the corner of the chair, threatening to slip. Violet suddenly became self-conscious that she still had light smears of Paul's blood on her pants.

Would Laurel be happy to see her? Would she want Violet to come, or would Laurel suspect Violet of the attack? The peace offerings in her hand lent Violet some confidence. She was glad they had taken the time to acquire them.

"Sorry to disturb, but we brought your clothes from before the wedding started…and some of the Caesar salad and a few of the tacos." Violet slid forward with her offering outstretched.

Laurel craned her whole body towards them, eager and urgent. She sandwiched Violet's hand and the stacked supplies with her two hands, then gave Violet's hand a warm little squeeze. She held on to Violet's hand as she sniffled. "Thank you so much. It means a lot to me that you came."

As Violet stumbled for words, Laurel tilted her head down towards the hospital bed to peak under the dividing curtain that blocked the door.

"Is that Detective Donnelly's legs? Thanks to you two, Paul will be fine in a few weeks! You saved his life! And treated me for shock to boot!"

Don stepped around the curtain, blushing and holding his head high. "Just doing the job, ma'am."

Laurel gushed. "No really, you two found him and stopped his bleeding so fast that he's-" Laurel turned to indicate Paul's hospital bed. "Already out of surgery!"

"How was surgery?" Violet leapt at the chance to ask.

"They said that his injuries weren't as bad as they looked, whatever that means." Laurel parroted. "The surgeon said that they were not all that deep, most of them hit his ribs, and that's what ribs are there for. He mentioned 'perforating his lungs' but those lacerations are closed up, the stitches will dissolve, and the toughest thing to get over will be the fluid in his lungs."

At Violet's disgusted face, Laurel stopped the narrative. Violet couldn't stand the thought of internal bleeding. You can't clean it up, you just have to live with it and wait for the body to mop up, disinfect, and get back in shape.

"I'll go ask the surgeon for details." The detective was still beaming as he swept the curtain aside and strode out of the room.

"Will you give him another thank-you for me? That seemed like it made his day." Laurel snickered to Violet as they both sat down.

"Sure thing, but Laurel, what happened? Who did this?" Violet changed gears.

"I don't know. I was hoping that you could tell me, since you were there."

"I wasn't there when he got…stabbed." Violet was reluctant to say the word. "But now that I think about it, I might have seen the door closing behind the person that did this."

"Detective Taylor thinks that either you did it or that you scared away the person that did."

"What? Well I didn't do it!" Violet may not have been surprised by Detective Taylor's assumptions, but she was still offended.

"I know that. But that means you scared off whoever did it. It might have been worse if not for you."

Violet and Laurel sat in silence for a moment, listening to the buzz of the nurse's station outside.

"Laurel, do you know of anyone that would want to hurt Paul?" Violet finally ventured solemnly.

"Well, I was thinking about that, and I think maybe-"

THWAP! The sound of Dr. Glenn's cane hitting the floor made all three of them jump and stare at each other with wild eyes.

"Oh, uh, how's the patient? Any-any changes?" Dr. Glenn's words tumbled out as he struggled to wake up the rest of the way.

"No, he's still out." Laurel rolled her eyes at Violet.

"When do they think he'll wake up?" Violet again pounced at the opening for one of her burning questions.

"They said any time now." Laurel was vague as she stroked Paul's hand.

"Well, he would probably know who did this, so we were hoping to ask him some questions."

"Ah, settle down, me duck." Dr. Glenn shuffled closer. "He may wake up now, but he still, uh, needs that endotracheal tube until morning."

Violet struggled to think of a way to find out what she wanted to from Dr. Glenn. *Are you a murderer* and *Did you stab him* didn't seem like the right avenue to take.

"Do you know of anyone that would want to hurt Paul?" Violet asked the doctor, skirting the subject.

"Paul had cost some people a few quid and made some, uh, some mistakes, but all those people still needed him around to-to clean up the mess."

"How about people at the party, Doctor? Were any of those people at the party?"

"Oh, lass, you don't need to call me that anymore."

"What, you mean Doctor?"

"Aye, I lost my medical license today." Dr. Glenn bowed his head and explained. "Seems the medical board already found out about my dealings with Lukie and struck me off. I suppose retirement is at hand."

"I'm sorry," Violet contemplated, then probed, "I guess that family has done a lot to you over the years."

"Lord bless you. I never got anything that I di-didn't deserve. I shouldn't have sold that plonker my prescription slips, but I was staring retirement in the face and-and I'm skint! I needed the-the money. Pauley didn't have a ruddy thing to do with it, though. He-he was always a good boy." Doctor Glenn slowly moved to pat Paul's free hand.

"What about his grandmother? Did you really used to date Francesca LeBaron?" Violet tried to make her question sound casual and even playful.

"Ah, we-we had a go of it, but it never amounted to much."

Dr. Glenn looked around the room at both of their faces. "You birds might have a hard time imagining it, but-but she wasn't always the old bat that you knew. And I-I wasn't the nutter you see before you! We had just been mates, but her--her parents wanted her to marry a-a doctor, so we went out to the pub a few times. We never could get it sorted. Love is a tricky business, you know."

Dr. Glenn seemed to get lost in his remembrances for a moment, then he chuckled and went on. "She was too-too ambitious for me, and I was too boring for her. I always tried to skive off of going out to the nice places that-that she loved so much. And-and she always wanted me to be doing more. We were trying to think of a-a way to break it to her parents, but then, she-she met that toff that was Paul's grandfather, and bob's your uncle!"

"Hm, and you guys went back to being friends?" Violet asked doubtfully.

"Well, uh, well I wouldn't say that. We didn't see much-much of each other until after my medical practice was--was all sorted. Then she decided that I was the-the only doctor she would trust and made her-her whole family come to me."

"That's nice that she brought you so much business, or didn't they pay you well?" Laurel wondered, puzzled.

"Blimey, yes o'course they--hey did. I just throw - threw a spanner in the works and never saved a dime! I was that git that thought it would last forever! No, my money problems are-are my own fault. I-I know that now."

Violet stared at him. His frailty made it look as if his career had indeed lasted forever. He was so old, but just now considering his retirement. How would hurting Francesca or Paul have helped with that? He wouldn't get any money from their deaths, he wasn't the type that anyone would trust with a paid hit, and Violet believed that he didn't have any hard feelings towards any of the family.

He could be lying, but even if he had loved Francesca LeBaron and lost her to Paul's grandfather, Violet still didn't see that as a motive for what had happened. If their breakup had made him want to kill her, why would he wait fifty years?

It's true that she found out about the drug racket that he and Luke had going on, but she had found out at the party and he would not have had time to make the poison. The poison did require some medical knowledge, but it didn't seem like a doctor's style to Violet.

If a doctor had wanted to kill Francesca, he could have given her something that would react to her medication or something that wouldn't be traceable. Would a doctor go out, collect a plant, make a tea, boil it down, strain it out, bottle it, and slip it into someone's drink? Violet didn't think so. He could have altered a pill or injected her with something. He could have done it without anyone ever finding out.

And then there was Paul's attack. That didn't seem to fit Dr. Glenn either. He was always so even-tempered, and even too batty! Besides, a doctor would know where to stab to inflict the most damage.

Violet had to take him off her suspects list, but that only left Pierre, or Peter, or whatever he wanted to be called. Having an alias didn't exactly lower Violet's suspicion of him, but she tried to recall what he had said about his feelings towards Mrs. LeBaron.

"Mm! Look at those shoes! I have to impress this one! We have a history, you know. She got me fired once," Pierre had told her at the rehearsal dinner. "Oh gurl. It all worked out though. She probably doesn't even remember me, so now I get to knock her dead."

Violet now dwelled on that statement. Had he wanted revenge? Had he come to that party with a vial of poison and a plan? Hadn't it been moments after that when he had been offended and alone in that back room?

Pierre could have planted something in there. He could have placed a glass of water laced with his homemade tincture sitting on a table, waiting for Mrs. LeBaron to come in and drink it.

"He is an old friend too, you know?" Paul's mother had said, "Yes…he used to be the wine buyer at our club, until my mother got him fired over a big misunderstanding. But now he is more fabulous than ever! He is even a major sommelier in

Paris during the tourist season!"

Would his new success erase his old pain? Was he over getting fired and presumably humiliated by Mrs. LeBaron? Violet had to keep all the timing straight in her mind. When Pierre was offended at the rehearsal dinner, it was too late for him to have been able to plan her death. The motive had to be solely based on things that happened before the party. Did Pierre have enough motive before the party to want her dead?

Perhaps she had misunderstood, but Violet had interpreted his comment in a totally different way. She had known what Pierre had meant when he said that he would "knock her dead" because Violet was in the same boat. He had wanted to impress her and piggyback on her influence to grow his wine business, just like Violet had wanted to do for her catering company. Why would he want Mrs. LeBaron dead? He wanted to use her, not kill her.

Besides, leaving a water glass in an abandoned room was a terrible murder plan. How would he even know that she would go in there? And who would drink from a water glass they found sitting around at a party? Mrs. LeBaron wouldn't. Mrs. LeBaron must have been poisoned before she walked into that back room, too. She went back there because she had already been poisoned and was feeling sick.

Nothing that happened in that back room made any difference in this case. The evidence from that room meant nothing. The half-eaten tart, the barfed out pill, nothing. It didn't matter that Michael, Pierre, Katy, Greta, Jake and Violet herself had all had their turns in that back room, because she was poisoned long before she arrived in the room.

The police's timeline even had her dying shortly after arriving in the room! She was not poisoned in the room and she was not poisoned outside, her drink was laced with something during the party in that main room. And it was done by someone with preparation and a plan.

Violet had since learned that digitalis would have tasted very bitter. Whoever had poisoned Francesca LeBaron would have had to put it in something that would have masked the taste. A water glass would have shown the taste of the poison standing right out in front. Wine would have too, especially to someone with refined taste buds like Mrs. LeBaron.

What then? The tartlet was barely eaten, and the herbal tea was too late, so the coffee? Espresso would mask bitter flavors enough to be a good delivery system, and Francesca had eaten nothing else.

Before Violet could ask her next question, Detective Donnelly re-entered the room. "Violet, can I talk to you for a sec?"

"Wait, please, Detective. I want to know everything that's going on. I can handle whatever it is that you found out." Laurel was standing now. Her resolution seemed to fill the room.

After a long contemplative pause and a glance at Violet, Don announced, "Alright, I don't think any of you could have had a hand in this, and you might be able to help."

Don strode in and took the last chair in the corner, queuing them all to sit down.

"I spoke with Paul's surgeon to get a better idea of the wounds and anything they would tell us. I also tried to retrieve Paul's shirt for analysis, but Detective Taylor already sent it with an officer to get tested right away." Don wiped his palms on the quads of his pants. "So, I called down to the lab to hurry things up and see if they had found anything."

"And?" Laurel prompted.

"The surgeon confirmed that Paul will be okay. There was enough fluid in his lungs that they intubated him, but he should be extubated in the morning if he has woken up. He's suffering from a trauma induced vagal response, which is really more like fainting, and more because he hit his head on the way down.

"Anyway, the important part is that Paul's wounds were shallow, and made with a kitchen knife as we suspected." Don paused and gazed around at all of them with his acute, droopy eyes. "Then he mentioned that the wounds were aiming down, like someone had been swinging down at the elbow."

Don pantomimed the classic Psycho-style stabbing motion, which made them all cringe.

"Anyway," Don said by way of apology, "he said that according to Paul's height, we should be looking for someone between about five foot and five-five."

Violet was taken aback. This couldn't be Pierre! He was six feet tall at least. He was towering, willowy, but had wiry muscles that showed when he moved boxes of wine. Even the doctor was Violet's height at five feet ten inches.

Who was a short man? Michael? Luke? Some obscure guest that no one had considered before? Were there any stairs where Paul had been stabbed? Maybe his attacker had been standing on a lower level.

"And." Don interrupted their streams of thought with more information. "The lab found two blood types. Paul's and someone else's. This is great news for us, but we have to be patient to find out whose it is. We don't have a lot of criminal masterminds in this case, so the DNA probably won't be in the system for us to look up, but it will help us nail our guy when we do find him."

"Luke would be in the system. But they couldn't tell you now?" Violet pleaded. "Not anything? Blood type? Gender? Anything?"

"No, I guess they are working as fast as they can, but the tests take time, and everyone had already gone home. They are under pressure from the mayor and his office too, so they will be called in and working all night, but they said they still won't know anything 'til morning."

This made them deflate and relax a little as Don said, "Everyone needs to go home, get some rest, and try to put all this out of your minds."

"I'm not leaving." Laurel stroked Paul's hair and squeezed his hand. "But I will try to rest. Thanks again for the clothes."

Don beamed again and Violet nodded. "Would you like us to stay while you get changed?"

"Oh, could you?" Laurel said with puppy dog eyes. "I don't want him to be alone if he wakes up."

Laurel slipped into the bathroom with her stack of clothes and Doctor Glenn walked out into the hall to ramble to a nurse as Violet and Don turned in their chairs to face each other.

"Who does that leave us?" Violet asked first.

"I'm stumped." Don smoothed his hand over the top of his thinning, dark hair. "A short, weak 'him', that would have had blood on his clothes moments after the attack, that has an injury, and that would have a reason to kill Francesca and Paul, and probably would want to ruin the wedding?"

Violet filled the detective in on the revealing conversation they had had in his absence. "So, I really don't think it was Dr. Glenn."

"No, I don't either," said Don. "After I thought about it, he came up to help with Laurel's shock right after the attack. He came from the opposite direction and he's too slow to get to both places in the right amount of time, and he had no blood on him."

"And he has no injuries!" Violet sighed.

"Well, that we know of..." Don sighed, resigned and defeated. "Are you still liking Pierre for this?"

"Nope." Now Violet was disappointed. "He's tall, and strong, even if he acts like he wouldn't be. Plus his motive is no good."

Then who was it? Violet could not stop asking herself.

"Like I said," Don said sighing. "We can all take a break until morning."

"Yeah, right," Violet said with sarcasm as she stood up to leave. "I have to get back to my day job. I left the crew cleaning, but I still need to get back as soon as I can."

Laurel rejoined them and they said their goodbyes.

"Right," Don segueyed as he stepped toward the door, remembering that he was Violet's ride. "Violet, I'll get you back to your magicians behind the scenes. I'm sure you're anxious to get back and help them clean up."

This rang true but triggered something almost eerie in Violet's mind. His comment hovered in the air and drove them to contemplation during the long journey back to the towering Laguna Gloria.

211

Chapter Seventeen

What Was That?

As Violet stood outside the villa, Don's car pulled away, leaving a smell of exhaust. Pierre was slowly loading boxes into his van. His trim arms showed his sinewy muscles, and his van had his company logo on the side.

There had to be something that they were missing. Violet didn't believe that Pierre or Dr. Glenn could be responsible, but that meant there was no one left! The list of possible suspects was now annoyingly blank.

Michael? He was strong and had no motive. Luke? Same story. Besides, both of them had been getting ready for the bride and groom to leave while Paul was stabbed.

"Do we know where Luke and Michael were while Paul was stabbed?" Violet asked Don during their nearly silent car ride.

After an informative call to Detective Taylor, who had been present during a lot of the party's aftermath, Don filled her in.

"It looks like multiple people can corroborate that the photographer and the best man, plus the fathers of the bride and groom, were out in front of the building at the time of the attack." Don struggled to get his phone back into his suit coat's pocket, drive, and talk at the same time. "They were out there with some of the other guests ready for the bride and groom to make their exit. You know, to throw rice or whatever. And I asked about Windsor, too. Turns out Austin police's vice unit caught wind of our case and wanted to make an example of him. He's been arrested so he definitely was not here tonight."

"Are you convinced now?" Violet tried to not sound too 'I-told-you-so.'

"Yes, alright." Don flopped his head back on his headrest but kept his eyes on the road. "You were right. It wasn't Windsor or Luke."

Those were the last words they had said to each other before arriving at Laguna Gloria and parting ways.

Now Violet could hear and smell the rustle of the cedar trees all around her and the lake ahead. The rain gently spit raspberries and the full moon peaked out to light the lawns and make the metal statues shine. The house now looked ominous and looming in the bright light cast on its glistening tile roof and awnings. The tall silver sculpture directly in front of the mansion sparkled as it stared up in relief at the break in the clouds that revealed the moon. This drew her gaze upwards as she thought back on recent events.

What could she be missing?

Violet had found a way to talk to almost everyone, at least everyone that could have had a motive, but she must be overlooking someone. Or something.

Laurel had seemed to be holding back. Early on, Laurel had been keeping a secret, but now Violet still felt as if Laurel had more to say.

"Hey Violet." Laurel answered the phone, trying to sound like she had not been sleeping.

"Sorry to call and disturb you again, but I realized that you were going to say something before we got interrupted."

"What was that?" Laurel was still groggy.

"In Paul's hospital room tonight," Violet prompted, "I had asked if you knew anyone that might want to hurt you two. It…well, it sounded like you were about to answer when Dr. Glenn interrupted your thought."

"Oh," Laurel chuckled, but without any mirth. "It's nothing. I just had something nagging at the back of my mind. Something that Doctor Glenn said."

"Please tell me," Violet said, realizing that her silence wasn't as persuasive over the phone. She was now sure that Laurel couldn't be the killer, so dropped her attempts at stealth. "I'm trying to help out, but frankly, the police are

213

stuck. Any idea, any little lead, would really help us out."

"I'm not even sure what it was that was bothering me, but something in our conversation right when he got here made me uneasy." Laurel broke off, pausing, then haltingly relayed the whole conversation she had had with Dr. Glenn upon his arrival in Paul's hospital room.

Violet listened over the phone; her attention riveted on Laurel's voice as she trotted inside to escape the rain as it picked up again. Violet was desperate for the tiniest clue. What had made Laurel uneasy? What could be nagging at her as a possible lead?

As Violet wandered in, she gave Jake, who looked like he was ready to fall over, a kiss on the cheek as he swept the front porch of discarded flower petals. Cups of petals that never got to be thrown on the happy couple. Inside, the air smelled like rain and finger foods and the tables were now bare. Greta must have dismantled ornate floral arrangements with almost manic zeal and now walked out the front door past Violet and Jake to go fill her van. At times like this it was obvious who was the night owl and who was the early bird. Violet pressed her ear even harder to the phone.

"Then, Dr. Glenn mentioned that at his last appointment Paul was talking about all the people that he had injured financially. He went off on this long tangent about how he could tell me this now that he wasn't a doctor anymore. Like no more doctor-patient confidentiality, blah, blah, blah. I guess those people were still depending on Paul to clean up the mess and get their money back, or something." Laurel finally paused to think. "Does any of that sound suspicious to you?"

Violet could hear dishes being washed as she meandered her way to the kitchen, still listening intently. Violet tried to sound encouraging, but she was suspecting that she was just wasting her time with all this talk. "Well, I'm not sure, was there anything else?"

Laurel continued with contempt for her subject matter. "Then Dr. Glenn talked about that tramp, Trina. He said that she said that she was still depending on him too. I guess they would need some help, her and the baby. She has some job that makes her stay on her feet for long periods of time, so she will have to stop working soon."

Violet swung through the doors to the tiny kitchen, barely aware of her surroundings and focusing on her conversation. Dishes were piled high on both sides of the sink and the room was full of the smell of dish soap. The rush of running water came to Violet's other ear, so she plugged it with her finger again.

"Then he was talking about how this would all turn out to be a good thing! Ugh!" Laurel scoffed.

Violet leaned on the opposite counter from the sink, finishing her conversation with Laurel before taking over dish duty.

"He was like, 'Antonia will love being a grandma! And it will be so good for Paul to be a father! And Luke might finally shape up with a little nephew looking up to him!' And how me being there for their family through all of this 'was the best thing they could have hoped for.' Oh, and then for some reason it really irked me that he said we might even get custody! I mean, I don't even know if I want custody! I hadn't even thought about fighting for it, like, in court?"

Laurel obviously expected a response to this, but Violet had frozen in place. "What did you say?"

"I know he is Paul's son, and we could give him a good home, but is his mom going to make it all a living hell?" Laurel had run away with her subject.

Violet stared in front of her. Her thoughts whizzed up as if in a blender, but now everything was settling into place. Violet's mental list now had one glaring name on it. It was not a name she had expected, and it was in a form previously unknown to her.

Laurel rambled on. "Violet? I know we were going to have kids right away, so it wouldn't be like, inconvenient. And I know that we would be better parents than that hussy!"

"Trina?" Violet said into the phone with a note of panic, but still watching for the response it created in the room. "Did you just say that she's having a boy? Have you ever met her?"

"Oh, right. Dr. Glenn said that. So, I guess she lied to us

about that, too. Ugh! I mean, I don't mind either way, but it just shows you even more that she is crazy and will say anything!" Laurel vented openly.

"What? And…" Violet interrupted with a dreamy voice as the sink's water turned off. "She's been in contact with Doctor Glenn?"

"I guess so, you're right. But no, I've never met her." Laurel still didn't see the importance of all that she was saying. "I thought she was far away, but Dr. Glenn was talking like she was a regular patient of his."

Violet heard a familiar sound. *What was that?* Violet pried her memory as the sound registered in the back of her mind. She realized with a start that it was the familiar 'shing' of her knife leaving the pile of dirty dishes as she told Laurel. "I-I think I have to go."

"Wait, I-" Laurel tried to steer the conversation back to her own troubles, but Violet slowly pushed the red button with her thumb.

Violet had to focus now. In this moment everything made sense. All the puzzle pieces fit together, and she marveled that she had not seen it before. She had never asked the right questions. She was looking for someone who had a long-term motive to kill Francesca, who would want to ruin the wedding, and who would have gone into a frenzy after Paul was married. It had to be someone who knew plants and had access to the fatal flower. She was looking for a small person, inexperienced with violence and weak, but not a man. A boy. A baby boy.

"Katy," Violet finally said, appealingly but barely audible. "How did you hurt your hand?"

Chapter Eighteen

How Could I Miss That?

For a long moment, Katy didn't answer but stood anchored to the spot. Her little body was now rigid and immovable.

Violet stood against the opposite counter of the tiny galley kitchen. Violet's mind whirled through her situation. A killer, alone, everyone else outside, no one to even hear her scream. If she even needed to scream. What would Katy do? Could she talk her way out of this?

Violet's feet angled out and almost touched Katy's as she asked, just above a whisper, "Is your name really Katrina?"

Suddenly, Katy whirled around, slashing out with a knife in her roughly bandaged hand.

Violet was so shocked that she only managed to throw her hands in front of her and yelp.

Violet's own kitchen knife, sharpened that morning and smeared with cake and pink frosting, split the skin on the side of her forearm in a clean line. Blood trickled to the floor as Violet doubled over, cradling her arm in more shock than pain. She looked up to again see the other kitchen door swing closed behind Katy's retreat.

Without thinking and without preparing, Violet lunged after Katy. Violet knew that she could lose her at any moment, so she pushed through the pain that throbbed in her arm and the whirling thoughts that might convince her to slow down or turn back. Katy could not get away this time, through the same door even!

Despite her pregnant waddle, Katy was moving fast. At every turn through a doorway, Violet would barely catch sight of which direction Katy had turned. Finally, they emerged out into the dark wind as rain lapped at their faces. Katy pushed

217

onward and downward, descending the stairs that traced the hill behind the villa.

Violet tried to call for Jake, but the wind dissolved her call. She had no time to go get him.

Violet leapt, taking the slick stairs two at a time to catch up, but slipped. Violet half caught herself, then continued to pursue Katy one tread at a time. She added a twisted ankle to the list of pains that she would have to ignore for now. Nothing else mattered. Katy had to be stopped.

They were both toddling on the straight away of the flight of stairs, but still yards apart when Violet made her first attempt at reasoning with the panicked girl.

"Katy!" Violet yelled as the wind carried her voice away again. "Stop! You don't have to do this!"

She did look like a girl. Katy was always petite, but now she looked lost, scared, and as pitiful as a sunken cake.

Katy responded in a sob that couldn't be heard or understood as she hit the bottom of the steps and took off towards a wooded area. She strode, visibly uncomfortable, with her dark hair plastered against her face and back.

Violet whipped her own wet hair out of her face and tried to watch Katy. They ran along the edge of the lagoon as the wind made waves lick at the craggy shore. When Katy disappeared into the trees, Violet was worried that she had lost track of her after all this.

Why hadn't she gone for help? Why hadn't she stayed where she was? At least in the kitchen she would have been able to stop her blood from trickling down her arm. Now she felt shaky as she looked at it. It was impossible to tell how much blood she was losing, but it looked like even more as it seeped into the raindrops that pelted her. Violet looked away and decided that she should call Jake and the police.

Violet felt the back pocket of her soggy pants and realized that her phone had been in her hand when Katy had come at her. She imagined her cell phone whipping out of her hands, clattering down, and now lying with blood droplets on the kitchen floor.

Violet wanted to scream, wanted to clean up the blood,

wanted to sit somewhere warm and nurse her injuries, but she couldn't. After bowing her head, cursing under her breath at her own stupidity, and watching the rain bolt off the end of her nose, she decided that the only thing to do was continue. She had promised to not do anything dangerous and her safest option would be to turn back, but she could not think of a way to lure Katy back with her. She had to push on and avoid looking at her arm. This was their best chance to catch Katy. Violet was the only one that knew where Katy was, and no one could help her. This was the only way to stop her, to secure her, to clear all the innocent people for good, potentially save Paul's baby, and to end all this madness!

Her bleeding wasn't bad enough to be dangerous, and she was finally reaching the answers to all her questions. *Besides,* she thought, *how hard could it be to catch one tiny, pregnant lady?*

She ducked into the trees and strained her eyes against the gloom. Violet wondered whether, if she even found Katy, she be able to hold her until help arrived. Would help arrive?

Violet could see almost nothing, so she tried to reach out with her other senses. She listened hard for anything. It was dark and smelled of rotting leaves in here, but at least the howling of the wind was muffled. The sheltering trees rustled and dripped huge, splashing bombs, but she would probably be able to hear the sound of running feet.

Violet froze. She heard nothing, and then, wait, was that the sound of a person talking? Was Katy ranting? Chanting? Babbling?

Violet walked as quietly as she could through the saturated oak leaves of the forest floor towards something that reflected the filtered, ambient light of the sky.

Was it moving? No, the trees cast shadows that moved across its surface as they swayed in the gusts, but this was the source of the sound. Perhaps Katy was on the other side of it and talking to herself. As she got close, a different sound started. It was melodious and obvious now. Violet realized that this was one of the artists' installations. It was a car playing oldies music!

Violet started to relax as a twig broke on the ground behind her.

Violet spun on a heel, revealing Katy swinging her arm up with the same knife, already tinged with Violet's blood. Without seeing and without thinking, Violet caught the arm as it paused at the top of its arc.

The two women stood together with their arms tangled over their heads. Violet fought with all her strength as she realized that Katy was tiring under her. Violet considered kicking her down, or kneeing her, or anything to end the fight, but Paul's words came back to her.

"I couldn't hurt him, don't hurt him," he muttered. Violet couldn't hurt him either. How could Violet stop Katy without hurting the innocent fetus that she carried?

These thoughts distracted Violet as Katy realized that she was losing the struggle and abandoned the knife to let it tumble to the ground. Instead Katy sucker punched Violet and ran again deeper into the trees.

Doubled over again, Violet revisited the question, *Why am I doing this?* This was not her job and not her responsibility. She wasn't trained in combat or police procedure, or even psychology! Her own pain was cutting its way to the surface. She wanted to stop, to leave it to the professionals, to quit.

With the word quit, she remembered just what she would be quitting. She wouldn't just be quitting a fight for her own pride, no. She would be quitting on doing what was right, on Greta's freedom, on Lindy's happiness, and on Laurel's justice. The professionals couldn't help now, only she stood between her family and friends and this crazed woman. Katy even seemed to be hurting herself and her baby as she hobbled on with surprising energy. Violet's resolve hardened as she asked herself whether Katy had been a runner. She again righted herself and pursued. Another pain had to be added to the list.

Thinking back, Violet seemed to remember conversations where they had talked about Katy's successful college career as a cheerleader and gymnast. Katy had been fitness personified before she had gotten pregnant. Katy, Violet, and

Greta had shared things about their lives with each other, they had worked shoulder to shoulder, they had even been friends in a way.

How could I have not known that she was a murderer? How could I miss it? Violet wondered. *How could I have not seen all the facts!*

As the indecisive Texas rain slowed to a drizzle again, Violet entered a clearing with more artists' installments. She could see that this was the end of the path that they had followed. The water of the lagoon now rippled in front of and beside Violet through another row of trees at either side.

"Please Katy!" Violet cried. "Stop this!"

The protected air of the clearing carried her voice and made it sound eerie. Ominous was the gnarled voice that came back to her.

"You can stop calling me that now!" Katy's words were garbled by anger and tears. "I never even told your overbearing witch of a sister to call me that! My name...is Katrina!"

The name was almost screamed with pent up rage.

"I'm sorry!" Violet called. "I'm sorry. I guess I never really got to know you. You have been going through a lot, and-and I don't think any of us even noticed."

Violet spoke to manipulate, but also with real emotion. Violet realized now that she had never really seen Katy. She had always glanced right over her to look to Greta, figuratively and literally.

"Exactly!" Katy was more coherent now, but her voice resounded around the clearing in a way that disguised her location. "You two with your perfect little lives couldn't be bothered to look twice at me. But that was okay! Because I had someone that loved me!"

"Do you mean Paul?" Violet ventured after a long pause.

"Of course I mean Paul. He loved me! We were going to be together until Laurel had to ruin it!" Katy's voice had turned into a gut-wrenching sob mixed with screams that was difficult to understand again. "He said that Laurel wanted to get back together and that she was the sort of person that his family, and

221

especially his grandmother, would approve of! He all-but told me that he was getting back together with her for his family! And for money!"

Violet realized that she could keep Katy ranting while she took the time to find her. Violet had to find Katy while she was distracted if she was going to be able to stop her without hurting her, but where could she be hiding? The sculptures in the clearing were small, so Violet slid clockwise along the tree line. She had to find Katy and cut off the only other pathway that lead away from their confrontation.

Violet prodded. "Didn't he really love her?"

"Of course not!" Katy snapped back. "That was obvious to anyone with half a brain! Paul needed his grandmother's money, so he needed to marry someone that his grandmother approved of."

Katy scoffed and went on. "If Granny was out of the picture, then Laurel would be out of the picture and no one would ever suspect me."

Violet felt the silence lengthen and encouraged Katy again. "So you got Francesca out of the way?"

"It's not like y'all will miss her!" Katy lashed out like a petulant child. Her voice whined and complained with contempt. "I think I did the world a favor! I definitely did Paul a favor, but then he married Laurel anyway! It's really just that he was too nice to cancel the wedding. I should have killed Laurel! That would have ended both of our problems!"

"But…" Violet tried to stall and get her questions answered at the same time. She was now almost a quarter of the way around the rough oval clearing. Violet had come to the leading edge of the other path out of the clearing, sure that she would find Katy here. She was still nowhere to be found. Katy's voice resounded around the space, but it was becoming clearer. Violet needed more time, so she went on. "Did you try to talk to him?"

"Ye-es." Katy was annoyed. "I talked to him last night. I never got my chance at the rehearsal dinner. He never even noticed me! But I finally got him alone so I could see him in person when we were setting up for the bachelor party. I told him everything! I showed him that I was still pregnant and that we had to be together now! I even showed him that I have dark hair now like his precious Laurel!"

Katy almost growled the name. The disgust that both Laurel and Katy could weave into each other's names was striking.

Katy groaned in what sounded like pain, then let out a few squeaky sobs. The new kinds of sound that she made carried differently in the air and Violet finally found her.

Violet had been searching the trees, but now she saw Katy's tiny frame crouched, huddled behind a metal sculpture in the middle of the clearing. Katy was turned the other way, looking over her shoulder and waiting, probably for Violet to come into view. Katy had been waiting for Violet to hear her voice and come walking straight down the middle of the lawn. Apparently Violet's location had been disguised, too.

Now that the knife was gone, Violet perceived that Katy was poised with a brick in one white-knuckled fist.

Violet was now afraid to say another word. Would her words carry differently now that she was on the same side of the sculpture as Katy? Would her voice give away her location? Would Violet be right behind Katy and elicit another attack?

"Even after I told him everything, he still married Laurel!" Katy went on without encouragement now. "How could he do that? Why would he do that? Marrying me would be the right thing to do! And that's what he really wanted!"

Violet stood silent for what felt like a long time as Katy continued in a childlike voice mixed with shuddering sobs. "I guess he really loved her...well, both of us. I couldn't stand that he married her, and I just lost it. I don't know, if Laurel had ever been alone, then I think I might have snapped at her first, but Paul was the one making all the wrong choices! He was the one who had lied and cheated and RUINED MY LIFE!"

Katy's frame shook with fury, then she was obviously seized by a moment of pain and cradled her baby-bump. Violet had to do something. She had to end this soon, but without hurting Katy or her baby. Now that Katy was screaming again, this had to be her chance. If Katy was distracted and loud, Violet could sneak up behind her and grab her without her realizing it until she was trapped.

Violet lifted one foot, rolled her ankle in the air to work out any popping before the crucial moment began, and took one smooth step forward. As she did the same with the second foot, arms reached out from behind her and snatched at her. The arms ripped her back and down onto the disgusting wet leaves. Silently, gently, but quickly.

Violet's nerves were so high, and she was so surprised that she let out a tiny squawk as she turned to see Don's face behind the arms. A finger immediately flew to his lips, but it was too late.

They both turned to see Katy charging at them. Her eyes were savage, and her lips were curled back in a devilish, satisfied smile. As Katy unevenly galloped towards them, she raised the brick in her hand. She was ready to take a swing and she was going to revel in it.

Don followed his training and popped to his feet with his hand flying to his holster, but he hesitated. His hand gripped his gun, but his face was stunned.

Violet was still on the ground from being pulled down and back, but she saw Don's tormented eyes rest on Katy's pregnant belly. That's when Violet knew, she was about to get hit with a brick.

Pure adrenaline coursed through Violet's veins as her legs curled up under her and her arms flew up. One stretched out and one did it's best to envelope her head. She instinctively clenched her eyes closed and waited for the impact.

Nothing came but a twisted, scream of agony. For a moment, Violet wondered if she herself had let out that strange, primitive noise, but as fast as the question came, she knew it must have been Katy. The brick thudded to the ground in front of Violet and briefly rolled down the embankment. Violet opened her eyes to see Jake towering over and behind Katy, holding her in a full-nelson with her arms stretched out and his arms hooked under her armpits and behind her neck. It was obvious that he had been able to do what Violet hadn't.

He had snuck up behind Katy, close enough to catch her mid-flight, then pounced right when he was needed most.

Violet's body relaxed as her muscles slackened, then she started to wobble like a custard. She shook from cold. She shook from pain. She shook from fear.

Only now did she feel the sear in her arm again, the twinge in her ankle, the dull ache in her stomach, the late hour pull at her bottom eyelids, and the bite of the cold wind that cut through her wet clothes. And the dirt. The mud, leaves, blood, sweat and tears mingled and made Violet's mind scream and her scalp wince.

Don stepped forward to handcuff Katy and recite her rights, so Jake was free to step to Violet and scoop her up. As she was still on the ground and shaking, she must have looked pitiful. He swept her up into his arms and carried her up the path behind her to a stone pillared gazebo to sit down.

The structure was beautiful but mournful, soaked with rain and draped with wet leaves and branches. He sat her on a frigid marble bench without a word about her breaking her promise and wrapped his coat around her. Then, he kneeled in front of Violet and pulled out the white apron that he had stuffed in one pocket. Jake deftly bandaged Violet's arm. He covered the slash with layers of apron, then trussed it all up like a turkey with the long apron strings. His hands were tender, yet firm, like perfectly cooked pasta. He then sat next to her, keeping one arm tightly enfolding her and rubbing her good arm for warmth with the other.

Violet's body was still coming down from its adrenaline high, but it recognized this gesture. It was Jake's way to say that she was safe now. It was now that she realised that he had been speaking this whole time in low, comforting platitudes. She had not been able to absorb his words, but his actions had finally broken through her fog. She now understood that it was all over and Violet let herself cry and lean into Jake's warm embrace.

Chapter Nineteen

How Did You Know?

Back at the villa, Don was busy guiding the now placid Katy with one arm and talking into his radio with the other. Jake followed at a safe distance, with Violet standing and holding his arm, huddled at his side.

"We got her! Meet back in front of the main building," Don said into his radio, then into his cell phone over and over. "You had a lot of people worried about you," he said when he noticed Violet's questioning expression. "Your sister, Jake here, Detective Taylor, lots of officers, and Laurel all needed to hear that you are safe and sound as soon as I found you."

Between calls, Don loaded Katy very gently into his car. She sat slumped and defeated with her arms handcuffed in front of her for added comfort, but sporadically a pang of pain would make her hunch and cradle her belly.

"Does she need a doctor? It looks like she's having contractions!" Violet asked with wide eyes and a shivering voice.

"Yes, almost definitely. An ambulance is about one minute out and they'll have something to stop those contractions, so we just have to wait. You need some medical attention, too."

"I'll live." Violet was prepared to argue more, but she realized what a state she was in. She pictured how she must look. Wet, covered with blood for the second time tonight, battered with grass and leaves, an apron tied in lumps on her arm, limping, hunched, shivering, covered with a police blanket and a jacket that was about ten sizes too big, and bone tired. She needed to rest, but mostly, deep down, she needed to feel clean.

226

As people started to filter in from all areas of the grounds, Violet asked, "How do they all even know what happened?"

"Well as soon as you got off the phone with Laurel, she called me," Detective Donnelly recounted. "She said that you sounded so strange that she knew something must be wrong. So, when she told me the questions you asked and the answers that she gave you, I finally put it together too. I was only a few minutes away by then, so I turned around and raced back. I ran in here, probably looking crazy, and everyone wanted to help out. Even Laurel said she was on her way over."

Don sighed, trying to return to his usual equilibrium, then continued. "Jake and I were able to set out first, and luckily the rain had let up or we wouldn't have been able to follow your slight blood trail to the stairs. After that, we had to guess. But if I were running, I would have headed down that trail and into the trees. Other people had fanned out in other directions and were talking like mad over the radio, so I turned it off when I heard you guys through the trees yelling to each other."

"You both knew it must have been Katy." Jake filled in the brief silence.

"Yeah." The detective sighed again. "When Laurel told me the stuff that made you freak out, I finally put it all together. I had looked at her a hundred times, but it just couldn't have been her, right?"

Violet agreed with a shiver. "I know what you mean. She didn't have a good motive, that we could find at least, and the only puny reason I could find was that she was offended by Mrs. LeBaron at the party. That was too late for her to plan to kill her! Plus, she hadn't actually been inside that back room, not really. She just took a half step in through the open doorway. She made a mistake there, at least. Anyway, it looked like she hadn't been anywhere near Francesca the whole night. Even the drinks that Francesca had during the party had not come directly from Katy.

"The fact that she is dainty and pregnant probably helped," Violet added. "And, there is just something about her! She's just so...sweet."

"Ch-yah," said Don. "She's sweet until you cross her! But

once you pieced it together that this Trina was actually having a boy and was in the area, then it was so obvious! How did we get so misguided?"

"I've been thinking about that," Violet explained. "All of the information about Windsor that made us suspect him, came from her!"

Violet shared the blame of being led astray, although she had never followed Katy down that rabbit hole. "Katy was the one that printed out the low-jack record, and probably tampered with it. Katy was the one that said that Windsor had threatened people, even though he had always seemed so harmless. And Katy was the one that made us believe that Windsor was capable of poisoning someone!"

Don was in deep thought and his words stumbled out. "So she altered the low-jack record, lied about Windsor, and tried to lay low."

Don seemed to snap back to the present. "But wait, you said she made a mistake. What was her mistake?"

"Hm? Oh, the timeline, and what we could hear from the kitchen." Violet continued when Jake and Don looked lost, "Mrs. LeBaron was supposed to have died right after going into the room, but according to Katy, she was alive and yelling at her just before the party ended. Plus, I didn't hear anything. I only realized it later, but I should have heard Francesca yell at Katy. Earlier when Francesca had an argument with Luke, we could hear it. Maybe not the actual words, but we could make out muffled sounds coming from that room as we were standing in the kitchen. When she said that Mrs. LeBaron was yelling at her, there was nothing. Francesca was already dead and Katy lied.

"She also shouldn't have gathered foxglove leaves for the tartlet that she gave Francesca, or shown that she knew the name of her heart condition." Violet went on. "The tincture that she put in her coffee was enough to kill her, she didn't need more. I guess she did that to frame me, but it was too risky!"

"But when did Katy put the foxglove in her drink? You're saying it was the espresso? I thought the only drink that she gave Mrs. LeBaron was the herbal tea…but that was too late, right?"

"Right! It wasn't the herbal tea which was delivered to her after she had already died, or the water or wine which wouldn't have masked the taste. It was the espresso! That espresso may have been handled by Paul and his mother before getting to her and abandoned on a table for anyone to mess with during her argument with Luke, but it originally came…from Katy. Mrs. LeBaron had ordered the whole room to get her an espresso, and I guess Katy was about to oblige. I thought she had been making herself a drink, but she must have altered it for Francesca when she said that she wanted one. I think that the fact that the drink changed hands several times on its way to Francesca, and sat unattended for a while, was just a lucky coincidence that threw us off."

Now Greta came running up and hugged Violet hard around the neck. "I was so worried! Are you okay? What happened?"

Violet gave the condensed version to the gathering crowd in hopes of getting back to her conversation with Don.

"Paul and Katy must have already known each other long before we even met her. I gather they were dating but keeping it kind of quiet because Paul's family wouldn't have approved of her. When Laurel wanted to get back together with Paul, he jumped at the chance. It was just bad luck that Katy had just become pregnant. I just can't believe we never suspected her!"

Greta hugged Violet again. "But you figured it out in the end! My sister, the hero!" she said.

"But it was really Detective Donnelly. He figured it out at the same time and saved my butt," Violet concluded to the onlookers, including his colleagues.

Don beamed and soaked up the praise gratefully but shot Violet a mischievous glance that seemed to say they both knew that wasn't true, but thanks anyway.

Violet only answered with a shrug and a wavering smile. She didn't want the praise, her business didn't need that kind of attention, and Don needed to make a splash for his self-esteem and his career.

Detective Taylor weaved his way through the crowd,

actually looking impressed. He stopped in front of Violet, piercing her with a firm but approving glare. His gray eyes bore down and his square jaw was clenched.

"Sorry I didn't leave it to the professionals." Violet smiled coyly.

"I gotta hand it to you," Taylor said quietly as his sneer turned almost friendly. "You figured it out but gave Don the credit."

"Well, he figured it out too, and…"

That was all Detective Taylor needed to hear. He stuck his hand out to Violet and they silently, firmly shook hands. Their eyes assessed each other for a moment before they both offered a slight, grudging smile. Then, Taylor turned around and got back to work as if nothing had happened.

"Wow!" Don exclaimed. "Even I've never gotten the Taylor handshake."

"I guess I made the right choice then, but I'm definitely a little worse for wear," Violet admitted as two ambulances and their radiating lights crawled up the driveway.

Katy was laid on a stretcher, still with handcuffs, and the two detectives went with her in the back of the ambulance. They left after having Violet agree to come in and offer another statement in the morning. Considering Violet had never been down to the station before this week, she was getting to know it pretty well.

Jake led Violet to the back of the second ambulance where she was allowed to perch on the back bumper and lean on one of the open doors. She hadn't wanted to lay down because she had wanted to stay in control. This blood loss felt a little like being tipsy, and she hated it. Violet's arm laceration and possible shock and hypothermia were being attended to by a bubbly young EMT who, wouldn't you know it, looked to be pregnant.

"Violet!" Laurel had just arrived and was running up from behind the emergency vehicles in her jeans and tee, which she made look effortlessly stylish.

"What happened? Did you guys figure out who did all this?"

"Yes, thanks to you," Violet said smiling at her friend. "You gave us the crucial evidence about Trina, so we finally figured out that it was…"

Violet nodded to indicate Katy as they closed the doors to the ambulance.

"Her? Your sister's sweet little assistant? No way!"

"Yep." Violet nodded again, but slowly to stave off the headache that was brewing. "I think it's time to put some real thought into whether you want custody of a new baby boy or not."

Laurel's face lit up and she said, "Well, I don't know. If no one were ready to fight it, then I guess he could really feel like he was mine! But, wait, go back. I don't get it! Walk me through it."

Violet checked on the progress that the EMT was making with her arm, decided she had the time to explain, and turned back to Laurel. "Are you sure you have time? Does Paul need you? And…there might be a lot that is hard to hear."

Laurel took a deep breath and said, "As long as it means this is all over, I want to hear it. Besides, Paul's dad is sitting with him for now, so I have time to step out and have a breather. I hate hospitals."

"Ok then," Violet acquiesced. "Well, do you understand that Katy was Trina? That she was Paul's girlfriend while you two were broken up?"

"Yeah," Laurel drawled, leading Violet to go on.

"As I understand it, she got pregnant right at the end of their relationship. She might not have even known that she was pregnant until after you two got back together.

"Well something about what Paul said when he was breaking up with her made her think that Paul was marrying you for his family and for money. I'm sure that's not the case, but she must have misunderstood, or he said it kinda like that to soften the blow. I don't know."

"Okay, sure." Laurel led Violet on again after the signature scoff and eye roll.

Violet continued. "So she tried to use her pregnancy to get back together with Paul, but when that didn't work, she

231

figured that she needed to remove the obstacles. Katy thought that Paul was marrying you to get his grandmother's approval, and her money. She concocted this plan to kill Francesca LeBaron in a way that wouldn't lead back to her, so that Paul could be free to marry her. She was convinced that he would come back if he no longer had to impress his grandmother and if he was financially independent.

"When that didn't work. It drove her crazy! The pregnancy hormones probably didn't help. After you guys actually got married, she just lost it and attacked him with whatever was nearby. Luckily, she didn't know how hard it is to stab a person, she's weak and tires easily because she's pregnant, and she wasn't able to do any long-term damage.

"Oh, but before that, she apparently confronted him on the night of the bachelor party while we were setting up the food. I guess he hadn't noticed her on the night of the rehearsal dinner. Now that I think of it, he looked surprised and confused at one point. Maybe he had only kind of seen her, or thought she looked familiar, but shrugged it off. She never went up to him that night, probably because she could never get him alone. She just kept her head down at the espresso machine.

"The one time Paul was alone and not on your arm, she tried to take a break. She couldn't get to him though. Instead, I think that's when she put the poison into Mrs. LeBaron's cup. Paul's grandmother had already announced to the whole room that she wanted an espresso, so Katy made one up for her instead of making one for herself like I thought. Katy was probably going to take it to her on her own, but it ended up being a happy coincidence that Antonia took it from her to give to Mrs. LeBaron. You see, it was that cup, not the later tea, that was poisoned all along. It was just like you said! She poisoned Mrs. LeBaron while she was still in the party and before anyone even knew anything was wrong. No one noticed her, not even Paul, in the middle of the party. No one thought anything of her messing with the coffee cups, because that was her job. No one saw her give Mrs. LeBaron the poison, because it changed hands several times on the way. I also gather she looks really different, so Paul didn't truly recognize her while she worked at the espresso machine. So that means he really hadn't known that she was still pregnant! Paul was telling the truth!"

Laurel let one tear fall from her eye, but prompted Violet. "Keep going, keep going. I want to know."

Violet grimaced, and went on in a kinder tone. "All along, she had been going to see Dr. Glenn and staying in Austin. I think she might have even been keeping tabs on you guys, maybe even using Greta to do it. She dyed her hair to be dark, maybe to look more like yours or maybe as a way to blend into the crowd and not be noticed while she committed the murder.

"It was that dark hair versus Trina being a blonde, the fact that she was having a boy while we thought Trina was having a girl, her apparent sweetness, and just everything about her made me not suspect her for a second. I'm so sorry that I didn't figure it out sooner! I could have saved Paul if I had opened my eyes! Mostly, I didn't see a motive. I-"

"Stop that right now." Laurel came to put a hand on Violet's knee through the police blanket and the soaking catering Dickies. "You couldn't have known, no one did! If Paul didn't even recognize her, then you certainly couldn't have seen through her. And you did save Paul!

"You interrupted the attack, you found the killer, and you stopped her without hurting that sweet, little baby. I can never thank you enough! You, too, Jake!" Laurel said, craning her neck around the edge of the ambulance.

Jake gave a little two-fingered wave from around the corner, showing that he was listening in.

Both girls had tears in their eyes now as they snickered at Jake and squeezed each other's hands.

Chapter Twenty

Why?

Excerpt from William P. Hobby Unit Interview, TDCJ Transcript 5 27 95
Completed by the University of Texas at Austin's Department of Psychology
Students Mark Payne and Jamie Shimizu

My momma always told me to find a man that would take care of me.

We were abandoned by my father as soon as she gave birth to me. After she gained weight and wasn't sleeping, my father disappeared without a trace. He was so determined to leave us behind that he has never even contacted his own mother. My father was my momma's high school sweetheart and they had always known that they were going to get married, so my momma never bothered to get an education. She had no marketable skills, she was uneducated, and she was bitter.

She could have been a better mother, but she always taught me what was important. She taught me to do the things that she had not. My momma taught me to be ambitious - to go out there and make things happen for myself. My momma taught me to go to college and learn everything I could about any field and then use that knowledge to be ambitious. And my momma taught me to love, but love a man who deserved my love, who wanted to be married and who would provide the right kind of life for me and my babies.

I found him.

While I was still an Aggie, he had come to use the agricultural extension's services for something that was affecting the grass on his ranch. I was in the office working part-time as their receptionist, learning as much as I could because my major was part of the College of Agriculture and Life Sciences. When he swept in the door, I couldn't even tell that he was a rancher.

He was so current and handsome. He was tall and thin, unlike all the men my mother had dated. He also seemed sad, the kind of sad that makes your heart pull right out of your chest and stick right to them. Immediately I could imagine cheering him up by putting my fingers into his curly dark hair and making his eyes light up with a smile. I had to say something, I had to do something.

I put on my sweetest smile and flipped my long, blonde hair. "Are you in town for long?"

"No, I just came for tonight, then I have to get back." His head fell and he continued. "My ex is coming to collect her things."

He seemed to struggle to say it, but it was obvious that he needed to get it out to someone. This was not a man that had done the dumping. This was not a man that had cut and run. This handsome, young, landowner had been in a committed, long-term relationship that had not worked out because she had ended it with him even though he had wanted to stay together.

"Come out with my friends and me tonight." I made my eyes big and inviting. "We are hitting Hurricane Harry's and we can show you the best place to go in College Station!"

"A club?" He scratched the back of his head. "Those really aren't my scene."

Even better, I thought.

"That's alright. It's really a country dance hall." I was worried I was losing him, so I touched his hand and went on. "Don't worry. I won't let you out of my sight."

With that, he smiled a little and agreed.

That night was a wonderful blur. He was draggin', so we started with drinks. He was tipsy by the time we started dancing close, then even closer. He kissed me once softly, but pulled back, closing his eyes with regret. After a few more

235

drinks, he didn't pull away anymore. I finally got my fingers into that hair.

At the end of the night, he was a perfect gentleman.

"When can I see you again, Cowboy?" I asked as he walked me to my car.

"I had a great time. But I don't come here very often at all."

There was a silence where I was scrambling to think of something. I couldn't let this man walk away forever. He was exactly what I had been looking for my whole life.

"I'm coming to Austin, to interview for a job," I lied.

He finally looked at me. "Then maybe I can show you around Austin. Here's my card."

Now I had to find a job that I could interview for in Austin! I searched for positions at UT, the big landscaping firms, and the small landscaping firms, but it was November, and no one was looking to hire someone that they would have to carry through their off-season. I was considering just going to Austin for no reason when I saw a commercial for fresh flowers. I could work at a floral shop! I had taken the floral arranging class and had the qualifications. Sure, it wasn't the kind of job that I would want forever, but they needed even more help over the holidays until other jobs would be hiring, or maybe I could even lock him down that fast and not need to work anymore.

I imagined being a kept lady. There would be farm chores, cooking, cleaning, and eventually kids, but that would be fulfilling and dreamy. I could be with a man that I think I already loved, and we could be partners in this big ol' crazy world. I wouldn't be alone like my momma.

I lined up some interviews and skipped Friday's classes to go to Austin for a long weekend. During the afternoons, when the floral work was slowest, I had some interviews, but every night I got to the real reason I was there.

His name was Paul. His mother called him Paulo sometimes. My half-Italian man. I called him Cowboy. I had him hooked. Sometimes when we kissed, he would even tear up. His cold tears would escape onto his cheeks, and he would apologize, which would make me fall for him all over again.

I visited him another weekend, and he visited once more before I was able to graduate in December. I had missed Thanksgiving floral arrangements, but I went to work for a floral arrangement supply company before the Christmas rush. It was a great job where I would be the only full-time employee amongst a sea of temporary help. I had a steady income and the perfect man. I didn't have to deliver the arrangements either. It was the type of place that produced arrangements wholesale, then a cute driver would deliver them to retail locations like grocery stores. I didn't even have to stay on my feet all the time! Mostly I directed and had power over the temporary help that the college students provided.

Everyday was relaxed and productive and every night was romantic. It was the perfect life and I would make it last forever. Nothing could come between us now. Sometime soon, Paul would ask me to move in, or just to get married right away. To move things along, I complained about my new apartment. He didn't get the hint. Then, I asked for a drawer in his apartment. He said that he didn't know if he had room, but there was a drawer that was entirely his socks and an empty hat box on top of his dresser! What could be more perfect? I moved his socks to the hat box, put a few things in the drawer that I had been keeping at his house anyway, then surprised him with it that night. He said nothing, but rolled with the change.

One day Paul met me for lunch, and I realized that he and my boss actually knew each other! Paul was one of those people that seems to know everyone though, so I shrugged it off. The part that hurt was that he pretended to not know me and he asked me to leave after him so that they wouldn't know that we were together.

"It adds to the fun," was all the explanation that he had given.

When I got back from lunch, I spoke to my boss, Greta. "So that guy who was here earlier, how do you two know each other?"

237

"We grew up together. Next door neighbors, in fact, but I haven't talked to him in a while."

So, of course, I had to ask the question. "Did you guys ever…"

"Well, it was a long time ago," she said, flushing.

I felt my cheeks burn, too, but with anger. I knew it was irrational, but I hated Greta for having dated Paul. He was mine and I was going to make sure that he stayed mine. I knew then that I really was in love with him, we were going to get married, and I was going to stop at nothing to make that happen.

I was starting to think about a fall wedding when Paul seemed to grow distant. A few evenings in a row he was late and lacked his usual energy, then when I asked what was wrong, he made me wish that I hadn't.

"My ex wants to get back together." Leaning on the corner of the dining room table and letting his head lull forward, this was the only thing he said.

"Aw, did you let her down easy?" I laughed.

"No, Trina I-I need to go back to her." Paul looked at me now with pleading eyes. "We've had so much fun. But I'm really sorry. I need to go back to her."

"Well, tell me why! We can work it out!" I could hear the squeak coming into my voice and the tears rising, but I didn't need to hide that. Not from Paul. "If she has some kind of hold over you, or if your family is making you, or-"

"It's not that. My family probably wouldn't approve of you, well my grandma at least, but I'm not worried about them. I need Laurel. I-I'm sorry if you thought that we were more serious than I did. But I need to go back to Laurel. I need to marry Laurel if she will have me. I'm sorry."

"We can figure something out!" I almost shrieked it this time. "I love you. We can work through this together! I know you have some debt, but we can work our way out of that. You don't need to go marry this rich girl just to-"

"It's not like that," he said, turning away from me.

There was a long pause as he said nothing more and I grew enraged.

238

"You love me! You can't do this to me!" I went on like that. Somehow I ended up just yelling at him for a long time.

He just sat there, taking it. He was saying nothing and not looking at me. I tried wrenching his face up and kissing him hard, leaning in. He very gently grabbed my hands and used them to push my whole body backwards till I was steady on my feet.

"No!" he said with determination.

I was out of ideas. I cried, partly to get his sympathy and partly for the heavy emptiness that was gathering in my stomach. I fell down crying on the couch. All he did was go to the kitchen to get me a glass of water. I wasn't hopeless yet, but I was so overcome, so angry at Laurel, and Paul, and Paul's grandmother and anyone else I could think of. I couldn't understand why I could not make Paul listen to me, or say more, or anything! I cried harder and harder until I was over the toilet heaving.

I got sick, then stayed queasy for days. I was so sick that I didn't want to eat. What was my new plan? How could I get him back? The swirling emotions and gut-wrenching anger made me nauseated.

Or at least I thought that's what was making me sick, until my period was late. I didn't notice at first, but when it was a whole week later than I should have expected, I wondered. I wondered whether I could be pregnant. We had been careful, but not every single time. According to the calendar, those had been okay times to forget though.

At first I was scared, but then I realized that this could be my tactic! If I was pregnant, Paul would come back to me! Maybe that was even why he had gone back to Laurel. Why had he needed to go back to her? Maybe it was to do the responsible thing and marry the girl that he had gotten pregnant. Well he loved me, so if I was pregnant, too, then that would level the playing field again! I could win him back! We could be happy again! He might end up with legal responsibilities to Laurel, but he could be with me again!

We had been apart for about two weeks and he had not answered my phone calls or texts. Even before this, I had tried leaving a message saying that we needed to talk or it was important and to tall me back. Nothing worked, so I waited outside his apartment one morning.

"I-I think I'm pregnant," I said, putting on my most innocent-looking face.

He had not seemed happy to see me, but now he started to turn a little green. His gaze flickered back to the door that he had just come out of and his apartment window above.

"Is she here? Is she up there right now?" I tried not to sound angry, but it didn't work. I was learning what true hatred really was. My life hadn't been perfect, but I don't think I had ever really loathed someone until then.

"She doesn't know about us, but I guess I will have to tell her now." He turned even more pale and sickly.

"This is a good thing!" I tried to convince him, but he just offered an empty laugh and tears rimmed his eyes. "Now we can be together again! Whatever hold she has on you doesn't matter now. She will let you go when you tell her that I'm pregnant!"

"That's what I'm afraid of!" He snapped the words at me like he was angry as tears shook down his cheeks. "I will have to tell her and hope that she can forgive me."

I'm pregnant and he is still thinking of her first?! *I thought. I couldn't believe it. I think that was when hate started to harden and turn to resolve in the pit of my stomach.*

He was going to stay with her because she had money and she was more his type of person according to his granny. I was his true love and was carrying his child, but his loyalties had to stay with her. They even offered me money to get an abortion and leave them alone. Can you believe they would bat me around me like that? I took their dirty money, but I was never going to get that abortion. That baby was the only way I was going to get Paul back now. I would think of a way to shift his loyalties back to me, but I had to stay close.

I kept the floral design job and bided my time, thinking. Paul and my boss were even kind of family friends, so I found out when he announced his engagement and hired us to arrange the flowers.

Even though this was horrible news, it could be turned into a good thing. I could see him again and convince him to be with me! If I could just find a time to talk to him alone, then I'd talk to him and he wouldn't be under that horrible Laurel's spell. I'd dye my hair to look more like Laurel, show him that I was still pregnant, and remind him of how much he had loved me! It was going to work!

He would come back to me and we would be happy. That was it! But I never found the right moment to talk to him at the rehearsal dinner, when I blessed his family. That was alright. Then he would never know that it was me. Then I finally talked to him at his bachelor party and said everything that I had been planning to say. He was just shocked, so I guess he needed a little time to think. Needed to sleep on it. When he actually got married anyway . . . I don't know. I just . . . I just lost it! I barely even remember stabbing him. It was like I was watching it from very far away. My whole body just wanted to hurt him, and I just grabbed whatever was closest.

Anyway, I wasn't thinking about that. In the beginning, I didn't plan to hurt Paul. All I was thinking about was how to get him back. I just wanted to love him and keep him all for myself. I wanted him to love me and look at me like . . . well, like he looked at Laurel. Like he had never looked at me before.

Doing the flowers for his wedding meant that I would get to see him again. I could persuade him and his family, and especially his snooty grandmother. I would convince them all that he should be with me.

Wait, I knew better than that. My momma had always been the perfect lady, but had still never been able to convince any of the fancy people that came in to her job that she was worth anything. None of them would even give her the time of day. They had judged her without even getting to know her. There was no way I was going to be able to convince them that I was 'their kind of people'.

What else could I do? Quit? No sir! I had to find a way to free Paul from these people. If he didn't need their money, then their approval wouldn't matter anymore. If he had his own money, then he wouldn't have to marry Laurel!

His judgmental old granny was the one that he had to please. She was going to leave him her money and she was the one running the show. She would probably be the one that wouldn't approve of a floral shop girl that was in the family way. She was probably the one that had convinced Paul to pay me to get an abortion and move away, too!

I'd never do it, of course. It's a sin! Besides, I was going to get Paul back and the three of us were going to live happily ever after. I could already feel her moving around inside of me. I felt like I knew her enough to even know that she was a girl, like my momma had known with me. I wasn't interested in no more boys. They just cause trouble.

That old witch had probably given Paul the money to get rid of my baby girl. Well, she wasn't going to kill my baby! She was the one that deserved to get knocked off!

Paul's granny thought she was so high and mighty, but no one actually liked her. They buzzed around her, worrying about her heart condition and trying to keep her happy, but they were all just waiting for her to die!

It's a sin to kill, but hadn't she wanted to kill my baby? Wouldn't I be forgiven for protecting my baby and helping my man? My momma always told me to find a man that would take care of me, and now I had to take care of him.

It would be a blessing really.

Chapter Twenty-One

Then What?

It was late February now, and it was drizzling again. The sky was bright but clouded over with a consistent white haze like frosting. Water spat sideways in an icy wind as Violet and Laurel sat inside Stella San Jac for their weekly Monday brunch.

Catering jobs rarely, if ever, interfered with their plans and Laurel had stopped working to be a full-time mom. Usually they sat outside on the quirky green chairs, but weather and the new member of their brunch party drove them inside.

"He's so cute. I can't stand it!" Violet cooed as she looked at baby Noah. "And he looks more and more like Paul every time I see him!"

Laurel let out a contented, yet exhausted, sigh as she pulled him out of his baby carrier. "I know, I'm so lucky."

Violet stared at Laurel out of the side of her eye. The comment had carried so much fatigue with it that she wasn't sure how Laurel really felt about her situation.

"How has it all been?" Violet asked while Laurel mixed a bottle of formula.

"Oh Violet, it's all so wonderful. It's like…it's terrible, but in a wonderful way." Laurel sounded dreamy and gratified. "Sure, I'm inconceivably tired, cuz like, he gets gassy and wakes me up, the other day he even shot poop onto the wall, but it's all mom stuff. None of the stuff has happened that I was afraid of, so he really gets to be all mine. It's all just normal baby stuff! Which is okay because it's part of the deal and I get to just stay home with my little squiggy pie!"

Laurel nuzzled her baby's neck, then got him settled in the crook of her arm for his bottle. Violet recognized the look that

243

Laurel gave baby Noah as pure contented but fascinated love.

"So, Katrina hasn't caused any trouble, you mean?" Violet asked.

"That's right!" Laurel chirped. "The adoption is final, Katrina has no rights, and she has gone away until this guy is at least twenty-five. She didn't even try to fight, not like she could from prison, but she didn't even try to hold on to Noah. Luckily, he will never know that. I send her pictures and stuff, but I'm not sure she even cares."

Katrina, as they had finally gotten used to calling her, was safely in prison and had gotten her 'twenty-five to life', but it had been a near thing. At first, Don and the police hadn't been able to get her to speak at all, she just sat hugging her belly and not making a peep. Even though Don said that they had all the proof they needed, and more, to convict her, it's always better for everyone to get a confession. To save everyone from the hassle, time, and scandal of a trial, Paul had insisted that he should be allowed to visit Katrina. He had convinced her to talk, to admit everything, in exchange for monthly visits from himself, not arguing with them over anything to do with Noah, and a few prison privileges. Katrina had agreed immediately.

Don had caught the killer in his boss's eyes and had started a sterling career as a detective like he wanted. Laurel had gotten a baby that was all hers without a fight or stretch marks like she had wanted. Unfortunately, Katrina had gotten a bit of what she wanted too - a little slice of Paul.

Love really was a strange beast. Especially Katrina's.

"How is Paul?" Violet asked Laurel between sips of her cranberry juice.

"He's doing great! Yesterday he said he finally feels all the way recovered, like it all never happened. Dr. Glenn finally cleared him to go running again, but I told him to still run on a treadmill on cold days like this."

Paul's wounds had recovered beautifully, and faster than expected, but the fluid in his lungs had turned into pneumonia this winter. With constant care from Dr. Glenn Jr., two courses of antibiotics, and his loving wife, he was finally getting back to normal.

"Great. But how about being a dad and having to visit Katrina?" Violet grimaced.

"He loves being a dad! And he has made the most of visiting Katrina. He actually got some master's students from UT to use their situation as a case study, so he doesn't have to be alone with her and he feels like some good has come out of it all. They even wrote down her side of the story in some long prison interview."

"Creepy, but cool! What ever happened with Luke and Dr. Glenn? All I know is that I was never asked to testify or anything," Violet wondered aloud.

"I guess there wasn't enough evidence to convict Dr. Glenn, so he has moved back to England for his retirement and . . . to avoid the scandal. He was able to neatly hand over his practice to his son. And Luke and his slick lawyer were able to plead their way down to rehab, probation and a lot of community service." Laurel gave Violet a devious smile, "He is hating it!"

Violet pictured Luke picking up trash on the side of the road in an orange vest, meeting with his parole officer and going through nasty bouts of withdrawal. She returned a vindictive grin. She was satisfied.

"How about you guys? Is Greta still mad at you?" Laurel asked, tipping Noah farther back as he neared the end of his bottle.

Greta had not been able to wrap her mind around Katy being guilty until she actually confessed. Then Greta had been so frustrated that she had partially blamed Violet. As a way to avoid blaming herself and freaking out about how close she and her daughter had been to a scheming murderer, Greta had lashed out. Greta had even known deep down that it was crazy to blame Violet, but it had been a necessary process in her grieving. That was how Greta had worded it when the sisters finally made up. After that, Greta had finally been able to deal with her feelings about being used by Katy to get into the wedding, and be grateful to Violet for clearing her name and saving their businesses.

"Nah, Greta's fine. This has all worked out for the best for her, too." As Violet said it, she truly felt it for the first time.

Things had worked out better because she had been involved. She was able to help those around her and the case. Her attention to detail could be a blessing as well as a curse.

"I think she finally stopped being hung up on it all when she found a new full-time employee," Violet said. "Get this! He's a straight floral designer who's handsome, strong enough to do all her heavy lifting, gets along famously with Lindy, and just got out of a relationship!"

Violet and Laurel gave each other knowing glances with raised eyebrows and pursed lips.

"Sounds like wedding bells to me!" Laurel teased. "Oh, that reminds me! Later today Paul and I are planning to reschedule our honeymoon!"

"That's wonderful!" Violet found herself volunteering. "I'll babysit while you are gone!"

Violet was not even sure where that had come from. It was true that their adventure had made her realize how lucky she was, and that life was short, but she and Jake had not revisited the topic of having a baby.

"Can I ask you a question?" Violet asked in a somber voice.

"I think you just did, but shoot!" Laurel replied while keeping her eyes on the baby and wiping milk out of his double chin.

Violet waited. A waiter set down their orders in front of them. Violet watched the waiter leave and Laurel watched Violet. While tearing a piece of her herbed biscuit with bacon and cheese, Violet asked, "How do you think having a baby has changed your relationship with Paul?"

When Laurel just squinted at Violet for a moment, she went on. "Jake has brought up that we could start a family now, and every other obstacle is gone, but-I finally figured out that what really scares me is how it will affect our relationship."

Laurel now beamed and reached across the table and around the cutlery to squeeze Violet's hand. "Oh, Vi! Don't worry about that. Having baby Noah has made our love grow. Sure, it has changed, but it's grown!

"We do need to get some time to ourselves, but Paul's mom has been surprisingly open to babysitting. She says it makes her feel younger!"

Violet could not imagine Antonia LeBaron Jorgensen with a baby, but she could imagine her own mother with one. Barbara had been a voracious babysitter, and still was, for Lindy and Greta. I guess being a grandma was funny that way.

Love was funny that way! The same force could make one person into a murderer and another person into a caring, devoted mother to another woman's baby. Matters of the heart could drive selfish, poised grandmothers and sweet, little maternal grandmothers equally. But mostly, love could grow. Violet finally understood that love wasn't a pie that had to be divided between a husband and kids, but a big bubble. It would grow and encompass anyone that she let in.

Violet let out a deep, contented sigh as she silently offered to hold Noah with outstretched arms. Laurel handed over baby Noah so she could get started on her smoothie and Violet held him up to her shoulder to burp him. He snuffled and brought his arms up while he nuzzled her neck with a bobbing head of wispy, fur-like hair.

Violet caressed his peach fuzz while he moved to make cooing noises and put his fist in his mouth. She sighed deeply again, this time with a shudder, and she closed her eyes while a smile hinted at her lips.

Violet yearned. It was time to make another batch of strudel.

THE END

Easier Apple Strudel with Phyllo Dough
(when you're in a hurry)

Buy gingerbread cookies and crumble them in a big sealed bag or pulse them in a food processor or blender until you reach whatever texture you prefer. This is a great use for leftover cookies or cake, but especially a picked-over, old gingerbread house!

2 ½ lbs Granny Smith apples, or another firm, tart baking apple (this can be 5 big to 10 small apples or about 1.1 kg)
1 Tablespoon lemon juice
⅔ cup (135g) sugar
1 teaspoon vanilla extract
Dash of salt
Dash of cinnamon
½ cup (75g) raisins
2 Tablespoons apple juice (or filling juice from your apples)
Old gingerbread cookies or cake to make 1 ⅓ cups of dry crumbs or 120g
8 oz. (Or half a 1 lb. box) Phyllo dough from the freezer section of the grocery store, thawed overnight in the fridge then set out to come to room temperature for about an hour. There are two rolls inside a box and this uses one of the rolls. Keep the other frozen for next time. (Internationally, use the entire 220g box of filo)
8 Tablespoons butter or 1 stick (125g), melted
Powdered sugar to finish

1. Before you start! Make sure your phyllo dough has thawed in the refrigerator over night. Now set it out for about an hour to come to room temperature.
2. Peel, core and cut apples to ⅛ to ¼ inch slices and drizzle with lemon juice. Mix in sugar, vanilla, salt and cinnamon.
3. As the apples release juices, pull out 2 Tablespoons and put it in a separate, small, microwave-safe bowl with your raisins. If your apples are especially dry, use apple juice, another fruit juice, or even water or your favorite booze. Cover this bowl with plastic wrap and microwave for 20 seconds. Let rest, still covered, on the counter until you are ready for them.
4. If you haven't already, turn some gingerbread cookies or cake into dry crumbs. Take an old gingerbread house, gingerbread cookies, ginger snaps, gingerbread cake, or even some cinnamon graham crackers and smash them up in a bag or food processor. If they are not especially stale and dry, lay the crumbs spread out on a cookie sheet and

dry them in the oven for about 10 minutes at 400 degrees F (200C). If they are crisp and dry, you can skip this step.

5. Now for assembly! Preheat your oven to, or keep it on at, 400 degrees F (200C) and have ready a large cookie sheet or jelly roll pan.

6. Lay two silpat mats or a large piece of parchment paper out on your counter and layer that phyllo dough in a big 16 inch by 22 inch (40 by 50cm) rectangle, making sure the pieces overlap. Use the whole individual package, so half the box, roughly brushing with your melted butter between layers. Stagger the seems and shingle the sheets to prevent leaks or splits in the final product.

7. Brush the layered dough with more of the melted butter. You can never have too much.

8. When your rolled strudel is finished it will be about 10-11 inches (26cm) long. So parallel to one of the shorter sides, lay the crumbs down in a thick line about a third of the way through the length of the dough. Crumbs should stay about 3 inches (7cm) away from the long sides and form a bed for your apples that is about 6 inches wide (15cm).

9. Now fold raisins into your apple mixture, then use a slotted spoon to pile the apple mixture on top of the gingerbread crumbs. Leave any juices behind in the bowl and do not add them to the assembly.

10. Fold the dough over the filling, starting with the inches left at the ends of the strip of filling. Gently press in and fold ends, then shorter side of the length, pushing the dough so it wraps tight but does not tear. Use the parchment paper or silicone mat underneath to gently roll the strudel onto and over the rest of the layered dough. Keep patting in ends and compressing it all into a log shape.

11. When done, keep rolling and position gently until the strudel is laying crumb-side down in the center of the silicone or parchment paper. Use the paper or mat as a sling and move the strudel with the parchment or silicone mat onto the waiting cookie sheet or baking pan.

12. Brush with the remaining melted butter and bake at 400

degrees F (200C) for 45 minutes to an hour. You'll know it's done when it's crisp and a deep golden brown.

13. It's okay if it leaked juice. Dust with powdered sugar to hide the imperfections before you slice and serve.

14. This can be served warm after at least 20 minutes of cooling or served cold after sitting at room temperature for about an hour and then refrigerating for about 3 hours, but I like to have it at room temperature. If you are waiting more than a couple hours to eat this, better cover and refrigerate it after about an hour of cooling on a wire rack.

Common Metric Conversions

US to Metric Volume Conversions

US Customary Quantity (English)	Metric Equivalent
1 teaspoon	5 mL
1 tablespoon	15 mL
1/4 cup *or* 2 fluid ounces	60 mL
1 cup *or* 8 fluid ounces *or* 1/2 pint	250 mL
2 cups *or* 1 pint *or* 16 fluid ounces	500 mL
4 cups *or* 2 pints *or* 1 quart	950 mL
4 quarts *or* 1 gallon	3.8 L
1 ounce (not fl oz)	28 grams
1 lb. (16 ounces) (not fl oz)	450 grams

When a high level of precision is not important, these basic equivalents may be used:

1 cup ≈ 250 mL

1 pint ≈ 500 mL

1 quart ≈ 1 L

1 gallon ≈ 4 L

Weights of Common Ingredients

1 cup flour = 120 grams

1 cup confectioners' sugar = 120 grams

1 cup sugar = 200 grams

1 stick butter = 113 grams

1 cup chocolate chips = 6 ounces = 170 grams

Common Temperature Conversions

300 degrees F = 150 degrees C

325 degrees F = 160 degrees C

350 degrees F = 180 degrees C

375 degrees F = 190 degrees C

400 degrees F = 200 degrees C

Fantastic Books
Great Authors

darkstroke is
an imprint of
Crooked Cat Books

- Gripping Thrillers
- Cosy Mysteries
- Romantic Chick-Lit
- Fascinating Historicals
- Exciting Fantasy
- Young Adult
- Non-Fiction

Made in the USA
Coppell, TX
30 September 2020

39086742R00152